Summer *at* Orchard House

ELLYN
OAKSMITH

Summer *at* Orchard House

bookouture

Published by Bookouture in 2020

An imprint of Storyfire Ltd.
Carmelite House
50 Victoria Embankment
London EC4Y 0DZ

www.bookouture.com

ISBN: 978-1-83888-751-3
eBook ISBN: 978-1-83888-750-6

To my clever, lovely Christine.

You truly are my sunshine.

CHAPTER ONE

I Quit

The phone rang at the worst possible moment in the history of bad moments. Hall of Fame bad moments. Carmen's presentation was the culmination of a bone-crushing year's work. Life at her firm was lived in dog years. Humiliation was routine. Families, lauded for their support at Christmas parties, studied photos on the fridge to remember what their loved ones looked like. She'd forgone a social life, regular meals and going to the gym (her version was getting coffee in her workout clothes) for her job. Her thirtieth had been spent eating ramen in front of her computer. Carmen, who couldn't commit to a houseplant, let alone a relationship, would let only one thing interfere with her chance at a promotion to marketing director: family.

Her father had taught them. Family comes first. Always.

The caller ID was a picture taken at the winery when they were all kids, laughing in the sunshine. That meant one thing.

One of her two sisters.

The Alvarez sisters didn't talk every week, but when they did, they dove in. There was no small talk, just life. A daytime call meant something was urgent. She had to take the call. It was painfully awkward staring at her ringing phone.

Carmen glanced at her Tyrannosaurus Rex of a boss. Felicity ate interns for breakfast. When she came out of her office, people scrambled to be otherwise occupied. Her unorthodox methods and borderline (or dead on) bullying were studiously ignored by those in charge for one reason. The usual one. She got results.

Right now, Felicity drummed her glossy nails on the gleaming conference table, her eyes narrowed at the interruption. A ringing phone was heresy. Answering a call wasn't a thing. It just wasn't. "Carmen, are we interrupting your social life?"

Carmen's colleagues nervously tittered, except Deena, the only person in the room who wouldn't push her off a ledge for this promotion. They'd sworn to watch each other's backs, as if they worked for the mafia. The comparison held.

Carmen swallowed. "It's my sister." *I should have lied*, Carmen thought, wishing she were the kind of person who lied without thinking. Who could stab a colleague in the back without a second thought. Maybe that was what was holding her back. Last month, Felicity had proudly pointed out that she never sent a Mother's Day card because then her mother would expect one every year.

Families were messy.

Felicity didn't do messy.

The ringing stopped.

Felicity rolled her eyes, waving a hand. "Your sister? Well, golly. By all means, stop the meeting."

Carmen's heart pounded in her throat. Felicity was not unlike a charging rhino. Impossible to stop or distract. You'd end up trampled. The words that came out of her mouth surprised everyone, even Carmen. Carmen normally toed the line. Felicity terrified her. That was the point. But still. The words came out. And they'd change everything. "Actually, I have to return the call."

Felicity stared with thinly veiled contempt while everyone in the room held their breath, thanking their lucky stars that they weren't in Carmen Alvarez's kitten heels right now. Why didn't Felicity say something? The tension was unbearable. Finally: "Of course. Because you have a contractual obligation to your family between the hours of nine to five, right?"

The rest of the room glanced nervously each other, reassured that Felicity was on point. Rules needed to be obeyed. Felicity's nastiness was a given.

Deena shook her head ever so slightly, eyes widening with a *don't do it* warning. Carmen tried to thank her with a look, then faced down the rhino.

Carmen pushed back her chair. "Sorry, I'll be right back."

Felicity looked at her watch. "Sure, why not? It's only your career." She swept her hand towards the door. "But you go. Swap recipes. Book manicures. Go be you. We'll be here. Waiting while you live your best life."

"This will take one second. I have to…" Carmen pushed open the door, pressing one of the favorites on her phone.

The door closed with an airless whoosh.

Carmen kept a worried eye on the conference room where the slightly stunned employees resumed their meeting. She whispered into her phone, stressed on multiple levels. "Adella, what do you want? I was in a meeting."

Her sister, a full-time stay-at-home mom with three children under the age of five, including twins, lived on the end of a rope. "Connor, that is the dog's food. Put it back. Angel, the cat is going to scratch you!"

"Adella?" A conversation with Adella always took ten times longer than necessary. Her children saw their mother with a phone and immediately unleashed havoc, like Pavlov's dogs. "Adella, I can't talk. Estoy en el trabajo."

"I know you're at work. Do you think I don't know how to read a clock?"

Adella had a chip on her shoulder about being a stay-at-home mother. No matter how many times her sisters reinforced her choice, Adella felt judged.

"Can I call you back?"

"No. Listen, I went home yesterday to check on Papi and Mr. Wilfrey from the bank was there. It's a total mess, Car. He's headed for foreclosure. Orchard House, the winery; everything."

"What?" Carmen must have shrieked because dozens of heads popped up from their cubicles, like prairie dogs. Carmen glanced furtively into the conference room. Felicity tapped on her watch, shooting daggers. Carmen hid behind a leafy ficus, crouching on the ground. As if a tree could shield her from Felicity's wrath.

"Papi hasn't been paying his taxes."

"I thought you were looking after that."

"Lola took it over for me."

"Lola?" Lola, a recent art school dropout, was allergic to responsibility. Adulting was for people other than Lola. As a kid, she began getting dressed in the morning when the bus driver started honking.

"You let Lola take over?" Carmen heard the mixture of hysteria and anger in her own voice, trying unsuccessfully to calm down.

Lola had the attention span of a fruit fly. She was easily distracted and perpetually late. Nobody asked Lola to bring an appetizer, always dessert.

There was a crash in the background. Adella scolded her kids before returning to the phone. "I was going to check on her, but things just got away from me. Anyway, they put a lien on the property. If we don't come up with forty-six thousand dollars, it's going into foreclosure."

Carmen staggered out from behind the ficus into the hallway. "Forty-six thousand dollars? Where are we going to come up with forty-six thousand dollars?" She looked around. Every single person in the office was staring at her. She mouthed apologies before crouching down again.

"I don't know, but it gets worse."

Carmen gave up crouching, sat down on the ground. "How could it get worse? Is Papi lost? Abducted by aliens?"

"Don't be a drama queen."

"You can't call someone a drama queen for reacting to bad news."

"You know that chico who moved in next door? The Microsoft guy with that stupid yellow Lamborghini?"

You couldn't throw a stick in Chelan without hitting some Microsoftie with cash to burn, looking for a second act as a hotelier, restaurateur or vintner. They ran around town talking to anyone who'd slow down long enough to listen to plans for their hotel with cats, tasting menu built around the seasons or organic winery that was truly revolutionary. All of it would change the known world.

The roads were clogged with European sports cars. The lake teemed with Cobalt boats. Pilates-toned women opened boutiques selling three-hundred dollar bikinis. Chelan natives found it highly annoying that it wasn't enough for these people to make one fortune; they had to keep going and rub it in your face.

Whatever happened to the good old days when people made their pile and retired to do good deeds? These people had to reinvent the wheel. And talk about it.

All.

The.

Damn.

Time.

Carmen remembered seeing the new owner walking the property line a few years ago. Hollister Estate and Blue Hills vineyard were on adjacent slices of land sloping down to the lake where they each had orchards. Blue Hills curved around the hillside, placing it at a lower elevation. The only exception was their winery, which stood on a small parcel carved from Hollister land by ancient water treaty. Carmen had been on the winery patio, working on her computer. She'd glanced up, vaguely noticed the new owner in his vineyard, looking down at her. He was young and tall, wearing sunglasses. He didn't wave or say hello. Just stood there, hands on hips, surveying his fields like the lord of the manor. Completely annoying and entitled. They all missed the family who'd sold the vineyard next door and moved to Florida, of all places. Alligators, bugs and hurricanes.

"What about him?" she asked.

"He wants to buy Papi's vines. All of them. When I went over, he was in Orchard House with the banker. They were ganging up on Papi, trying to convince him that selling was the right thing to do. That he couldn't possibly come up with this year's vintage on his own. You remember Robert, Papi's winemaker?"

"Of course I remember Robert. He gave us that kitten."

"Well, he left because Papi couldn't afford to pay him."

Carmen felt like she was in a maze and running into one dead end after another. "Wow, I can't believe he left. He was there a long time. Like, since we were in high school."

"Es malo, Carmencita. You have to do something."

There it was. The big ask. She knew it was coming, but still. Carmen's voice was tight and high. "*I'm* going to have to do something? Hang on, Adella, last time I checked there were tres hermanas Alvarez."

"You're the only one who can do it. If you don't do something, this guy is going to work a deal with the bank."

"No, no, no, no, no, no." Carmen was sitting on the carpet, oblivious to the small crowd of staff at the end of the hallway staring at her. People didn't sit on the floor and hide behind trees in this office.

"Carmen. Think about it. Papi has Alzheimer's. That guy can swoop in and write a check for the whole thing before we even know what's happening. Papi doesn't know what he's signing. He needs someone there. Orchard House is in bad shape. It needs painting and cleaning. We need the next crop to make wine. Good wine. I have three kids. Lola is Lola. I mean, Papi is in no shape to run it on his own, but what do you think will happen if he sells? It's his life. His history. Everything." Adella paused to stop a fight between the twins, promising extra TV time. "I don't trust this Microsoft guy as far as we can throw him. He could be over there right now, promising Papi he's going to plant something on his hill, so the spring rains don't flood our driveway. They could be signing the papers and all Papi's hard work will be gone. It's our heritage. We can't just let it go. Please, Car."

"I can't come up with that kind of money."

"If we can get wine from this year bottled and sold, we can give the bank enough to back off."

Carmen's head was spinning. She'd seen Papi and the wine master in the shed tasting from the barrel, testing the brix level, ensuring that the mix of grapes brought out the quality they were looking for in each wine. She'd seen the bottling machine filling each bottle. Seen labels pasted on with the distinctive Blue Hills label, with the sketch of the dusky blue hills that surrounded their property. But she'd never done any of it herself. "I don't know anything about wine." Kind of a pathetic statement from someone raised on a winery.

"None of us do, but if we want to save the vineyard, we've got to learn."

"And by *we*, you mean me?"

Adella sighed. "Car, believe me, I'd love to check my kids into school and pick them up next month. Saving a winery would be a vacation for me pero no puedo."

"Okay. I'll be there as soon as I can."

After promising her sister she'd call with a plan, Carmen hung up the phone, looking up at the people at the end of the hallway. "Thank you, I'm fine." Because people that were fine sat on the ground. She got up, dusted herself off and tried not to panic.

This was bad. How could they have let this happen? Why did it have to fall on her? First Papi's Alzheimer's and now some predatory millionaire with his eyes on the family vines. Some dilettante who had no idea that Juan Alvarez had worked his way up from a picker who got by on one meal a day to save money. Who'd worn a rope to keep up his pants rather than spring for a belt. (The first gift from his young fiancée? A belt.)

The vineyard wasn't just land, it was his American dream.

What on earth was she going to do? *Forty-six thousand dollars!* The number loomed in her head in flashing neon.

Without realizing it, Carmen had strayed back towards the glass wall and the conference room. Felicity was staring at her with her arms crossed.

Great. Carmen felt like she'd been hit by a truck.

A rising panic clutched at her throat.

Blue Hills Vineyard wasn't just where she'd been raised. It was eighty-seven acres of prime Lake Chelan realty that her father had spent his entire life acquiring, painstakingly planting it with vines until they took root in the soil, like his family in the United States. Blue Hills was situated on a sloping hill leading to the lake. Situated in a gap between two foothills of the Cascade mountain range, yearly erosion resulted in grapes that were unlike any other. They made prizewinning wine. The land, and its mineral rich soil, was literally priceless.

Carmen's father had come from Mexico as a penniless teenager, staggering across the border so badly dehydrated he had been hallucinating. He'd made his way to the Pacific Northwest by train, working in the vineyards in Eastern Washington until a vineyard owner had recognized the young man's potential and offered him an apprentice position in Chelan. Carmen's father had immediately fallen in love with the lake, the small town and Mercedes, the woman who was to become his wife, a checker at the local Safeway. They'd sacrificed everything to buy their first plot of land and plant their first grapes.

Losing Blue Hills wouldn't be losing a piece of land, it would be losing their father's dream. Their part of America.

Without his vineyard, Carmen's father would wither like a raisin. Carmen wouldn't let that happen. Adella was right. It was up to her.

The only thing in her way was a Tyrannosaurus Rex.

CHAPTER TWO

Microsoft Money

It was nearly lunch and Carmen hadn't yet come up with a solution. She gnawed her on her fingernails, weighing her options. She could call Adella back and beg her to talk to the banker. She knew how that conversation would go. She'd hear how the price of daycare for three kids was like buying a new car every year. Nobody understood how grueling it was to chase three niños locos, let alone find a babysitter. How going to the bathroom with the door shut was me-time. How teaching thirty-one fourth grade kids was a vacation compared to her current life.

Carmen smiled, thinking of how she and Lola imitated their older sister. If they went to get a manicure, they'd say, "Why bother, it will just get ruined changing diapers and washing sippy cups. A glass of wine afterwards? ¿Estás loca? A babysitter for three children is twenty-five dollars an hour!" Adella was an easy target. She saw herself as the only responsible person on the planet.

Carmen kept an eye on Felicity in her glass-walled office, waiting until she was on a phone call and safely plugged into her headset with her Prada-clad feet on the desk. Always a sign that she would be a while.

Carmen called her best friend, Stella, a hairdresser in Chelan on Main Street. Stella was naturally nosy, sociable and had the perfect job for keeping her finger on the pulse of all things Chelan. If you wanted to keep a secret in Chelan, you didn't go to Stella's salon.

Stella answered on the first ring. "Hey, I'm with a client. Can I call you back?"

"Adella called me. Papi's in trouble."

Stella didn't miss a beat. "Of course she called you. Why doesn't *she* go check on your dad?"

"She's busy with the kids."

"Last I heard, kids were portable. Why can't she throw them in the car and go see your dad? Why do you always have to be the one she asks, just because you don't have kids?"

"I'm thinking about asking the Dragon Lady for a week off."

Carmen could hear Stella suck in her breath. She wondered what color her friend's hair was this week. Stella, like most hairdressers, like to mix it up. A lot. "Ohhhh. It's been nice knowing you. Can I have your Levis?"

Carmen peered over her cubicle. Deena looked up from her computer, smiling kindly. "This isn't making me feel any better, Stella."

"Sorry. But everything you've told me about her makes her sound like Cruella de Vil. But listen, it's your Papi. Go in there and explain things. Maybe she'll grow a heart."

Carmen thought of when Ben, their administrative assistant, had wanted time off to go to his grandmother's funeral in Alaska.

Felicity had said Ben couldn't possibly have known the old lady very well if she lived way out in the sticks.

"You're right. She has the mindset of a hungry crocodile, but what choice do you have? I mean, I can go check in on him if that'll help."

Papi loved Stella, but that wouldn't help. Only family could dig into finances. "He's thinking of selling the vineyard."

Carmen heard the clattering of Stella dropping her phone. She could hear her friend yelling and a client asking what was wrong. A moment later Stella came back on. "You scared me. For a second I thought you said that your dad was thinking of selling the vineyard."

"That's what I said."

"It's like the end of the world."

"Exaggerate much?"

"No, I'm totally serious. Your dad is like one of those old-world guys who's completely connected to his vines. He's like some walking, breathing advertisement for the American dream. Why would he sell?"

Hearing Stella say what was on Carmen's own mind made her realize the severity of the whole thing. "The millionaire next door is trying to talk him into it."

"The guy with the mid-life crisis yellow Lamborghini?"

"Yep."

"That's a shame. I don't want to hate that guy because he's seriously hot. And seriously rich."

"And seriously trying to take advantage of Papi."

"He just got fifty percent less hot, but he's still rich."

"Stella, I'm stressed out here. Could you not?"

"Okay, and I seriously have to get back to my client before she starts throwing brushes at me. Listen, this is what you're going to do. You're going to march into Dragon Lady's office and explain to her that your dad just had a heart attack and you need to go home for at least a week."

"But that's lying."

"Minor detail. Alzheimer's and the hot guy next door trying to buy the vineyard is too much detail. Keep it simple."

"On what planet is lying simple?"

"I've got to go. As soon as you know when you'll be here, text me. This is going to take some Chardonnay and beach time."

"Wait, I have one more question."

"Go."

"Even if I stop the guy and keep the winery, it's obvious that Papi can't do this on his own anymore. Who's going to run the winery?" Carmen and her sisters, despite their father's many attempts to interest them in viticulture, had wandered into other careers and motherhood. Except Lola, who had just wandered.

"You can."

"Be serious. I don't know anything about running a winery."

"You think I knew anything about cutting hair before I opened a salon?" Carmen heard Stella talking to her client. "Of course, I went to cosmetology school."

She hadn't.

That was Stella. She threw herself into things and figured them out later. That was not Carmen. She was a deliberate, steady list-maker. Her lists of pros and cons were famous in her circle of friends.

"I can't run a winery."

"One thing at a time, Car. Go see Dragon Lady. Call me when you're done. Also, what kind of flowers do you want at your funeral?"

*

Evan Hollister sipped the 2016 First Crush blend with his eyes closed. It's not that he believed closing his eyes made a difference to his taste buds, it just made him look like he knew what he was doing. Evan's wine master, Paolo Gentillo, was a fourth-generation wine master from the Piedmont region in Italy. With his tousled curls and Roman nose, Paolo had been born to sip Barolo in a town square whose buildings were older than America. Evan, however, had lured him to his winery in Chelan with a challenge: make a prizewinning Chelan wine to rival those of the big California vineyards. The First Crush blend was their third attempt. A challenge, and a big fat salary that grew the longer Paolo stayed.

It took a lot of money to keep one homesick Italian. Seattleites might flock to Chelan and pay big bucks to rent homes along its shores, but the Italian vintner might as well have been working on an oil rig. He hated it that much.

The men looked plucked from stereotypes of their respective countries. Paolo was wiry, dressed in a perfectly wrinkled linen shirt and thin cotton pants. His dark brown eyes looked sad beneath lush lashes. Evan looked like the high school quarterback, sharp-eyed, slim, broad-shouldered, his thick hair cut neatly. A polo shirt and aviator glasses completed the look.

Evan and Paolo were in the winery, the large warehouse-style barn that Evan had built of salvaged wood to house dozens of oak and steel casks, a tasting room and crushing vats for harvest time. It was up a winding dirt road from the vineyard estate where Evan lived—and increasingly, hosted weddings as a surprisingly necessary component to his winemaking business. Wedding guests drank the vineyard's wine, returning home to spread the word. It was, according to Evan's PR consultant Mandy, a necessary evil.

Weddings, Evan thought as the last sip of wine slid down his throat, were a tough business. Coming to this five years ago, Evan had thought that winemaking would be the challenge: keeping the vines healthy, the winery clean, the chemistry stable and timely. Getting the science right.

Hosting weddings seemed far more daunting. From what he'd seen at his friends' weddings, they were a circus of moving parts, freighted with so much emotion. Overwhelmed, nervous brides, bossy mothers, fed up fathers and unruly children. When he'd first completed the remodel of his house, he'd agreed to host a college friend's engagement party at Hollister Estate.

It was an unmitigated disaster. Someone broke a wineglass that his dog stepped on, necessitating a visit to the vet and a carpet cleaning. A couple brought their little child, who locked himself in the bathroom. Barry, Evan's leggy, excitable rescue mutt, ate all the appetizers fifteen minutes before the guests arrived and then barfed them up into the pool. The steak entrées were trapped in a truck delayed by wildfire road closure. Two drunken guests got into a fist fight that ended up in the pool. A cat strolled across the patio with a mouse in his mouth, proudly depositing the bloody offering on the foot of the tipsy bride-to-be, slumped on the back stairs, sneaking a cigarette with her maid of honor.

The whole experience had made Evan wish for the old Microsoft days, when he'd been a rat on an endless wheel of deadlines and travel.

Almost.

One look out the winery door at the turquoise blue lake, the dusty sage hills, the orchards dotting the edge of the lake. This, this right here, Evan thought, was heaven. Blue sky, fragrant June orchards, a kiss of summer in the air.

"No, no, no, no, no!" Paolo broke his reverie.

Evan lowered his wineglass, opening his eyes. His wine master's face was wrinkled into a disapproving frown. "The bouquet. It's full, but missing the minerals. We cannot taste the land."

Evan always had to think before he responded to Paolo. He didn't want to sound stupid, but… *tasting the land*? He didn't want his wine to taste like dirt. He wanted it to taste like sunshine. Like the smell of lake water drying on hot skin, like watching clouds. "It's not bad."

Paolo didn't look convinced. "No. But do you want to kiss a woman who isn't ugly? Or do you want to kiss a woman who is beautiful? Who smiles at you from her eyes?"

This was the problem with dealing with Italians, Evan thought. Why couldn't the guy just say what he meant? Why did everything have to be compared to something else? Did it really take a poet to make wine? He was a businessman. And very good at solving problems. But comparing wine to dirt and women? No. He couldn't do that.

"What would make it better?"

Paolo marched outside into the buttery June sun. Evan followed. After the cool dark of the cavernous winery, it took both men a moment to adjust their eyes. Below them, the lake curved around the northern hills, disappearing as it continued its way twenty miles further, stopping at the North Cascades mountain range to a land of breathtaking beauty. The sloping hills undulated with neat rows of grape vines hanging with ripening fruit, carefully tended as far as the eye could see. The neighboring vineyard to the west, separated by a stony path, belonged to Evan's neighbor, Mr. Alvarez, who had come here from Mexico, working his way from a field laborer to winemaker to landowner in fifty years. The old guy was a legend, and rightly so. His vines were the oldest, most established in the valley, with rich soil eroded from the mineral hills that fed into a crevasse above the vineyard, leaching valuable acidity into the soil with each winter snow melt.

"Those vines." Paolo pointed at his neighbor's field. "You need the old vines to bring depth. Old vines lift minerals deep in the soil. Those vines will make you a real vintner. It's in the land. It always comes back to the land."

Evan frowned. Old Mr. Alvarez had promised to sell him the fields, then changed his mind multiple times. Every time they agreed on a price, the old man went incommunicado until Evan hunted him out at the Apple Cup café in town where he met his cronies for coffee and donuts after church. Compared to those grizzled old guys, Evan always felt like the shiny city slicker with his Patagonia gear and carefully groomed hair. The Apple Cup was a homey café that served biscuits and gravy, down Lake Street, four blocks away from the establishments all the tourists and city slickers like Evan frequented. Although Evan always drove his least flashy car, a Tesla, to the Apple Cup, it still stuck out like a sore thumb amid the beat-up Chevy pick-ups and Sunday-best Tahoes.

When Evan approached the booth at the back of the café, he always asked Mr. Alvarez to speak privately. Mr. Alvarez always said the same thing, waving with his hands around the booth. "Mis amigos can hear anything you got to say."

Mr. Alvarez's friends would look Evan up and down like he was an overpriced heifer on the auction block. Toothpicks shifted in mouths. Expressions remained stony. Evan knew they'd gossip like old women the second after he left but for now, they were Mount Rushmore.

Standing there in the worn café with its decorations of dried flowers and rusted farm implements, Evan felt solidly out of his element. He was never invited to sit down. Never offered a cup of weak coffee in a chipped porcelain mug. Evan would explain that he wanted to buy the vineyard. That they'd agreed on a price and that he'd been trying to call, but Mr. Alvarez wouldn't pick up the phone.

Mr. Alvarez always looked genuinely surprised. "Sell my vines? The fruit of my labor? The fields that paid for my family to get an education, paid for Adella's wedding? The land on which my wife took her last breath?"

"We talked about that, Mr. Alvarez. I don't want to buy your entire estate, just the vineyard."

Mr. Alvarez would laugh at this point. "My estate. You hear that? Like I'm some rich man."

The old men would laugh, although Evan guessed that some of them had apple farms whose land was now worth millions, if they wanted to sell to developers eager to cash in on timeshare developments. Thanks to people like Evan, who drove up the prices, these men were now millionaires on paper.

Evan would point out that the price he offered Mr. Alvarez would, by most people's estimates, make him a wealthy man. But the conversation would inevitably deteriorate into the old geezers lamenting how Chelan had changed since all the Microsoft money had poured into the land, as if Evan wasn't standing right there, hat in hand, the living embodiment of all they despised.

"My daughter says I got to have weddings at the vineyard just to keep up!" Mr. Alvarez crowed. "She's got a few lined up for next month."

Evan felt his pain. Who needed weddings when you had grapes to crush in the fall? Pickers to line up. A festival to coordinate. The Fall Crush festival. Another thorn in his side. Evan wished he could talk to someone about the anxiety of helping plan the Fall Crush. Another thing he'd signed up for, hoping to get to know some locals. But all it meant was more work leading up to harvest time. He was supposed to get permits, sign up sponsors. Assign spaces for the food trucks. What a headache. So far, all the locals he'd met were ones hitting him up for donations for little league teams, the Fourth of July parade, the 4-H youth club and a myriad of high school teams, from mathletes to cheerleaders, when he'd knocked on their door hoping for sponsorship.

For a moment, Evan longed for an invitation to sit down. To commiserate with these men on the difficulty of running an ever-changing business. One that forced you into odd relationships with wedding planners, caterers and people who did things like make ice sculptures for a living and demanded space in your driveway for their refrigerated truck.

All Evan wanted to do was make wine. Prizewinning wine. Evan would love to talk to these men about his own struggles. Learn from them.

But Evan fell on the other side of the divide. He was new money. An interloper. He didn't belong at the table at the Apple Cup, complaining about newcomers. He was a newcomer. So, he always left. Inevitably, before he even reached the door of the Apple Cup, he'd hear the loud guffaws of Mr. Alvarez and his cronies. It always made Evan angry—and maybe just a little bit lonely. Every Sunday a table of friends waited for Mr. Alvarez, eager to talk about the good old days. Before people like Evan showed up and ruined everything.

*

Felicity's office was stark minimalist white with a view of gray Fifth Avenue skyscrapers. The joke was that she had a secret window opening to push out wayward employees.

Carmen looked at the tiny cars crawling through the Seattle traffic. It was a long way down.

Felicity tapped her blood red nails on her glossy white desk. A staccato noise that made Carmen even more nervous.

"Felicity, I have a situation—"

"Stop!" Felicity held an arm out, inches from Carmen's face. Her skin was so paper white Carmen could see the blue veins on her wrist. "Stop right there. I'm so sick of you millennials whining about your rights. Your needs. Your tender little snowflake hearts. When I was your age, I was the first in the office and the last one out." Carmen was the same, but didn't think this was the time to point that out. "If a senior partner told me to pull an overnighter for a campaign, I didn't blink. I kept a change of clothing in the office for just such an occasion. That's how careers get made." Felicity narrowed her eyes to a sliver, raising one perfectly arched brow. "Now, what do you have to tell me?

Carmen gulped. Her heart was beating so fast she could feel a vein pulsing in her throat. "My dad had a heart attack. I have to go to Chelan to take care of him for a week."

Oh no. It just came out. That wasn't what Carmen had meant to say at all. She'd panicked and blurted out a lie.

Felicity blinked three times, tapped her long red nails on the white lacquered desk. "Is he in the hospital?"

Carmen felt her face burning. "Yes." It came out with a squeak.

"And do you have a medical degree that I don't know about?"

Carmen tilted her head. Was Felicity really this mean? "No."

"So, your father is in the hospital being well looked after and you, a person with no medical training whatsoever, are required by his bedside? Not a doctor, or a nurse but a thirty-year-old marketing manager? That's what you're telling me?"

"Yes. I mean, he is my father."

"I understand that. But how exactly is you being there going to make a difference?"

"I'm his daughter."

"Understood. I have a father who had a triple bypass last year and miraculously, the hospital staff managed to perform the surgery without me."

"I'm sorry about your father."

"Don't be." Felicity sighed, gazing hopelessly out the window as if Carmen were a slow student who just didn't get the concept. "I hate to burst your bubble, but this is a business. We work. We do not take vacations in the middle of work unless we schedule them with HR."

"It isn't a vacation."

"A week in Chelan sure sounds like a vacation to me." Felicity pointed to the outer office at all the staffers pretending to work, but tuning in for Felicity's inevitable explosion. "We'd all like to bounce off to Chelan, take in some summer sun, maybe visit your dad while someone else takes care of him, leaving everyone else do the heavy lifting, wouldn't we? I love Chelan as much as the next person, but I have a company to run, don't I? Clients to serve, which right now I can't because you're interrupting me. Again."

How could it go sideways so fast? "My dad *lives* in Chelan. He has Alzheimer's."

Felicity's eyes flashed. "I thought you said he had a heart attack?"

Carmen shook her head miserably. She couldn't keep up the lie. "I did. I thought you'd be more sympathetic to an emergency."

Felicity threw up her arms. "You lied?"

Carmen nodded glumly. "Yes. The truth is that my dad has Alzheimer's and his neighbor has talked him into selling his vineyard, and I'm pretty sure if my dad lost his vineyard it would kill him."

"This doesn't make any sense."

"I'm sorry I said he had a heart attack. I was nervous."

"And nobody else can help your father?"

"No."

"Don't you have two sisters?"

It shocked Carmen that Felicity remembered anything about her family, although she'd probably filed it away for a moment like this one.

"Yes."

Felicity tilted her head. "Sounds like you have a little bit of a Jesus complex."

"There's nothing wrong with wanting to help my father."

"Of course not. But you have responsibilities here and I want you to think long and hard about them before you ask me to take a week off. If you want to schedule a week off in advance with HR, like everyone in this company does, that's fine. But if you keep wasting my time asking for special vacations, you won't have a job. Do I make myself clear?"

Carmen thought about pointing out again that it wasn't a vacation, but Felicity wouldn't listen. There was no point. This had all been decided before she'd even opened her mouth. "Yes."

Carmen's heart was thumping. She swallowed and stood, nearly tripping on a chair on her way out the door.

Deena gave her a sympathetic look as she sat down, tears blurring her vision. Taking three deep breaths, she called Stella.

"How'd it go?" Her friend's voice was reassuring.

"She said I had a Jesus complex."

"I wish. Then you could make water into wine. Did she give you the time off?"

"She threatened to fire me."

"Carmen, come home. Come home and be around semi-normal people. You can help your dad and go out with me. We'll get tipsy and gossip about who's gotten fat since high school, present company excluded."

For a half hour Carmen sat, staring at her computer screen, thinking about Papi signing away the vineyards. She called him three times, but he never picked up the landline that rang in the winery office and Orchard House. Calling again, she listened to his voice message, still thick with his Mexican accent. Imagined him sitting across the kitchen table where she'd done her homework, facing that Microsoft millionaire and his slick attorney, signing papers he'd never bother to have checked by his own attorney. Being duped out of millions on the vines he'd labored his entire life to bring to fruition. Making up her mind, she went back into Felicity's office.

Felicity looked up from her computer. "Seriously? Another fake illness?"

Carmen didn't bother sitting. "I know you won't understand this, but my dad is losing his memory and I have to go take care of him."

Felicity sighed. "We're back to this?"

"He's my father."

"And this is your job."

Carmen shrugged. "Then I quit."

"You can't quit, because I'm firing you."

"You can't fire me, because I just quit."

They looked at one another for a long second. Carmen could hear the traffic, cars honking, in the distance. She felt let down. This was a big moment and yet it felt… blank.

"You finally grew some balls," Felicity spit out.

Carmen was incredulous. "That's a completely sexist thing to say. You're a bully, Felicity. Grow up."

Felicity turned sheet-white. Carmen stood up, clenching her fists to stop trembling. She couldn't believe the words that had come out of her mouth. They were the kinds of things she normally thought of on the way home.

Carmen strode out of the white office with her head held high.

Felicity yelled behind her, "You're going to regret this!"

Deena stood up, smiling broadly. "No, she's not!" She sat down, whispering to Carmen across the half wall. "I'm so jealous."

Every eye in the office was on Carmen. People with whom she'd shared triumphs and failures. Her team. Late night cram sessions and bleary morning meetings ticked through her brain. Blood pounded in her temples. She'd poured years of her life into this place. Her career. What had she just done?

CHAPTER THREE

Alvarez Wines

Five boxes. That was all it took to leave Seattle after six years. Carmen had paid her rent until the end of the month. Her roommate, whom she barely saw, had left Carmen a note, scrawled on the back of a grocery receipt. *Good luck.* At least, that's what she thought it said. Her handwriting was worse than Carmen's. Hard to believe she could live with someone for two years and this was the first time she'd seen her handwriting.

Carmen had parked her car in a loading zone. She'd packed everything into her Toyota within the allotted half hour. Her car was dusty with lack of driving. Two hundred and fifty bucks a month for a parking spot for a car she never drove.

Goodbye Seattle, I can't afford you anymore, she thought as she pulled into the city's infamous traffic.

By the time Carmen reached Blewett Pass, winding her way into the green foothills of the Cascade mountains, the tightness in her shoulders had loosened. She'd stopped seeing Felicity's pinched face every time her mind drifted. Stopped imagining the worst when she reached home. Whatever greeted her when she walked in the door to the old Alvarez house, she'd handle it. How was it that the three sisters hadn't managed to keep better track of their father? How was it that they'd all gotten so absorbed into their own lives that they'd assumed someone else was watching Papi? How was it that it that they'd let their father drift so far into his disease that he might have sold his vineyards?

After crossing Blewitt Pass through the Wenatchee Mountains, she took the freeway exit to the 97, the cloverleaf loop that circled around, passing through an industrial stretch of apple warehouses and RV lots until the Columbia River stretched, jade green and swollen, on the right. Canyon walls bordered the river and the railroad was visible, sometimes spotted with mountain goats. The grassy lawns at Rocky Reach Dam were damp from early evening sprinklers. Under the shrubs, Carmen could see the shapes of little brown bunnies waiting for dusk.

It was all so familiar, so comforting. Carmen rolled down her window, smelling the minerals of the river; the dry, sage-scented air.

Carmen and her sisters used to play a game when they were kids, coming home in the back of the car. First one to spot the lake. Even when she was exhausted after a shopping trip in Wenatchee or a longer excursion to Seattle, she used to squish into the middle seat with her sisters' long black hair blowing into her face, eager for the first glimpse. The road rose up the mountain, passing through the tunnel where they held their breath for good luck, through the scrubby patch of farms with barking dogs running the fence. Once they'd crested the hill and began the long, slow descent, before they hit the vineyards, they'd all search the spot above the road for the first peek of Lake Chelan. Her sisters would push toward the middle of the car.

"I see it! I see it!"

The game never got old. The blue of the lake was their reward, glittering like a turquoise gem in the distance.

"I saw it first!" one of the sisters would scream, even when Carmen knew she'd seen it first, holding it like a secret.

It meant they were home.

Carmen remembered all those trips, the thrill of spotting the lake.

Today was no different. The lake was there for her, glittering, inviting. Signaling life lived at slower speed. Time for swimming. For lazy picnics. For burgers at the Lakeside. For the shared craziness of the harvest.

Home.

She took a left at Pat and Mike's gas station, where they used to jump out of the truck, hopping their way across the hot asphalt, and push into the cool store to sweet-talk Papi, paying at the register, into buying them cones. To the right was the fruit stand where each girl used to pick out a free piece of fruit. The lake shone on Carmen's right as the road hugged the shore. When she was a kid the houses had been much smaller, but as Washington State—and Seattle in particular—had grown in wealth, the lake houses had been snapped up and remodeled, growing up and out. Someone once told her that it was a status symbol to have a lake house nicer than your Seattle house, confirming that these new people were loco.

At night, the southern part of the fifty-one-mile-long lake lit up more every year with house lights. But no matter how crowded the lake grew, every winter the summer people left, the vines were pruned, and everyone settled into a deep snowy calm.

This was, for Carmen, when the lake revealed its true self, whispering its wintery secrets into the ears of those who stood still long enough to listen. Every winter, to give his wife some peace and quiet, and then, after she died, Papi would take any of his daughters willing to hike through the snow up to the trails past the snowmobile park. He'd park his truck, fortifying his girls with a small cup of steaming cocoa from his huge thermos, promising more after their hike. They'd set out on a trail heading for a ridge, keeping an eye out for snowy owls hunting in daylight, for eagles, red foxes like flames against the snow. By the time they'd worn themselves out, they'd reached the ridge. Below them spread the lake, rimmed with ice, sparkling in the winter sun. It ran the length of the valley, disappearing as it turned, outlined with forests and hills, majestic in the weak winter sun.

"Qué hermoso," their father would always pronounce, a slight catch in his breath. *How beautiful.* They'd stand quietly for as long as three little girls could possibly stay still, watching their breath puff in the brittle air. Carmen had known her father was sharing something important. His love of the land. Love of place. The beauty of the lake that was for everyone. Far from the hot Mexican sun.

Now, the turquoise lake glittered in the late afternoon sun. It was as if she'd never left. Five cardboard boxes, a lifetime of bad boss stories. She'd been so busy working, logging long hours at Felicity's whim, eating lunch over her keyboard. Still, it had felt strange leaving with nothing before her but an ailing father, a vineyard piled high with debt. She'd never quit a job in her life without two weeks' notice. She'd worked twelve-hour shifts in freezing cold apple warehouses during high school and college, washed dishes in her dorm dining hall at Washington State University, and never once called in sick. Since she'd been a teenager, she'd always had a job, a regular paycheck.

She'd had to call Stella several times to reassure herself she'd done the right thing.

Running the vineyard was out of the question. As much as she loved Chelan, Carmen couldn't imagine returning to small town life. Or running a complex agricultural business full of seasonal variables and challenges. Drought. Wildfires. Pests. Stiff competition in the Washington market with large vineyards. A small grower had to produce stellar wines that would attract notice by merit alone.

But.

Her father wouldn't even consider selling the vineyard if he were at all capable.

So, who could run the vineyard?

The question nagged her as she drove the last mile home. It was her favorite part of the drive and she barely noticed the scenery. Who could run the vineyard? Who would her father, a perfectionist with high standards, tolerate running the business he'd spent his life cultivating?

She ran down a shortlist of possibilities in her mind. She couldn't come up with one person who could do it.

She enjoyed wine, but her palate wasn't sophisticated. She knew next to nothing about her parents' life work.

For someone who had grown up on a vineyard, it was embarrassing.

*

Every year, like clockwork, Carmen's father repainted the Blue Hills Vineyard sign on Lakeside Drive. It was a rendition of the now iconic Blue Hills label. It was the first impression; he told his daughters. And first impressions were "muy importante." As a girl, Carmen had trailed her father down the drive, holding the paintbrushes, listening to his lecture on appearances. Of course, the first thing was the wine. Always the wine. Then, he'd say, holding up a paint brush layered with just the right amount of paint, came appearances.

Carmen loved when he'd tell the story of hiring a famous local artist to sketch the label for their first wine. She had been very well known, more than they could afford. "We'd eaten beans and rice for weeks to pay for it," Papi laughed. But when he offered her the hefty check, the artist ripped it up, telling him that she could tell she was talking to another artist. She took her commission in wine from their first harvest.

The first thing Carmen noticed when she slowed to take a left onto their property now was the faded sign. She'd always taken the blue and gold sign for granted. One of the million things her father took care of, that nobody thought to question. He just did them. Carmen drove up the long driveway through the apple orchard. Potholes, typically graded and filled every year, pocked the drive. The grass under the trees was overgrown. Some of the tree branches touched one another, the neat rows looking scraggly. Carmen continued up the hill. The flowerbeds flanking Orchard House, normally overflowing with blossoms, were empty. A few dried weeds poked out. The lawn furniture was dirty, left outside over the long winter.

Carmen got out of the car, turning to look down onto the lake. Normally the view cheered her, but today she couldn't enjoy the beauty. The house didn't look right.

She heard voices and walked around the gravel path, opening the squeaking metal gate. Weeds poked up between the flagstones. As she rounded the corner, she saw her father, still in his work clothes, sitting at a dirty metal table. Across from him was a handsome man in his thirties. He stood, looking Carmen up and down with appreciation. Her father stood, too.

"Carmen! You didn't tell me you were coming!" He stepped forward.

"Papi, I did."

Her father shook his head, looking puzzled, his eyes slightly clouded by confusion. He wore the same style of indestructible Carhartt pants he'd worn since she was little, fabric so strong she remembered seeing them half-standing on their own in the laundry room, caked with dirt. They were the exact color of the soil in his vineyards. "You did? When?"

"I called you this morning." *And last night.*

A rush of love overcame Carmen. Her father, the man who answered all the questions, who had swung her from his solid arms, was failing. The weight of it made her want to collapse on the tile floor.

"Oh." He sounded so sad.

Carmen hid her feelings, her longing to share what had happened at work, and smiled brightly, squeezing his hand. "Never mind." She stepped forward to give him a hug. His mustache was a little grayer, his thick wavy hair longer.

Her father looked down at his clothes. "I'm still in my work clothes."

She gave him a solid hug anyway, relieved by his bulk. At least he was still eating.

The younger man stepped forward, offering his hand. "I'm Evan Hollister, your dad's neighbor."

Carmen gave him a cold look, pretending not to notice his proffered hand. Still, Stella wasn't wrong. Evan Hollister was tall, broad-shouldered and green-eyed. A fat Omega watch encircled his wrist. He looked like a man used to getting what he wanted. *Well, sorry, Evan Hollister, this vineyard isn't for sale.* "I know who you are."

Evan raised one eyebrow. He lowered his hand, seemingly not bothered by the obvious snub. "I see."

"You're the one trying to buy the vineyard out from under my father."

Evan scratched his forehead. "Out from under? Where'd you hear that?"

Carmen's father went to fetch another glass from the kitchen. As he passed his daughter, he gave a hushed reminder, "Be nice, daughter. He's our neighbor."

Evan watched the exchange between the two with silent amusement.

"This is a small town, Mr. Hollister. Word travels."

Evan Hollister pulled out a chair for Carmen.

She stayed standing. "I'm fine," she said. "Long drive."

"You're the daughter from Seattle."

"And you're the neighbor who wants my dad's vines."

Evan took a conciliatory tack. "Carmen, look, I know you probably think I'm taking advantage of your father because of his age."

Carmen snorted, making sure her dad was inside before she spoke. "You live next door, watching Blue Hills slowly deteriorate. You notice that each harvest there's fewer and fewer pickers. You hear that the wine master that's worked for my dad for years has left. What would make me think that?"

Evan gazed out at the lake. "I'm not trying to displace him. Just cultivate his vines. I don't know if you know, but your dad is having a hard time managing all this. I thought he might want to retire."

"Blue Hills isn't for sale."

Evan took a sip from his wineglass, his voice low and annoyingly calm. "That's not what your father says."

It was, Carmen thought, the voice of someone with nothing to lose. No skin in the game. A rush of hate flooded Carmen. Sure, it was easy to come in here with millions, taking what you wanted and not bothering with the little guy who'd spent his life building up those vines. They could easily be bought. A lifetime of work disappearing in the time it took to write a check. Suddenly Evan Hollister, with his fancy car and his expensive aftershave, stood for everything that was happening to Chelan. Carmen's small town was changing, and she wanted it back. She wanted to be able to walk into restaurants and know people. To cross the street and not worry about being run over by some sixteen-year-old in a BMW.

Evan Hollister wasn't just a symptom. He was the problem.

Carmen's father returned to the patio from the back door. Orchard House, like everything else, needed painting. Carmen waited until her father had poured her wine to finally sit, pointedly, to join him—not Evan.

The level of disrepair was staggering. Her mother would be rolling in her grave. Even the flagstones under her feet were cracking. Everything about this place needed work. And love. It would take a mountain of effort. But if it would defeat this slick man and his fat checkbook then it would be well worth it. It wouldn't just be a victory for the Alvarez family, it would be a victory for every Chelan County resident who'd been on the receiving end of a newcomer's sneer. It was high time they stuck up for themselves.

Carmen took her time, swirling the wine, enjoying its deep ruby hues as it caught the afternoon sun, just cresting the vineyard hills.

She made a point of looking directly at Evan as she finally responded. "Well, Mr. Hollister, things are going to look a little bit different now. I'm here to look after my father and his land. Whatever it takes."

Evan gave her a long penetrating stare, raising his glass in almost a *touché* gesture. The funny thing was, Carmen thought, he looked like he was enjoying this.

Game on, Mr. Hollister, Carmen thought, as her father looked between the two young people, wondering what he'd missed.

"Carmen, please sit down." Stein Wilfrey had been the family banker for as long as Carmen could remember. He ushered her into his office with the pleased demeanor of a man who'd been there at family occasions and signed off on loans that had helped the Alvarez family achieve their dreams. He was, Carmen realized, part of her father's success.

"Thank you, Mr. Wilfrey," Carmen said, smoothing the skirt she'd worn to make herself seem more businesslike. Less like the kid Mr. Wilfrey had seen sliding on the hardwoods in her stockings at his daughter's wedding. On his desk was the jar of suckers she'd helped empty over the years.

"Oh please, I think you can call me Stein, young lady."

Carmen gulped. *Here goes nothing*, she thought. "Thank you, Stein." It felt strange, but she was here as an adult. Might as well act like one. "I'm here on behalf of my father." The words felt formal and awkward in her mouth.

"How's he doing?" asked Stein, throwing her off with his concern. Of course, she thought, he was Papi's friend.

"Oh, he's fine." Carmen's voice wavered. "Mostly." It was a fine line, since her father was the one with the debt. She certainly didn't want to make it seem like he couldn't run his own business, but she did want to let Mr. Wilfrey—Stein—know that her father had extenuating circumstances.

"His memory?"

Carmen's heart sunk. Was it that bad? She wished for the hundredth time that she'd paid more attention. Not let things get to the stage where Adella had let ditsy Lola take the lead. Lola wouldn't notice a sink hole in her backyard.

"Yes," she said firmly. "It's not so bad that he can't run the winery, but I'm helping him. He's teaching me the business and we'll hire a vintner when we're back on stable ground. I just wanted to see…"

Mr. Wilfrey's eyes clouded over. His fingers tented as he looked out the window at the arid hills, dusty brown in the summer heat. Main Street in Chelan was skirted with pocked roads that quickly gave way to the steep foothills of the Cascade Range. "You wanted to see?"

"To see if, since my father has been such a good client over the years and has some very valuable land, we can have more time." She clasped her hands in her lap to stop herself from fidgeting.

"Ah, yes." Mr. Wilfrey looked truly miserable.

It took every ounce of self-control she had not to apologize and walk out of the bank, head across the street to the Three Horses and day-drink herself silly. Or at least have one very ill-advised glass of wine. But she couldn't. She owed it to her father and her sisters and herself to stay in this plush chair, making this very nice man miserable.

"Carmen," Mr. Wilfrey met her eyes with a pleading stare. His hair was fighting a losing battle with baldness. He looked older than she remembered, and tired. "I'd love nothing more than to give your father an extension on his loan. But this isn't my money. It's the bank's. And your father has defaulted on his payments. Been late. I personally have stretched the limits of what's possible. But we can't run our business this way. We need at least thirty thousand dollars by October first at the very latest. The remaining sixteen thousand would be due in early December."

Carmen grasped her hands until they were white. "I'm not sure we can make it. I don't know how we're going to come up with the harvest this year."

"Can one of your sisters take out a line of credit? Maybe on a house?"

Carmen shook head. "Adella is the only homeowner. She has three children who might need braces or college tuition."

Stein shook his head. "I'm sorry. Nobody wants the Blue Hills Vineyard to stay in business more than I do."

Carmen stood, shaking his hand. "I know."

"If anyone can keep things running, it's you girls." His voice was strained with emotion. "Your dad raised some very fine young women."

"Thank you, Mr. Wilfrey." *Stein.* She didn't bother correcting herself. There wasn't any point.

Carmen walked out of the bank into the breathtaking heat. It shimmered off the sidewalk as a gaggle of tweens with damp hair and ice cream cones passed, blissfully absorbed in their own drama.

Buoyed by the vision of happy girls, Carmen steeled herself. She was going to have to learn how to run a winery and beat Evan Hollister at his own game. He might have money, but she had history and a tough family on her side.

Her car was achingly hot. She couldn't stand it. Instead of taking a left down to the lake, Carmen turned right and then right again, driving through the oldest homes in Chelan. Built a century before the word "McMansion" arrived, these Victorian beauties were in various states of disrepair. Her mother's favorite was still the same soft purple-blue with pink and white trim. The yard was thick with blooming white lilacs and gladioli, a flower that had fallen out of fashion but her mother had loved. On the freshly painted white porch were three large rockers. Her mother always used to say "One for the wife, one for the husband and one for the cat."

Funny, the things she remembered.

Mama used to walk her up here after shopping, sharing a bag of licorice, just to visit her homes. She had her own nice home, but liked to visit her "ladies." She only took one girl at a time and Carmen had always felt special when it was her turn.

Carmen reached her destination, rolled down her window and said a silent thank you for the breeze. The cemetery seemed to catch a breeze on even the stillest day. Her father had chosen a beautiful spot overlooking the lake. She sat down at the bench near the grave, looking at her mother's tombstone. *Another fine job, Papi,* she thought. Thirty-five years old. Five years older than Carmen was now. The sweet smell of ponderosa pine blew through the graveyard, refreshing her. The flowers that Papi brought every Sunday were still fresh. Carmen poured more water into the vase.

"Don't worry, Mamacita. We'll take care of him. He's going to be showing his grandchildren how to trim suckers. Papi is going to be fine."

Carmen patted the gravestone, hoping she wasn't making an idle promise.

She'd have to come through. For herself, for all them. It wasn't just land. It was their history.

Standing in their way was a very attractive obstacle. Evan Hollister. The embodiment of everything wrong in Chelan. Entitled, spoiled, arrogant and ambitious.

Hating him was going to be fun.

CHAPTER FOUR

Wedding Belles

"He's like a poster for privilege," Carmen snapped, wiping the sweat from her brow, smudging her flushed skin with dirt.

"Or, like, the cover of a romance novel. I wonder what he looks like without his shirt on." Stella tilted her head as if admiring a fine painting or view.

"I don't," Carmen snapped. "Doesn't it bother you? We're here sweating our butts off and he's sipping iced tea while his minions do the work for him."

"He's providing a valuable service."

"By standing there?"

"You have to admit, he improves the view."

Carmen rolled her eyes. Stella had always been like this and normally it was funny. But why couldn't she find Evan Hollister as thoroughly annoying as Carmen did? Although Stella was certainly putting in some serious labor helping her. The salon was dark today. She'd arrived at nine to help. It was three o'clock, eighty degrees and they were both exhausted and covered in a fine layer of rich red dirt.

It was Monday. Carmen had four days to get the patio, the pool and the main floor of Orchard House in shape before the first wedding planner came. She wasn't at all sure she could do it in time. She was having dreams of walking outside with a snooty bride and finding a sink hole in the back yard.

Stella dropped a heavy flagstone in the dirt, looking up the hill at the two figures on the Hollister patio, highlighted in the sun, peering down at them. "Is that his girlfriend?"

"Who cares?" Carmen offered her friend a glass of cold water. If she was perfectly honest, though, she was curious. What kind of stuck-up woman would Evan drag over from Seattle? She'd be the kind to complain that her rosé wasn't chilled enough. Carmen knew the type. They dressed for other women and bought competitive handbags.

Carmen sipped at her water. The ice chips floating on the top reminded her of opening the freezer and finding it nearly locked in ice. Her father must have left it ajar at some point. It was like peering into a miniature Antarctic. The first two days back Carmen had spent indoors, cleaning out the freezer and fridge, going through the house systematically, making lists of what needed to be done. There were three pages of repairs. Anything that wasn't directly in front of her father had been ignored. If she thought about it too long, Carmen felt a weight pressing down on her. At times, she'd been tempted to pick up the phone and call the number that jerk Evan had left. Tell him she'd changed her mind. It was too much. She'd go back to Seattle. Find someone who wasn't poisoned by the rumors Felicity had surely floated. Start at the bottom in a smaller firm.

But when she imagined someone else harvesting the vines or her father without his acres to walk through, she changed her mind.

His nightly walk through the vineyard was an accounting of his life. His accomplishments. No. She'd persevere.

She'd wake up and begin the endless and seemingly insurmountable amount of work. The more she worked, the more she noticed new things. A broken irrigation system. Barrels that smelled of mold. A vineyard was a mountain of chores at the best of times. Her father had fallen so far behind, it would take years to catch up.

Stella gulped down the entire glass, pulling Carmen back into the conversation. "Hello? I care. An eligible millionaire moved in next door. Are your eyes working? He's gorgeous. And rich. What about that combination doesn't work for you?"

"Stop looking at him," Carmen hissed.

"He can't hear you."

"He probably has listening devices planted on the hill."

Stella gave her a weird look. "Okay, what's up?"

Carmen took a long drink from her own glass to give herself time. "What's up is that he's one of those super aggressive types who thinks he can barge in here and take Papi's land."

"Last I heard, he offered you a bunch of money. He's not a pirate, although that is a super sexy image."

"Do you know what's going to happen if Papi doesn't have those vines? That land is his history. It's ours."

Stella sat down on a pile of broken flagstones, uncharacteristically somber. They'd been at the tail-end of fourth grade during Carmen's mother's illness. Carmen had been at Stella's house when Mercedes died, two weeks before spring break. Stella had composed filthy songs about cancer and distracted Carmen with facials made from honey and oats, rainbow manicures and thrift shopping for denim. Raiding cherry orchards by night. Anything to keep her friend busy.

Juan had poured his grief into the dirt, the grapes, the wine. Everything he cared about was right there. His girls. His land. There was nothing else.

"Fair point."

"Exactly. And that guy"—Carmen pointed up the hill—"isn't the kind of guy who will quit. He'll figure out a way to get our vines, no matter what we do."

Stella finished her water, setting the glass down on the table. She picked up another broken piece of slate, admiring the mica glinting in the sun. She looked up at her friend, grinning. "Then you'll just have to stay here and thwart him."

Carmen smiled broadly. "That's the plan."

Stella lifted her glass. "Let the thwarting begin."

*

"It's so much worse than I thought," Carmen said, looking around the Three Horses wine café, seeking familiar faces. She'd brought Stella here as a small thank you for all her hard work. The place was jammed with tourists sipping local wines, eating cheese platters, and comparing tans and dinner plans.

Stella's wrist jangled with an armful of bracelets as she put down her glass of rosé. "Yeah, I was surprised."

Carmen gazed into her glass, swirling the wine absentmindedly. "Did I ignore it?"

Stella shook her head. "Maybe, a little? You were on a pretty tight leash, Car. Arriving late at night, leaving early. Remember that

Christmas I drank champagne with your sisters while you wrote that stupid proposal?"

Carmen sighed. "Yes, it was awful. Orchard House needs about five years of back maintenance, if not more. Paint, roof. You saw the orchard. It would be totally fine if the wedding theme was Zombie Apocalypse, but anyone who thought a wedding would work there now is out of their mind."

"That would be your sister."

"Lola," they both said at the same time.

Lola was a jump-first ask-questions-later kind of girl. Carmen had found a brochure for Blue Hills weddings that had Lola's fingerprints all over it. Weddings at wineries were a solid thing now. Winter was a time for the vines to grow, the fruit to cultivate. In the meantime, wineries produced no income, excluding wine sales. Blue Hills Vineyard hadn't produced a vintage in two years. They'd need money to pay the harvest crew, the warehouse workers, the bottlers, everything.

Weddings were the obvious choice. Chelan had become a wedding destination. Blue Hills Vineyard had breathtaking views. Local rental and catering businesses flourished. The problem was that Lola had booked everything, then, without so much as a backwards glance, returned to art school. She was enrolled in the Art Institute of Seattle, racking up student loans, and as usual, had left someone else holding the bag.

"The problem is we can't get ready in time for those weddings and we can't *not* do them. Papi owes everyone. My heart goes crazy just looking at his books. If we aren't a wedding venue, we can't hire pickers. He can't even afford to pay his wine master. I have no idea how we're going to make the wine this year. We can't afford anyone. All the wine masters have been hired for the year. But if we don't harvest, we don't have a prayer at paying the back taxes. It's a disaster."

Stella scratched her head. "That hot millionaire next door has a master vintner he brought all the way from Italy. The man is yum on a stick."

Carmen laughed despite herself. "Yum on a stick?"

Stella nodded enthusiastically. "Yes! Totally. Don't get me started on his accent." Stella pulled out her shirt, blowing lightly into her cleavage.

Carmen rolled her eyes. "What good does that do me?"

"He's next door. Get to know him. Do your research. You might not be able to hire him, but you might be able to pick his brain."

"And what about the weddings?"

Stella rolled up her sleeves and flexed her biceps, poking one and frowning comically. "They might not be much, but they're all yours."

Carmen tilted her head, teary-eyed with gratitude. "Have I told you lately that I love you?"

Stella smiled her crooked grin. "I'm so happy you're back. We can do this. The two of us make one superhero."

Carmen nodded. "But weddings, as in plural?"

Stella counted on her fingers. "You've got Adella, Lola, your dad, and"—she raised her eyebrows—"this fine specimen here. You're the organized one. Make a list."

Carmen's face lit up. "My three favorite words." She opened notes on her phone. "First we text my sisters."

Stella finished her wine, signaling the waitress for another round. By the time their glasses were topped up, the girls had a plan.

*

"The ice sculpture can go over here. And—wait—no, over here."

Evan had thought he'd met fast talkers in his life, but this wedding planner put them to shame. The woman tumbled from one thought to the next like lemmings off a cliff. Now she was gazing off into the distance with a dreamy look on her face that made Evan rolls his eyes. What he wouldn't pay to shut her up and hustle her off his property.

Oblivious to his distress, the wedding planner kept babbling. "I love that people can look at the view through the center of the sculpture. Isn't that so gorgeous?" The woman didn't walk, she flowed, waving her arms through the confusion of white gauze cascading from her belled sleeves.

Why does anyone need such big sleeves? Evan wondered.

Bored out of his mind for the last half-hour, he'd counted how many times she'd said the word "gorgeous". Thirty-five and counting. "It will melt," Evan said flatly. "No shade."

The wedding planner, whose name was Maura or Mavis or something mumsy, gave him an exaggerated sad look, trailing her fingers from under her eyes like tears. "Can't we put up a canopy?"

"Sure, if you want it to blow into the field."

Evan's pricey PR person, Mandy, shot him a look. She was the one that was so hot on this wedding thing, insisting that weddings drove the wine business and you couldn't replicate the word of mouth from five good weddings hosted on the vineyard property. Evan had insisted that he hadn't gone into the wine business to host weddings.

"Did you go into the wine business to fail?" she'd shot back. She knew exactly how to manage her high profile, type-A clients. Threaten them with failure.

Evan trailed the bubbly wedding planner around his own property as she insisted that eighty-degree weather wouldn't melt an ice sculpture and wind coming off the lake wouldn't hurl a canopy into the air. Clearly the woman had never heard of physics. But, as Mandy would tell him, that wasn't his problem.

Maura or Mavis asked if she could float flowers and candles in the pool.

"No!" Evan said crankily just as Mandy said, "Sure."

Maura or Mavis frowned, looking like a toddler who'd just lost her cookie.

"Excuse us," said Mandy, dragging Evan into a shaded corner of the pool patio. "You're going to scare her off and if you do, the other wedding planners will follow suit. Buck up, tell her can you do things and stop acting like I dragged you into this."

"You did drag me into this."

Mandy continued scolding, but Evan stopped paying attention. He was watching the two women on the Orchard House patio in the distance, working hard with brooms and shovels, cleaning off the debris and broken flagstones. Carmen was staying. Despite her annoying attitude, she was attractive in that plucky way Evan found irresistible. Now all he had to do was convince her to sell off the vines that he needed. All this stupid wedding stuff wasn't going to make a bit of difference if he didn't have a medal. His bottles needed those little gold stickers if they were going to fly off the shelves. The First Crush medal, awarded by fellow vintners, would, if things went as planned, belong to Hollister Estate Winery. Losing wasn't something Evan Hollister did.

He was so close. If he could just harvest the vines on the next hill, he'd be there. He could hire any master vintner in the country and get rid of smarmy Paolo. He'd be right on track, producing award-winning wines. Carmen Alvarez was the only one standing in his way.

"Evan!" Mandy was yelling at him. "Are you listening to me?"

"Yes." *No.*

Mandy stepped closer to the edge of the embankment, bordered by arctic willows blowing in the breeze. The sharp scent of oregano drifted up the hill. She peered down below, catching sight of the two attractive women working on the bordering estate. "Liar. Who's that?"

"Carmen Alvarez." He watched the way Carmen wiped the sweat off her face, not minding the dirt. She'd take a break to gaze down the length of the lake, stretching her back before lifting another heavy piece of slate. Carmen would remember the woman's name. She'd easily answer all the silly questions. He wouldn't ignore Carmen if she was talking. Even if the subject was weddings.

Mandy looked more closely at her employer. "There are two women down there. How did you know which one I was talking about?"

Evan woke up. "I didn't. Listen, I'm sorry." He turned around, dutifully trotting over to the wedding planner, who was pouting near the rose garden.

Evan turned on the charm, smiling broadly, waving at the expanse of fragrant budding roses. If there was one thing that powered Evan to the top, it was his ability to close the deal. It was a switch he flipped that lit up a room. This ability had decimated the competition within and without Microsoft. It had allowed him to retire at thirty-five and buy up fifty-eight acres of lake view property complete with a budding vineyard, as well as a thirty-five-room mansion with a flagstone patio on the Lake Cuomo of the Pacific Northwest. "This will be completely ablaze with roses during the wedding. We can put the ice sculpture there"—he pointed towards the house—"under the canopy to protect it. I promise you, it'll be an amazing wedding. You have my word."

Maura or Mavis lifted off her kitten heels, clapping her chubby hands, completely under his spell. "Oh, goody. My bride will be so excited. I'm bringing her here next week. For champagne, correct?"

"Correct," said Evan, trying to keep his enthusiasm from flagging. He had no idea how he was going to survive one wedding, let alone five.

What on earth had he gotten himself into?

*

Entering the overly air-conditioned Safeway from the baking heat of Chelan was always a challenge. Carmen remembered Mami, who used to work here, bringing a sweater every time she grocery shopped. Carmen always forgot. She was shivering and rubbing her arms when she spotted Evan, perusing the aisles like a lost toddler. He had that deer in the headlights look worn by men who had never been forced to grocery shop. Someone else was always there to feed them. She backed her cart out of the aisle, hoping he hadn't seen her.

Was he stalking her? This was the third time Carmen had seen Evan in town. Sure, Chelan was tiny, but three times in one week? This was more than a coincidence.

The first time, he'd been sitting at the Three Horses Wine Café. Carmen had nodded as she passed him on her way to meet Stella. He'd looked up eagerly, but she hadn't stopped. Perhaps it came off as rude, but she didn't care. She was tired of his seeing his lean profile every time she looked up from the patio, sweaty and tired. Inevitably, he had a glass of wine in his hand and a pretty woman nearby. She was always sweaty, dead tired and running behind.

The second time, she was able to cross the street and avoid him. She'd been on her way to the bank to talk about her plans for Blue Hills Vineyard. She looked up and there he was, walking down the sidewalk on his phone. A quick detour had prevented the encounter.

But this time, at the Safeway, her dodge didn't work. He came around the corner pushing his cart, practically bumping into her, eager as a puppy. His chipper mood made her feel sour. Of course he was happy. He was gloating. He hadn't spent the week doing backbreaking work, dealing with painters who demanded to be paid up front—in cash—and then showed up with the wrong color paint insisting it was what she'd ordered. He wasn't worried about money or facing a deadline that seemed impossible to meet. The man was a walking advertisement for prosperity. Even his white teeth bugged her. Would it kill him to have a tiny little imperfection?

She hated him.

"Oh, hi neighbor!" Evan was walking on sunshine. *Blech!* Carmen forced a smile. "Are you having guests over?"

Carmen looked down at the steaks in her shopping cart. "Yes." When he waited for her to share more information, she reluctantly added, "My sisters."

"That's great. I only have one brother. He's a lot older. We hardly see each other."

Carmen wasn't looking forward to having her sisters spend two nights. They'd both complain about Carmen's plan to mess with Hollister Estate wines. And argue over the direction of the vineyard. The one thing the Alvarez sisters had in abundance, besides great hair, was opinions. They'd all talk at once, agree on nothing and end up arguing until their father took his cigar to the fields for some peace and quiet, telling them they were all crazy, but he loved them anyway. Carmen was dreading it. She had five good ideas her sisters would pick apart like vultures.

"I heard that you're planning to host weddings this summer?" Evan asked.

Carmen nodded, annoyed that he had a bead on her. "Yep. We're gearing up."

"Yeah, so that's actually what I wanted to talk to you about."

"Me?" This took Carmen by surprise.

"Yes. I need help."

She raised her eyebrows doubtfully. Surely this man could hire any help he wanted. Evan wore fitted khakis, a spotless white Lacoste shirt. His Ray-Bans were propped up on his wavy, damp hair. Carmen was glad she'd taken a shower, applied lotion and a flick of mascara, then felt agitated with herself for caring. "With what?"

Evan tilted his head, wincing. "Everything." He looked around the grocery store aisle as a mother with three children hanging from her overloaded cart approached. "Look, would you mind coming over to discuss things? I could make you dinner."

Here was the enemy asking for help. Carmen's first instinct was to laugh in his face, tell him she was busy and keep walking. However, her father had always told her to keep her friends close and her enemies closer. Besides, if she knew more about what Evan had planned, it would be easier to thwart him.

Maybe this was a prime opportunity. This could be a way to meet the Italian vintner. So far, she hadn't engineered a conversation with Paolo. Evan seemed to be everywhere, but she had yet to lay eyes on the elusive foreigner. Carmen was waking up at six just to deal with the mountain of paperwork and taxes her father had stuffed in a drawer, and staying up until three trying to figure out how they were going to make wine without a wine master. Her father knew the rudiments of wine making, but he'd relied on his wine master. It took so much attention to detail. The growing of the grapes, which he'd learned as boy, was imprinted in his memory forever, but the intricate steps of fermentation, decanting, and the tasting of the new wine was something he'd always hired an expert to handle. Even if they had the money for a master wine maker, they'd all been snapped up.

Carmen and Evan moved their carts to the side of the aisle to let the beleaguered mother pass them like a tropical storm.

The aisle smelled like Cocoa Puffs and canned coffee. Evan was still looking at her hopefully. "Dinner? I'll grill something?"

Carmen took a deep breath. Perhaps he did know how to cook. Maybe his look of confusion was just shopping in an unfamiliar store. She caught a whiff of expensive aftershave. Something green and masculine. She didn't want anything wearing down her distaste for this man. He was everything that was wrong with Chelan. The price of real estate. The obnoxious boats on the lake, polluting the serenity. The entitlement.

Suddenly she felt tired. She wanted this harvest to be over. To get the vineyard back on its feet, find someone to live with her father and move back to Seattle. She couldn't see herself in Chelan, running a vineyard.

"It's only dinner," Evan said, as if he could read her mind. "This woman I hired to help me manage the weddings is driving me crazy. Half the time I don't know what she's talking about. I need a system and she's talking about naked cakes. I didn't know cakes were supposed to wear clothes. I need someone to look at the space and tell me how it should be set up, so all these wedding planners don't drive me off the deep end."

He was speaking her language. A system. Maybe that's what she needed for her wine. Besides, Evan had a master winemaker. A plan hatched in her mind. She smiled broadly. "Yes, I'd love to come to dinner. I'll bring the wine."

"Great. It's a date."

They both blushed scarlet.

"I didn't mean that." His face flushed darker under his tan. "I mean, I did. It's a time to come over and eat food. But not like a date-date. Just a…" He gripped the shopping cart until his knuckles were white. "Okay, I'm going to leave now before I say more stupid things."

She couldn't help but smile and immediately regretted it. "You do that."

He pushed his sunglasses over his eyes, wheeling down the aisle, whistling. She watched him for a second, thinking it wasn't fair for a man to look that good. He reversed himself until he was parallel with her. She hadn't moved. "I didn't tell you a date. I mean, a day."

"You didn't." Was that pine in his aftershave? Still, she hated him. She did.

He covered his eyes with his hand, taking a deep breath. "Okay, I'm going to stop humiliating myself and put it out there. Saturday. Does Saturday work?"

They were both thinking the same thing. *Saturday night.* For a guy who claimed this wasn't a date, he sure chose an odd night.

"It's a cake with the frosting scraped off," she said.

He raised his eyebrows. "What?"

"Naked cake."

He frowned. "No frosting? Why have a cake?"

"Exactly." She couldn't help but grin, quickly reminding herself that this man was out to ruin her father. There was something enormously appealing about someone so obviously in charge in every other area of his life completely losing it over something as silly as having a neighbor over for dinner. "Saturday works."

"Okay, it's not a date. It's a time to eat."

"And drink."

He grinned, delighted. "Yes! Six o'clock?"

"See you at six."

He waved. "Bye, neighbor."

"Bye, neighbor." She forced herself to stop watching him, pushing her cart down the aisle. Tension crept into her shoulders. *Breaking bread with Evan Hollister?*

It's not a date, she said to herself. *It's a mission.*

CHAPTER FIVE

It's a Date

"You have a date with the millionaire next door!" Stella chortled. They were in Stella's salon, Twig, an airy space Carmen loved. Stella had decorated with squat white pots overflowing with lovingly tended plants. The woman in Stella's chair, Esther, eyes blinking like a baby bird under a crown of tin foil, was her last customer of the day.

Esther, who worked in the pharmacy and had known the girls since they were teens, was peering over her People Magazine, eager for hot gossip. The whole town adored rumors about one of the entitled newcomers. There were two Chelans. The people who served the drinks, bagged the groceries, cleaned the hotels, taught the children, served the burgers; and the ones who swooped in from Seattle and bagged the brand-new mansions growing like weeds along the shores of the increasingly crowded lake. Ten years ago, the summer people decamped back to their Seattle mansions immediately after Labor Day. Now they stayed to run their wineries and overpriced restaurants, catering to each other in a tightly knit closed circle. Sure, they might say hello to the people who cleaned their houses and serviced their hot tubs, but they weren't inviting them over for dinner.

"It's not a date," Carmen insisted, again.

Stella checked the color on Esther's foil, unwrapping a strand, glancing quickly at it in the daylight streaming from the storefront window. Stella's bright modern salon had three chairs, but the other stylists had left early. Although Carmen had to get home and prepare for the dinner with her sisters, she'd found herself driving past. When a parking spot had opened in front of the salon she'd seen it as a clear sign for her to pop in and share the latest news.

"He invited you over for dinner on a Saturday night. He's cooking. At his place. What do you call that, Esther?"

Esther looked up from under her headful of tin foil. Her eyes watered from the bleach. "A date."

Carmen shook her head. "He wants to get advice on his wedding planning business."

"He's planning weddings?"

"Not planning them, hosting them all summer. At his winery."

Esther nodded. "I heard he's been booked for months. His place is gorgeous. I heard that Bill and Melinda Gates will be at one of them. Their friend's daughter is getting married. They'll have security."

Stella was studying Carmen with intensity.

"What?"

"We need to add some caramel highlights to your hair."

Carmen backed up towards the door. "Oh no. You're not fixing me up for a business meeting."

"It's a date," Stella said.

Carmen pushed open the door. "Stop it."

"I'll stop it if you admit that he's the hottest thing to set foot in this valley."

"He's the most egotistical thing to set foot in this valley. I'll give you that."

"I'll squeeze you in tomorrow," Stella shouted as the door closed.

Carmen waved as the door shut, rushing back to her car. She'd better get those steaks in the fridge and steel herself for her sisters. The Alvarez sisterhood was strong, fierce and always something of a battle zone.

*

Juan Alvarez knew something was up the moment he walked onto the patio. His normally chatty daughters, always arguing and laughing, were strangely subdued. Bats swooped over the vineyard, dining on mosquitos. Adella asked about his visit to the cemetery.

Juan filled his wineglass, helping himself to steak and salad, saying a quiet prayer for the family before answering. He took a moment, savoring a small sip of wine. "The usual. Quiet. Nice. I talked to your mother. She listened." He took a bite of the meat.

Lola nudged Carmen under the table, but he saw it. He'd forgotten what the girls had told him about their gathering, but there was a reason. It was palpable.

"Papi," Carmen began. "Do you want to sell your vineyard to that gringo next door?"

Juan had to smile. It was funny hearing his American daughter call anyone a gringo. His daughters spoke Spanish with American accents. Thought nothing of spending what used to be a day's wages for him as a teenager on a cup of frothy coffee. They knew little of the life he'd had in Mexico and his youth in the United States. Which is exactly the way he wanted it.

Juan shook his head. "No. Of course not mi corazón. I want to walk those fields until my boots turn up. But we can't always have what we want, can we? You girls don't want to grow the wine. I can't hire anyone no more. That gringo, as you call him, wants to expand his fields. Maybe it's time."

Adella and Lola glanced at Carmen. Her eyes glittered in the growing dusk. They hadn't yet turned on the patio lights. The night sky faded from pale magenta to deep purple. His girls looked so beautiful, all of them. Grown women. Maybe this was good time to give them their inheritance. What he could squeeze from the fields. The man next door had offered him a good price.

"Papi, do you trust me?" Carmen asked.

Juan smiled, placing his hand over his heart. "Con todo mi corazón."

If it weren't for these girls, each so like their mother, he didn't know what he would have done. They'd saved him.

"Do you trust me to run the winery?" Carmen asked.

Adella scratched her throat: a sign, Juan knew, that his eldest wasn't quite comfortable. He studied his middle daughter. Carmen had been gone so long, had shown little interest as a child, a girl. But she was his best bet. Unencumbered by family. A head for business. All the work she and her friend had done to the house, the patio. They were planning on hosting parties of some sort. He couldn't remember what kind. They needed Orchard House back to its original splendor, like when Mercedes ran things. Casa Huerta.

Orchard House. Mercedes had chosen the name the day they'd signed the mortgage. He'd let it get so run down. Days slipped away before he remembered what he'd planned. He'd go to bed with big ideas only to have the next day fly away, a kite with a snipped string.

Although he wasn't quite telling the truth, Juan nodded. "Yes. Sí. You want to try and get through this harvest? We can sell the crush, have someone else make the wine."

Carmen looked at her sisters before responding. Although she didn't know much about wines, she knew that the price of the unfermented crush, basically grape juice, was vastly different than casks of Blue Hills wines. "We have to make it ourselves."

The old man shook his head sadly. "We don't have a wine master."

"I know one." Or she'd get to know one. Even if it meant spending time with Evan Hollister.

Juan studied his daughter. He remembered the feeling of wanting something so desperately that facts had no bearing on what burst from in his heart. He could see the spark in her eyes. She wanted this very badly. What was the worst thing that could happen? She'd find her task impossible. Learn that you could desperately want something but that the world wouldn't bend to your will. Grapes don't ripen, land doesn't produce, casks aren't properly turned, wine sours, insects invade, fires burn, and it has nothing to do with the effort, sweat, hours, days and months of your life. All of it could amount to nothing. She might discover that life doesn't care about your passion.

He owed it to her to let her find out on her own. It was one of the hard and beautiful lessons of making a living off the land. She was young. It wouldn't break her. And if she got a taste for it, the Alvarez name would continue in the wine world.

"Do you know what you're taking on?" Juan asked his middle daughter.

She nodded.

She didn't. How could she?

Juan admired her surety. Saw something of himself in her firm nod. "Then I will help you." He raised his glass, thinking of his wife. How many years had it been since they named their fledgling winery? Too many. "To Blue Hills Vineyard."

The three Alvarez women raised their glasses in the purple dusk. "Blue Hills," they repeated, each of them smiling at their own thoughts.

This, Juan thought, was about to get interesting.

*

Evan's dog whined to be let out. Evan had thought about an evening swim and went to check on the water. He heard them when he stepped out onto the patio. Laughter. Cackling, if he was honest. Coming from Carmen's patio. Evan knew he should turn on a light, let them know someone was listening, but he couldn't help it. Carmen had fascinated him from the moment he'd laid eyes on her. Smart, serious, charming and sexy as hell. Pursuing her would be impossibly difficult. Wonderfully challenging.

Life-altering, perhaps.

He padded in his bare feet to where the dog was sniffing the wind. Three women sat around one of the patio tables, the wind whipping their hair, their faces shadowed by the light coming from hurricane lamps. Each of them held a round goblet of red wine. One of them talked and the others laughed hysterically.

They all gestured with their hands, adding to the conversation with glee.

It wasn't your typical late-night hushed gathering. Evan bent over the embankment, trying to hear what they were saying. He could only hear individual words, whipped away before they made sense by the wind rushing down the lake. Carmen's sisters. Even if he hadn't recognized them, anyone could tell from their shadowy silhouettes that these women were related. Their dark hair, mannerisms and familiar intimacy left little doubt.

The three Alvarez sisters were all home. Evan was sure that they had gathered for a reason. He shifted uneasily.

Those women were up to something.

CHAPTER SIX

Up the Hill

A guttering candle flickered on the patio table. This table had hosted more family dinners than Carmen could count. Summer birthday parties, first communions and quinceañera parties that confused the neighbors until Lola had insisted that her invitation said "Sweet Fifteen". Mami's funeral feast with enough food to feed the entire town. Tonight, four wineglasses stood nearly empty as the evening wound down. Stella had arrived late, enjoying the cool night air after waiting two hours for the air-conditioning repairman to arrive at the salon.

Papi had fallen asleep hours ago with his window open. Carmen smiled at the thought of him drifting off to his favorite sound: his daughters and his honorary hija, "bonita Stellita," as he affectionately called her, chatting on the patio. Carmen knew he thought it was a shame her parents had moved to Arizona. Juan never understood people who willingly left their adult children.

Leaning back in her chair, Carmen looked up the hill, noticing Evan's dog sniffing the night wind. Her stomach ached with laughter. Adella had told a hysterical story of a squirrel who'd run up one twin's leg and back, chittering angrily from atop the poor boy's sunhat while the other twin screamed for Mommy. Sister stories were the best.

Stella dropped an ice cube into her first glass of wine. "Do your sisters know that you have a date with Mr. Microsoft tomorrow night?"

"Exaggerate much?" Carmen sighed. It was wonderful, sitting down. The muscles down her back and legs ached from weeding and pulling up heavy slate.

Adella frowned. "I'm so confused. You hate him, but you're going out on a date?"

Carmen shook her head. "Stella is the one calling it a date. I'm getting to know his weak spots."

Lola speared a tomato with her fork, popping it into her mouth as she gazed at her phone. "Such as?"

"His hotness," Stella said. "Just looking at him you'd assume he was dumb, but clearly he's not if he's inviting Carmen for dinner."

Adella's eyebrows arched. "What if Carmen is his weak spot?"

Carmen shook her head, annoyed. "I'm right here. Don't talk about me in the third person."

Adella nodded. "That's one weak spot, what's another?"

Lola flipped her phone face-down. "Being one of those annoying people showing off their Stratus Rewards Visa." Adella gave her an arch look. "Okay, maybe he doesn't, but he's probably been invited. It comes with a concierge service and a jet share."

"I'd get one," Stella sighed. "In a heartbeat."

Carmen ignored them. "His vines are newer and weaker. Shallow roots."

Adella nodded. "Which is why he wants ours..."

Carmen nodded. "*I'm* using him, he is *not* using me."

"Why can't Carmen take one lousy night off and enjoy the company of a hot, rich dude?" Stella objected. "And a free meal?"

"Says the girl who decorated her salon to attract wealthy people. You haunted Pinterest before you chose a lick of paint," Carmen pointed out. "You wanted to charge a hundred dollars a haircut."

Stella shrugged. "I like money. Everybody does."

Adella glanced at her phone, mumbling something about her children and needing to wake up at the crack of dawn to drive home. "We need a plan."

Carmen glanced up the hill while Stella topped off their glasses. There was a dark shape beside the dog on the Hollister patio. Was it a shrub, a sheathed umbrella or Evan, spying on them, eavesdropping? She kept her voice low. "Stella and I thought..." It was surprisingly hard to say in a group, even to her sisters. "Sabotage? Nothing terrible, just enough to slow him down."

Stella nodded. "Mess with the business."

"Oooooh! So dramatic," Lola said. "We could snip his vines. Bleed them."

Adella winced. "Lola! We're not *those* people."

Stella waved her arm at the dark, rolling Hollister Estate vineyard hills. "Too many plants. We'd definitely get carpal tunnel syndrome."

"We'd be the first suspects," Carmen said.

Adella drummed her short nails on the iron table. "We could mess with his irrigation system, but it's probably illegal."

Carmen shook her head. “He’d have it fixed within two hours. He’d reprogram some computer system and bam, back in business.”

Stella sighed. “And we’d be in jail.”

“Sabotage,” Lola whispered theatrically as she scrolled through her fellow art students’ Instagram feeds. “Such a fun word.”

Carmen sat up. “I’ve got it. We make our business more attractive by default. Whatever he’s doing to attract customers—wine tastings, hosting events, winery tours, whatever it is—we subtly ruin it.”

Lola lifted a finger. “We do it so that even if he suspects something, he can’t prove a thing.”

Carmen blinked, opening her mind to the possibilities, already making a mental list. “Okay, okay, let’s brainstorm.”

Stella wrapped an arm around Carmen, hugging her. “You’re insane and I love you.”

Carmen gazed up at the celestial view that had informed her childhood. Her small corner of earth. “We can’t let him win.”

Adella pushed her chair back, heading into the house. “We need more wine.”

Lola nodded, biting her lip. “Car, what would you think if I dropped out of art school and stayed here to help? My student loans have run out. I can’t make tuition, and this seems like a lot more fun.”

Carmen resisted the urge to lecture, to warn her that this wouldn’t be fun and games. It was business. “I think that would be awesome.”

Lola grinned happily. “This is going to be the weirdest first date ever.”

Carmen’s lips tensed. “Not a date.”

Stella uncorked the next bottle. "Keep protesting, Car. It's totally believable."

Carmen finished planting the last anthurium and took a long, hot shower, digging out an old toothbrush to get the dirt from under her nails. There wasn't time to paint them, but at least she'd get them clean. As she studied her closet, she could hear her father whistling below, getting himself dinner in the kitchen. Orchard House, with its thick Spanish-style walls and tile roof, stayed cool and dark, even in summer.

After dinner, Papi would carry the remains of his wine to the patio and smoke a few puffs of the cigar that lasted him all week. He seemed happy to have her home. He'd stopped eating in front of the television. They made salads and grilled steaks. He'd told her that he was happy that she was going out tonight. His whistling meant that all was well in the world.

Sometimes it was easy to forget that her father had Alzheimer's. Then she'd find him staring at a plate of tomatoes, wondering who had cut them. Or returning from a trip into Chelan without the items he'd gone to fetch. Calling from his truck, asking for a reminder of who he was supposed to meet or where he was supposed to be going. One night when he hadn't shown up for dinner, she'd hiked up into the fields, finding him wandering and hungry. He hadn't eaten lunch. His blood sugar was perilously low. He'd been confused, disoriented. As they'd strolled through the packed dirt fields between the curling vines, Carmen had felt grateful she'd found him. Someone should always be there for him. Maybe that person should be her.

As she'd left him in his bedroom, his eyes had cleared. He took her hand. "The vines."

"¿Sí, Papi?"

"They need trimming."

Carmen had added it to her long list.

Trimming the vines, she knew, took some expertise.

Hopefully she'd get to talk to Evan's mysterious vintner.

Carmen stared into the mirror. Her office pallor had disappeared. Working in the hot sun had returned her skin to its golden hue, her cheeks pink. Running her fingers through her curls, she was glad she'd let Stella work her magic, telling herself it had nothing to do with Evan. She'd seen him on his patio, his long legs up on a table, talking on the phone. His voice carried over the distance. He was arguing. Unlike her, he didn't sound defensive or raise his voice. He was self-assured and confident. Someone accustomed to negotiations. She felt admiration, before tamping it down.

Evan Hollister was used to maneuvering people into chutes. He knew how to pull levers and get people to commit to things they didn't want to do. It was his bread and butter. She'd have to watch herself.

After experimenting with a few hairstyles, Carmen frowned into the mirror. "This isn't high school and it's not a date."

Still, it felt fun to be getting a little dressed up. *Presentable*, her mother would say, patting her cheek before church. *Fancy*, when they were younger and wore glittery barrettes and hairbows. Since she'd arrived home, Carmen had barely had time to shower, let alone choose an outfit, apply make-up and spend time on her hair. She'd chosen a black gauze dress with short fluttery sleeves and white embroidery around the neck. Summery and attractive, but long enough to send an *I'm not flirting with you* vibe. She was glad she'd bought it in Seattle last summer. It was her first chance to wear it.

After kissing her father on the head while he ate dinner at the kitchen table, Carmen debated driving to Evan's house. It was a little ridiculous to drive the quarter mile down the orchard road to the street, take a right and immediately turn into Evan's drive and right back up the eastern side of the same hill through virtually the same orchard. The steep embankment between the two houses had once had a switchback path but it had eroded years ago, leaving rocky dirt, wild sage and few scrubby ponderosa pines.

Fifteen minutes later Carmen was climbing the slope, scrabbling in her low sandals, arms flung out to keep her balance. Halfway up the hill, she realized it was mistake. For every step she took, she slid backwards on the rocks. She looked back, weighing her options. Should she go back down and get the car like a sane person? Plant the bottle she was carrying in the hill to free her hand for better balance? How stupid, she thought, to be climbing a hill in a dress, a bottle of wine in one hand. She prayed Evan wouldn't be standing on his patio. The only thing worse than sweating and sliding backwards down this hill would be having Evan witness the spectacle.

A few seconds later, a large dog appeared on the patio, sniffing the cooling air. Carmen's back foot had slid down the hill on a cascade of pebbles. She was holding her arms out beside her, feeling the wind lift her dress, praying she didn't lose her balance. The dog walked the perimeter of the patio, his hackles rising when he saw her. A slight growl came from deep in his throat.

"Oh no. Nice doggy. It's just me, your neighbor. No worries."

The dog erupted into a series of sharp warning barks, quickly escalating into hysteria as he ran back and forth.

"No!" Carmen wailed to herself, acutely aware of the spectacle she was creating.

She was stranded in a dress on a steep slope between two of the valley's most storied wineries.

A few seconds later, Evan appeared, springing into action. "Barry, be quiet."

His dog's name was Barry?

She reminded herself not to appreciate Evan's whimsy. Ridiculous dog names were an easy thing. People did it all the time.

Evan didn't hesitate. He shushed the dog, and scrambled down the hill, oblivious (and Carmen had to admit, handsome) in his crisp white shirt. It was impossible not to enjoy the chivalry as he used the ideal approach to avoid covering her in dust and rocks.

In moments, he was a few feet above, offering his hand. "Nice of you to drop by."

His smirk wiped out her hero fantasies. His shoulders could be as wide as an aircraft carrier. He'd still be a rich, entitled guy. "Maybe I should have taken the car."

"More fun this way." He gained a few points for that one. Maybe this evening wouldn't be torture.

Maybe.

"I keep sliding backwards."

He frowned. "You should take off your shoes."

"My sandals?" Carmen thought about all the sharp rocks, and more importantly, arriving dirty-footed at Evan's mansion. Her mother had had a strict rule about going barefoot and keeping one's feet clean when going to anyone's house. Dirty feet were a sign of bad manners.

"Your sandals," Evan pronounced gravely. As if he could read her mind, he said, "Don't worry. You can wash your feet and put them back on."

Satisfied, Carmen took them off.

Even held out his hand. "Here."

Carmen hesitated. Give him her dust-covered sandals? This was not the way she'd wanted this night to start. Still, his logic was irrefutable. Reluctantly, she offered them up.

"Take my hand." He leaned forward. His sleeve was rolled up. The veins popped on his arms, strong and ropy with muscle. Not the hands of an office drone. He's spent some time outside. Papi would approve.

She shook her head. *Stop it.*

"It's okay, I've got you." He took the bottle she was carrying, freeing both hands.

There was no choice. Either take his hand or gracelessly tumble down the hill while he watched. His hand was cool and smooth. He gripped her arm firmly, pulling her slowly towards him. She found her footing a few feet away and stood up straight.

They were inches apart. She looked up into his face. He smiled, his teeth straight and white.

"Hello, neighbor." His breath was hot against her skin. She turned away.

"Lead the way."

"Hang on a second. Look at that." He turned her shoulders gently toward the lake.

The lake could always surprise her. No matter how many times she thought she'd seen every mood the water could throw, it could seem completely different when the sun went behind a cloud, or a bend in the road revealed a waterfall, or the turquoise depths turned black.

The low summer sun cut a glittering path off Wapato Point, slanting across the blue velvet of the lake, seemingly headed straight towards them.

Carmen's breath caught. The shimmering blue and gold was stunning. Lake breezes ruffled a stand of aspens atop the hill and cooled her skin. She was acutely aware of Evan behind her, his solid height. If things had been different… But they weren't. She steeled herself for the night ahead. She couldn't let the wine, or Evan, mess with her head. All Papi's work would be for nothing. The land, she knew, was everything. It had never occurred to her that one day it would all be resting on her.

She didn't move. Her thoughts raced as she enjoyed the view, listening to Evan's steady breathing. How amazing would it be to enjoy a single night without worry? To be a summer girl. Barry paced anxiously on the patio, his tags jangling, eyeing them. A few pebbles broke free from her heel, skittering down the hill.

"Are you all right?" Evan's voice was different. Warm, inviting.

"Yes. It's beautiful. This is different from the view at Orchard House. Higher up."

"The first time I came here, I swam out to a rock and lay on my back watching the sun go down. The sky must have changed to a hundred colors. I never wanted to swim back to shore."

"I know the feeling."

For a moment, she felt like they were out on a rock. Between the complications, on an island of solitude, if only for a moment.

"Yeah. When you're a kid, you think you're going to have it all figured out by the time you grow up. Then you realize you knew it all when you were a kid. Swim, play, eat, repeat."

"Isn't that the truth?" Carmen sighed.

"It's nice. Being here. When I think of my life in Seattle, the traffic, the meetings, the complications, I don't miss a thing. This view is worth everything."

Carmen got the feeling he wasn't looking at the lake, which was silly. Her back stiffened. This was business. "We should get going." Thinking she sounded rude, she added, "Thank you. For coming down to help me." It came out overly formal.

"Ready?" He called out to the dog, reassuring him they were coming. "Look at him, pretending he's worried. It's only because he hasn't eaten dinner."

She loved the way he talked to his dog.

Stop it, Carmen. We're enemies.

This was business, Carmen thought. It was hard to remember with Evan rolling up his sleeves to grill the steaks, chatting casually, pouring the wine she'd brought. He was so sure of himself, so comfortable cooking and talking. Carmen could either cook or talk. She couldn't do both. She didn't understand the magazine spreads featuring people in the midst of a dinner party, chopping and sautéing while their guests mingled in the kitchen. Evan was a natural. He checked on the steaks, squeezed lemon on the grilling vegetables, and tossed a salad while telling her about his decision to buy the vineyard.

"I'd come out here as a kid, you know, to sail and water ski and play on the beach while my parents socialized, but we didn't have a second home here. I'd always loved it. As soon as we arrived, before we unpacked, I'd dive off the dock and swim out, right to that rock. It was my tradition. I'd sit out there until it was getting dark or my mom got angry enough to yell. Whichever came first. I was king of the castle." He laughed. "I guess that's what I'm playing at up here."

And you want to invade the neighboring castle, Carmen thought to herself, along with, *No, we didn't sail or water ski, we worked and went to school. While everyone else sailed and water skied.* That was life in a resort town. You led your life while everyone else goofed off. You never let your feet get dirty for fear that someone would call you a dirty wetback.

"One time, I came with this girlfriend," Evan continued. "She and I were sort of over, but we had this trip booked with friends and I didn't want to be the bad guy. She ended up spending half the time at the pool and the other half chatting up one of the single guys. I took these long drives and ended up stopping at some open houses on the lake. I was coming back from one of them out by Twenty-Five Mile Creek and I came around the corner and noticed this place up on the hill. You know how you can't see it when you're driving north? I'd never really noticed it. I thought it was the most amazing location. The tasting room was open, so I stopped. I didn't think much of the wine, but the view just blew me away. The house wasn't really the thing that got me. It was looking down the lake. I left the guy my business card and told him to call if he ever wanted to sell. Then I went home and started learning everything I could about making wine."

He stopped for a second, shaking his head at the memory, removing the steaks from the grill. "I just thought, you know, if I could live in a place like that, I'd never want to leave. I'd never had a single thought like that. Of permanence. Of thinking, yeah, I want to settle down. Put down some roots. Make wine I could be proud of. I even imagined kids splashing in the pool. Which was kind of funny because I was all of twenty-five and basically single, particularly since my date was making the move on someone else. And here I was having these crazy thoughts."

"Not so crazy," said Carmen, taking a sip of her wine. He'd opened the Blue Hills wine she'd brought. A special bottle that tasted of chocolate, pepper and plums. It reminded Carmen of the reason she wanted to keep the winery in her family. Miracles like this bottle. Wine that tasted of moonlight, velvet and the bite of winter wind. Wine you couldn't forget.

"If you worked at Microsoft back then, you'd think it was crazy. We barely had time to breathe."

"That sounds familiar."

He looked back at her with raised eyebrows. She stayed quiet, nodding for him to continue.

Evan brought the steaks to the table, followed by the grilled vegetables. "The money made up for it." He slapped his hand across his mouth. "I'm sorry. That sounded terrible."

Carmen grinned. "I get it."

"No, I know what I am. I'm that Microsoft guy who comes here and ticks off everyone." His hand swept the valley. "We raise the land prices, drive too fast and insult everyone."

Carmen smirked. "You said it, not me."

Evan took a sip of his wine. "Wow. This wine." He swirled it around in his goblet, holding it up to the glow from the house lights. "The color, the depth. Everything. It's like the perfect wine."

Carmen glowed with pride. "That's my dad. When he wasn't in the winery or the fields he was talking to people about viticulture, reading reports from WSU on winemaking. There was never an endpoint, but at the end of the day, you could always share this wine. It made up for all the hard work."

Evan unwrapped the garlic bread he'd toasted. It was striped with grill marks, drenched in olive oil and butter, rubbed with pungent garlic. "I'd love to talk to him more." Evan served them both steaks, pouring more wine. He was the perfect host, solicitous without being overbearing.

They ate for a moment, savoring the food and the view. A coyote howled in the distance, calling to his pack. "My dad has forgotten a lot. Makes me wish I'd paid attention." She chewed for a moment, trying to decide how to broach her main objective for the evening, unsure if this was the right moment. "Don't you have a wine master?"

Evan leaned back, crossing his long legs, clad in faded Levis. "Oh, Paolo. The prince of Lake Chelan."

Carmen nearly snorted wine out of her nose. "Sorry. What?"

Evan shook his head. "I'm doing everything I can to keep him here. I pay him a fortune. I've rented him a house on the lake. He has a cleaning lady, a gardener who tends his organic garden. He's still miserable." Evan waved his hands around theatrically. "It's not Italy. No kidding, pal. You take a job in Central Washington State, it's not Tuscany. He's the worst kind of snob."

No, Carmen thought, Evan was the worst kind of snob. Mr. Center of the Universe. Paolo was probably just homesick. Carmen decided to be blunt. "I'd love to meet him."

Evan frowned suspiciously. Or maybe jealously. "He's a little crazy."

"I have some questions about my vines."

Evan tilted his head. "That reminds me. I have some questions about hosting weddings."

Carmen took another bite of steak. When she was finished, she took a sip of liquid courage. "Maybe we can make a deal."

Evan studied her over the top of his wineglass. "What kind of deal?" He spoke slowly, looking out at the lake. Carmen couldn't read his eyes. Which made it easier to keep this on a business footing.

Part of her missed their lighter, easier tone. She wiped that thought out of her brain and kept going. "A mutually beneficial deal."

"I'm listening." His eyes were far away, locked on the lake as it vanished into the blue hills.

Liar. His mind was elsewhere. He was motionless, knuckles taut around the fragile wineglass. She spoke anyway, hoping he would agree to her plan. Because everything was riding on his answer.

CHAPTER SEVEN

The Plan

"I'd try and talk her out of a champagne fountain, if you can," Carmen said, moving to the corner of the patio with the best view. Saturday night boaters cut white wakes across a swath of peachy light from the setting sun. A white sail flapped in the breeze. Evan moved towards her, so she crossed back towards the pool. Nothing had been overtly spelled out in terms of helping one another. She'd wanted to offer her help, in exchange for a promise that he wouldn't go after a single acre of their property. Adella thought it unlikely that he'd agree but Carmen hoped to persuade him. Now she wasn't so sure. He was an ambitious man who exuded confidence. His proximity only confused the issue. His aftershave. His hair, curling up at his collar. The way his eyes crinkled when he smiled. Evan Hollister was a confusing man.

"Because Hollister sparkling wine isn't as good as the Blue Hills sparkling rosé?" Evan finally stayed put, tracking the sailboat.

Carmen shook her head. "Because they're tacky."

Evan nodded. "That's what I told the wedding planner, but she said it was all about the bride."

Carmen nodded. "From her point of view, it is. She wants word of mouth. You have a brand to protect. No winemaker worth their salt is going to put their wine in a fountain." She waved her hand across the air, including the Hollister Estate vineyard and palatial Mediterranean house. "It's not just the wine, you want every experience to reflect the same image, the style. People can have a beautiful wedding at a city park if it's done right. You want a wedding that is personal and stylish, yes, but also reflects the world of your wine. A sophisticated wine that not only works for every occasion, it elevates." Her years slaving in marketing were finally paying off.

Evan nodded. "Where have you been all my life?"

Carmen gulped. "What?"

A small grin. "I'm joking."

Carmen's face flushed as she nodded briskly. "Right. I knew that. I just assume that's what every vintner is shooting for."

"Like your dad. He's brilliant!"

Everyone in the winemaking community listened to Papi, or at least they had before he had started shutting down. When he had an opinion, it counted. "Right? He spent his whole life learning this business and to him it is much more. It really is about family."

Evan nodded in agreement. "Every time the wedding planner came up with this stuff—the champagne fountain, the ice sculpture, the miniature horses…"

Carmen's eyes went wide. "Seriously?"

"Little horses carrying baskets of flowers. With lace braided into their manes. I kid you not. Anyway, every time she opened her mouth, I knew that it was all kinds of awful, but I felt trapped. I'd signed this contract and I had to meet certain obligations."

"Miniature horse obligations?"

"Thankfully, no."

"But..." Carmen's eyes narrowed. *Here goes nothing.* "I do have some ideas."

Evan moved towards her. "I'd love to hear them, but you're so far away. Maybe I can come over there?"

He took a step closer. Then another. Each time Carmen felt her heart beat a little faster. *Time to implement phase one.* "What about goats?"

Evan raised his eyebrows. "Goats? Now that's romantic."

"Miniature goats. They're trendy. People love them."

Evan made his way slowly towards her. "Cloven feet and creepy eyes. What's not to love?"

"Unlike miniature horses, they won't poop much."

He swirled his wine. "Not much. Just a little. What's a wedding without a little poop, right?"

"They'll add some whimsy."

His eyebrows shot up in a look that was mischievous and sexy. "And poop."

"Now I know what you were like in kindergarten."

The corner of his mouth lifted. "I made everyone laugh."

"By saying poop?"

"It's a great word."

She couldn't help but smile. "I bet you were a funny little boy."

He was close enough to stop. But he didn't. One more step and they'd be nose to nose. "Stick around. That kid is still there." He tapped his chest lightly.

She could smell his cedar-scented soap, earthy and fresh. He was a collection of opposing forces. Hateful and lovable. Complicated and simple. Ambitious and down to earth. Why couldn't he just be slotted into one category or the other? "You still like to cause trouble."

He lowered his voice. "With the right people."

"I don't like trouble." Carmen took a step back.

"Maybe this isn't the kind you're used to."

"You're pretty flirty for a businessman."

He raised an eyebrow. "I'm not all business."

"Maybe we'd better get back on track."

He leaned into her. "Watch it, Carmen."

"You'd like that, wouldn't you?"

He nodded, raising his eyebrows, looking, Carmen thought, hatefully adorable. "I would."

"Then you'd be able to take over everything."

"Not what I was thinking."

"Oh sure!"

He moved so close the toes of their shoes were touching. His breath was a heady mixture of wine and berries. "Do you want to know what I was thinking?" he whispered.

She took a small step back, then she was falling. Her arms spun in windmills as she tried to right herself. It was no use. Evan tried to grab her, but his hand caught air. She fell backwards into the pool, emerging from the lit marine blue seconds later, blinking through her wet eyelashes. She gasped, pushing her hair from her face, furious.

He crouched down by the side of the pool, waiting to help. "Now do you want to know what I was thinking?"

She scraped her hair off her face as she treaded water. One sandal bobbed up beside her. She grabbed it before swimming to the edge. "No, I don't."

He leaned onto his stomach, reaching for her with a long, muscular arm. She ignored him, swimming for the ladder. "I was thinking that you'd better not step backwards."

"Now you tell me." The skirt of her dress floated around her in the blue light.

"It was pretty adorable."

"I'd rather be dry than adorable," she snapped.

He stood up, wiping his softly wrinkled khakis. "I'll go get you a towel. And a robe."

"A towel will be fine."

Evan's face softened. "Please don't go."

As Carmen climbed from the pool, she stood on the ladder, furious that he'd clearly known that she'd fall into the pool and didn't warn her. What a colossal jerk. It was time to instigate the plan she'd hatched with her sisters. Ruin his weddings. This one. All of them. Leave his reputation in tatters. Cause so much mischief and have a great time doing it. The Alvarez sisters would wreak havoc on the entitled Microsoftie who thought he could buy his way into a life that took decades to build. Who thought a fat checkbook gave him rights to the best growing land in the valley. Land that took a lifetime to cultivate.

Wrong.

Meet the Alvarez sisters.

"I'm soaking wet. I'm not getting a thing from you. I still haven't met Paolo, the prince of Chelan. Give me one good reason that I should stay here and help you."

Evan crossed his arms. "What do you want Carmen?"

She twisted her hair, wringing the water from it, exasperated. "I want you to promise that you won't, under any circumstances, buy our vineyard."

He lifted his hands as if pushing her back. "Carmen, hang on. If, and let me be perfectly clear, this is *not* what I want, but let's say *if* the bank does put it on the market—"

"You're the only one in this valley who could afford it."

"Better to do business with the devil you know." He waited for her to react, but her face stayed stony. "There are other buyers out there, trust me."

"Promise me Evan."

He sighed. "I can't do that. If it goes on the market, it wouldn't make sense for me to abstain. Carmen, I'm a businessman. If you were in my shoes, you'd feel precisely the same way."

She hated that he was right. Despised his sound reasoning. "Give me one good reason why I should help you."

Evan spread his hands. "I need you."

Carmen looked up at the night sky, at the stars twinkling. It was the sky of her childhood: open, bright and full of promise. Everything she wanted to save. Miles and miles of promise. She had him exactly where she wanted him. He offered her his hand. She took it.

Shouting with laughter, she pulled him into the water.

*

"Keep it together, dude," Evan said to himself in the shower. He'd promised himself, after seeing the Alvarez sisters on the patio that night, that he wouldn't let himself get emotional about Carmen. From the first moment he'd seen her, he'd known it was going to be tough. That hair. That smile. That determination.

Everything.

He'd never fallen so hard, so quickly.

But.

She was clearly up to something. The very thing that attracted him, her willingness to leave her life in Seattle to keep the land in the family, throwing herself at something so hard; it was very hard for him to resist.

And yet.

She was devious. She'd do anything to keep her father's vineyard going, including poaching his annoying wine master. Evan wouldn't put anything past her. To a man with a competitive nature, she was catnip, but also dangerous.

He had to stay sharp, he thought, as he shut off the shower and grabbed a towel. He had to keep his wits. He could win, let the dust settle and see where they stood.

Carmen Alvarez was adaptable.

Even if she lost, Evan could tell that she probably wasn't going anywhere. The woman obviously belonged to this town. If anything, she'd become more beautiful since she'd arrived.

By the time Evan had gotten dressed he'd convinced himself that Carmen Alvarez would be much happier helping her father invest his windfall from the vineyard in a little business in town. Something she could run. Something much easier than running an entire winery with all its complexities, at the mercy of rain, weather and pests.

He would be doing her a favor.

He could wait, he decided, until she'd realized it was for the best.

Evan was a patient man.

And he always got what he wanted.

*

Carmen watched Evan as he entered the kitchen fresh from the shower, a towel slung around his neck to catch the drips from his hair. An old surf T-shirt clung to his damp torso. His bare feet padded over the worn tiles as he poured wine, chopped fresh mint on a checkerboard block built into the marble countertop and generally showed himself to be at home in the kitchen. Men who cooked always reminded her of how Papi had rebuilt their life meal by meal, making Mami's recipes, forcing them to gather when they felt like scattering.

Evan dug in his freezer, holding up a pint of Snoqualmie Ice Cream. "They make this Smooooth Bourbon flavor," he said, pronouncing the extra "O." "You have to try it. I'm completely addicted."

"Booze and ice cream. Sure, why not?"

He scooped pale, creamy mounds into white bowls, sprinkling it with mint. "Raspberries?" She nodded. "I'm not too sure about the mint, bourbon and berries combo but it's already on there. Pick it off if you don't like it."

While Evan busied himself with dessert, Carmen perched on a padded barstool, listening to the dryer hum expensively as she wrapped the robe more tightly around herself. She took a sip of the fresh wine, wondering if it was one of Evan's or part of the cellar he'd purchased with the estate.

She didn't want to ask. They'd had such a great time after she'd pulled him into the pool. While they splashed there had been, in her mind, a ceasefire. It had felt like high school. Just a guy and a girl yelling, "I can't believe you just did that!" and, "You totally deserved it!"

Her cheeks hurt from smiling.

She'd forgotten how much fun flirting could be.

Life in Seattle had gotten away from Carmen. She'd been buried in office work, competing in a job that eliminated any romance with the people she saw daily. A few guys at the nearby Starbucks had smiled at her, but she'd always grabbed her coffee and left. She didn't have time.

Now she'd spent a good chunk of the night outdoors in the sage-scented air, watching the bats swoop low over the pool, flickering around the torches. It was a perfect place for weddings. For anything, really.

Evan had kept the basic lines of the house and patio, not going overboard like many relocating or summering millionaires. Some lakeside homes had terraced patios, tennis courts, parking for fleets of cars, elaborate water features, pools, docks. Evan had chosen his improvements carefully to match the existing house, the Chelan vibe. Although much had changed, Chelan was a town that prided itself on its rural values, its small-town character.

Carmen watched him sprinkle mint and raspberries carefully onto the ice cream. He would be fine, Carmen thought, once he'd settled on something else to pursue besides winemaking. Clearly, he was a man of many interests. Or maybe, Carmen thought guiltily, she was justifying her actions to herself.

Shaking her head to clear any doubts, Carmen offered Evan a bright smile as he handed her the pretty dessert and took her wineglass.

"Let's eat outside."

She climbed off the barstool in her bare feet. "Good. I have more ideas about the wedding."

He turned to face her at the kitchen door. "Still all business?"

The white bowl, bright with berries, was cold on her hands. "Still all business."

He pushed the door open with his back, letting her squeeze past. "Even after pulling me into the pool?"

"Especially after pulling you into the pool."

They walked outside into the inky night, carrying their bowls to the table with the best view of the moonlit lake. Another coyote howled on the plateau.

Evan scraped a chair back for Carmen. "That was the first time I swam in the pool."

Carmen laughed, taking a big bite of her dessert. It was delicious. The mint worked, adding a fresh note to the creamy ice cream and tart berries. "You're kidding me?"

"Nope."

Carmen spooned another bite. "Maybe you should slow down and enjoy things more."

Evan nodded, lifting his glass towards her. "Maybe you should do the same."

Carmen shook her head. "I've got a family business to run."

Evan seemed to think for a moment. He nodded. "It's a lot of work." He sipped from his wineglass, letting his ice cream melt. "Now, please tell me you were joking about the goats."

A name popped into Carmen's head: Mrs. Huttinger. Papi's eccentric friend who raised goats. As kids, they'd called her the goat lady. Did she still have a herd? Carmen took another bite, savoring it with her eyes closed. "This ice cream is delicious."

Evan was so relaxed. He looked genuinely happy, eager to please. When they weren't wrapped up in competing, he was interesting, chatting easily about food, wine, his life in Seattle, which he didn't seem to miss one bit. He confessed that he wasn't sure, early on, if Hollister Estate was going to make it. He'd given himself three years to turn a profit and was shocked when it did. "My friends thought running a winery meant sitting around and tasting wine all day. I've never worked so hard in my life. It was brutal."

Their hands brushed when she handed him her ice cream bowl and he blushed like a schoolboy. His eyes were bright as he listened to a childhood story about Adella and Carmen getting so annoyed with three-year-old Lola one winter, they'd strung her up on a tree branch by the straps of her snowsuit. Then, when she'd started to cry, they couldn't get her down. Their solution was to undress her, rushing her home in her long johns. He couldn't stop laughing. Kept asking her if she wanted more ice cream or tea, as if he didn't want the evening to end.

Which was strange, Carmen thought. What on earth was Evan Hollister thinking?

CHAPTER EIGHT

Sisterhood

Paolo walked the rows of vines of Blue Hills Vineyard with his small silver pruning shears, clipping curling pale green shoots from the plants. Evan had repeatedly avoided an introduction, but Carmen had seen her window. She'd spotted Paolo in the Hollister Estate vineyard and coaxed him onto the Blue Hills property with ice water and a smile.

"These and these. You see? They run away from the fruit. They have no leaves. They are not part of the family." He stopped to sniff. "Alone." Snip. "Lost." Snip. Snip.

It was, Carmen thought, more than a little theatrical. "Maybe if the vines went into town and mingled?"

Paolo shot her a dirty look. "The vines need their own kind."

She returned the look over the top of her sunglasses. "Maybe the vines need to adapt."

Paolo held himself up to his full height, snipping violently. "Does the sun adapt? Does the moon adapt? Or do they stay true to their nature?"

Carmen rolled her eyes. The man's ego clearly wasn't suffering.

It was starting to make sense, Carmen thought. If there was one personality Evan couldn't tolerate, it would be the suffering artist. Clearly Paolo thought himself the Picasso of the vineyard, stranded in this provincial backwater. She trailed behind the melodramatic Italian, trying to match his steps on the incline. All this hyperbole would drive Evan nuts. A vine wasn't a vine to Paolo, it was a child. A leaf was a home.

Carmen stopped to study an errant vine, curling pale green up to the sun. "What you mean is that the vines aren't feeding the fruit."

Paolo paused, holding his fingers up in the air. "Exactly, they are selfish. They have to go."

Carmen dumped the leftover ice from Paolo's empty glass into the dirt. "So, we clip anything that isn't supporting the grapes?"

Paolo nodded. "At this time of year, yes. In the fall, it is a different story."

"What about the fall?"

Paolo wiped his face with a snowy linen handkerchief. "You are exhausting me."

Carmen crossed her arms. "All I'm doing is asking a few questions."

Paolo threw his arms up in the air, yelling. "You have lived on a vineyard your entire life! How do you not know this? Were you blindfolded, wrapped in gauze, kept in the stables? The fruit is the thing that we are serving. The fruit is the wine. The soil is the fruit and the land is everything. Have you been kept in a nunnery?"

Carmen frowned. "I went to college."

"College? What did you study?"

"Hospitality."

"And is winemaking not part of hospitality?"

Finally, Carmen could show herself to be an intelligent person. "No, it's more like hotel and restaurant management, travel, that kind of thing."

Paolo looked up at the sky, muttering darkly in Italian. From the sound of it, much cursing streamed from his mouth.

Carmen, busy trying to make out a single word of Italian, didn't notice Evan descending the slope of his vineyard, crossing the gravel path between their properties. He moved between the vine rows, startling her with his appearance. It was the first time she'd seen him since their non-date.

He nodded, slightly out of breath from the hike down but not, Carmen noticed, winded. "Is there a problem?"

Paolo stopped ranting long enough to roll his eyes. "In Italy we have people trained to do this their whole lives. That is all they do. They trim the vines. They work all year long keeping the vines in shape and they know exactly what to do and when. This one spends her whole life living on a vineyard and now, only now, does she want to learn." Paolo accentuated this speech with a tornado of angry gestures.

Evan raised one eyebrow. His shirt was unbuttoned just enough to catch a glimpse of curling hair. "What's wrong with that?"

Paolo threw up his arms. "Everything! You cannot learn a lifetime of lessons in one day."

Evan crossed his arms, staring at Carmen as he lifted his sunglasses onto his head. "Sometimes you can."

Carmen flushed at his intensity, shrugging. "I'm just trying to take care of my dad's vineyard."

Paolo waved his arms. "You have to hire a master vintner. You cannot walk up a hill and expect to learn everything. It cannot be done."

Carmen hated herself for tearing up, gritting her teeth to stop it. She pushed her sunglasses firmly over her eyes as she shook a rock from her sandal. "I don't have any other choice."

Paolo threw both arms wide. "Then, you sell."

Carmen shook her head, furious. "Is that what this is? Are you just a mouthpiece for your boss?"

Evan stepped forward. "Carmen, no."

She stopped him with a raised hand. "No. I get it. Asking me to dinner. The 'I'll help you if you help me.' It's very clear to me what you've been playing at. I say I want to meet Paolo and the next thing you know, he's telling me I have to sell the land."

She turned back to Paolo. "You're feeling sorry for yourself because you flew here with a job waiting that included a house, a cleaning lady and, oh yeah, a gardener?" She pointed down the hill towards Orchard House. "My dad came here with nothing. Nothing but the clothes on his back. Yeah. He was literally a wetback. He tried to swim across the Rio Grande and almost drowned. He wanted to leave his country and make something of himself so badly that he threw himself into the water without knowing how to swim. He nearly broke his back buying and working this land. Making it into something we could all be proud of. Cry all you want about missing Italy. My father made this place his home. In one generation, we became landowners. College educated. He gave us wings. Do you honestly think I'm going to let him down now just because some big shot moves next door and wants to add winemaker to his resumé?"

"Carmen, please!" Evan said.

Carmen's eyes flashed. "You made a big mistake, Evan. Huge." She hurried down the hill alongside the rows of vines, her eyes blurring with tears, stumbling over rocks.

"You idiot!" she heard Evan yelling at Paolo, but she was rushing down the green corridor of grapevines. She'd been so furious, she had little idea of what she'd just said.

She just knew it had been too much.

Evan Hollister had no idea what he'd started.

No idea.

Carmen could hear Evan yelling at her to wait but she didn't stop. She just wanted to escape into the cool of Orchard House, get a drink of water and rest.

Evan caught up with her at the end of the row, on the short path to his driveway bordering the house. She was poised to continue down the hill to Orchard house. "Carmen." He held up a finger for her to wait while he caught his breath.

"We have nothing to talk about."

"But we do. The weddings. I need your help."

"Nice, Evan. Pretend like you didn't set me up."

He held up both hands. "I didn't. I swear. That was all Paolo. I can't help it if he's a raging prima donna. I told you he was crazy." Evan pointed at the Italian in the nearby driveway, who was climbing into his low-slung sports car, gunning the motor. The sound reverberated across the lake. "Case in point."

"Please leave."

"Carmen, listen to me."

Carmen fumed as Evan crossed his arms. A hawk floated on a vector in the cloudless sky. The lake shone, cut by the wake of a few boats. "This is just one more nail in the Alvarez coffin."

"No, it's not."

She shook her head. "It's a waiting game for you, isn't it? Sooner or later the bank is going to tip things in your direction. You're waiting for me to fold, aren't you?"

Evan shook his head. She could read his face now. He was annoyed. "No."

"Sure, you are. This is what you do. It's part of your whole executive mentality, isn't it? When negotiations stall, just wait it out. See if the other guy blinks. Guess what, I'm not blinking." She opened her eyes abnormally wide. "See?"

"You look pretty adorable when you do that."

"Oh, there you go. Diminishing me by commenting on my looks."

He crossed his arms. "It was a compliment."

"I'm talking about losing my home and you're telling me I'm cute?"

"One," he held up a finger. "It was never about your home. I have said that from the beginning." A second finger went up. "Two, it doesn't detract from anything you've said."

"Spoken like a man."

"Which makes sense, give that I am, in fact, a man."

"This is all a big game for you, isn't it?"

"No. It's a business."

"Which is a game. You don't need the money. Why don't you find something else to do?"

"Oh hey, yeah. What a crazy idea. I have a bunch of land with grapes. Maybe I should make wine? And no, I don't need the money, but here's a wild thought. I find it interesting. Unlike you, I find the chemistry and, yes, the art of winemaking fascinating."

She hissed. "That is a low blow."

"And 'why don't you retire like a good boy' isn't a low blow? You seem pretty good at telling other people how to live."

They were eye to eye, so close she could feel the heat coming off his body. She could see the blue flecks circling his iris, the color of the deepest part of the lake. "You seem pretty good at telling other people to throw in the towel."

Evan threw up his hands. "Why am I the bad guy here? I am offering your father enough money to retire. An inheritance. And somehow you make me out to be this evil money-grubbing loser."

Her smile took on a devilish glint. "If the shoe fits…"

Evan shook his head. "You think that anyone who wasn't raised here doesn't have the right to own property. Look in the mirror. You left. You're the one who chose to leave."

Carmen shot him a withering look, pushed past him and marched down the hill, moving so fast she almost fell.

Her first wedding was in four days.

"I hate him! I hate him so much I can't think of all the ways I hate him." Carmen said, drinking her wine like it was water.

"Sounds like love to me."

"You've seen too many movies."

"True. But sometimes life mirrors art."

"And sometimes a hate story is just a hate story." Carmen motioned to a passing waiter for more wine. "I can't believe he set up Paolo."

"Wine master. What a great job title. Almost as good as 'your royal highness' right?"

"Would you listen for one second?" Carmen snapped.

"I am listening. So far, you've mentioned a millionaire who wants to give you money and a homesick Italian with a fat paycheck. Both handsome. Both young. Both single. Remind me of the problem."

"One wants to run my father out of business and the other is a colossal idiot."

Stella sipped her wine carefully. "Oh. Right. It's kind of hard to remember what with all the money and swarthiness."

At least three different tables in Sol, the appropriately sunny restaurant, were eavesdropping. The story of the handsome young winemaker and the Alvarez girl had reached a frenzied pitch, thanks to the Olympic level gossiping of Stella's client Esther, who had left the salon the previous week with beautiful highlights and juicy tidbits. For five years, they'd all waited patiently for details about the private young Microsoftie (although weren't they all young?) who'd bought the Folkner place for an obscene amount, then plowed crazy money into it. There were rumors of light fixtures flown in from Paris. A marble bathtub. A Dale Chihuly chandelier. Nobody would have cared if he'd been some pot-bellied retiree with a bad weave. But Evan Hollister had a way of attracting interest.

Stella studied her friend with her fork poised in the air. Carmen was grateful that Stella had canceled her two o'clock balayage appointment, praying her client wouldn't spot her in town. She was supposed to be at the vet with a sick cat. "Are you sure Paolo is really that bad?"

"They're two of a kind. They both have one thing on their mind. Making me feel inadequate and stealing my father's land."

"That's two things."

"You get the point."

"Buying is not exactly stealing."

"Whose side are you on anyway?"

Stella studied her friend's wineglass. "Maybe I should give you a ride home."

Carmen arched her eyebrows. "Excellent idea." She took a sip. "I know you're trying to help, but a wedding is a well-dressed military operation with crudités. And this weekend, I'm trying to beat my opponent."

"You both have weddings booked for this weekend?" Stella raised her eyebrows.

Carmen nodded. "At almost exactly the same time. Hopefully he'll put a sign on his driveway." She put down her empty glass. "I don't know why I thought he'd help me in the first place. His goal is to put Blue Hills out of business. Do I seem like I've lost it?"

"Before you started drinking like a sailor you seemed perfectly rational."

Carmen accepted another glass of wine. "Thank you." She took a sip. "That man is driving me to drink."

"He likes you, Carmen. Accept it."

"Now you sound like the crazy one." Carmen raised her wineglass, dismissing her friend's comment with a shake of her head. "To covert operations and subterfuge."

Stella lifted her glass, clinked and took a small sip. "It's going to be an interesting weekend."

The bride was drunk. Not tipsy. Blasted.

Her well-intentioned mother had brought the nervous bride several seemingly innocent flutes of champagne, not knowing that the make-up artist carried bourbon in her kit for exactly this purpose. Bourbon got many a skittish bride down the aisle—unless that bride first gulped champagne.

The untouched cheese and fruit platter, along with a comment about a missed breakfast, gave Carmen all the information she needed.

The girl needed food.

Stat.

Luckily the bride in Evan's winery's first wedding had proved to be a poster child for movie bridezillas. Evan had called that morning, begging for help. It was incredibly satisfying, hearing his rising panic and profuse apologies for his previous behavior. She'd listened with growing sympathy as he described last-minute wedding frenzy. When the best laid plans fell like dominoes. Where could he find a two-foot-wide pale pink satin ribbon? The caterer was threatening to quit. His voice trailed off as he described the bride, who'd woken up on her wedding morning not with gratitude or thoughts of her soon-to-be husband. Her first thought was that her wedding menu was boring.

"She's serving deconstructed foie gras." Evan had sounded tired.

"Is that edible?" Carmen had asked.

"It's strips of pâté on duck fat," Evan had sighed.

"First of all, yuck, and secondly, nobody wants to eat that. Simplify it. Tell the caterer to put the pâté on a bun. Simplicity is chic."

"I don't think I can use the word 'chic' in a sentence and not spontaneously explode."

"You just did."

Thankfully, the two winery weddings were staggered by one hour, in a sequence which favored the Alvarez sisters. Adella had arrived late the night before to help. Lola, accustomed to her recent art school life, was sleepy but eager to help. While Carmen poured cups of coffee for the tipsy bride and ransacked the kitchen for Cool Ranch Doritos, the only snack the bride would eat, her sisters were available to help pass hors d'oeuvres.

The caterer had dashed into the kitchen half an hour before the guests were slated to arrive, cussing her head off about two waiters who both said they were sick.

"They're water skiing!" the caterer had screeched. "I can see them out on the lake!"

Adella, an elementary teacher until she had the twins, had chided her for using such language on a job. Lola had grabbed a platter and started scattering it with parsley, gulping coffee, confiding that she'd been fired from three catering jobs in the course of her life. By the time the bride had devoured the Doritos so quickly she nearly choked, the guests were arriving. The make-up artist repaired the damage from Doritos dust and Carmen ran downstairs to make sure the wine was properly decanted.

As she walked up the short path edged in flowerbeds to the heart of the Blue Hills Vineyard—the tasting room, cave and winemaking room, all housed in one glass-fronted building overlooking the lake—Carmen felt a tinge of regret. Evan stood on his patio, waving his arm, yelling into his cell phone. Carmen couldn't hear him, but guessed it could be wedding guests calling from up lake. If they'd followed the signs to the wedding, customized with the last names of the bride and groom, they might have been led astray. Each flower-festooned sign was mysteriously pointing to the Twenty-Five Mile State Park. Once inside the park, guests could potentially drive in looping circles looking for the wedding for hours. Especially if they saw more signs.

Lola, thought Carmen as she entered the cool dark blue cave, might have had a little too much fun with that one. In fact, Lola had seemed a little too thrilled with all this from the get-go. As if she never wanted it to end. Carmen couldn't wait for it to end. Despite her very strong desire to stop Evan from buying Papi's vineyard, she couldn't help but relate to his struggle.

All thoughts of Evan and his Alvarez-related troubles disappeared as soon as Carmen slipped into the cave. The beauty of the room, shadowy with flickering fake candles in tiny white votives, took her breath away. Her father had worked until midnight last night with Adella and Lola to turn the dark, barn-shaped cave, flanked on both sides with walls of oak casks, into a fairy land. The oak cask tables, which a friend of Lola's had made for a song, were topped in white tulle, leftovers from another friend's wedding. Each table had a mason jar of wildflowers. Fairy lights swung from the rafters, crisscrossing to highlight the natural wood beams.

It was magical. Like stepping into a dream. A shiver went across Carmen's skin as she inhaled the familiar scent of oak, pine and hay from the bales tucked into the corners, covered with canvas for seating. Carmen walked between the tables, her sandals quiet on the stone floor. She heard a noise and saw her father in a white shirt, a string of fairy lights illuminating his face. He studied the lights, as if searching for something.

"Papi?" Carmen called.

Papi turned, surprised. "Oh, mija. It's you. I keep expecting your mother."

Carmen's heart clenched. "Papi, Mama's gone."

He walked slowly towards her. "Oh, I know. It's just, this is where I feel her the most. She'd come here when you girls were little." He smiled. "To get some quiet. Cool down." He reached for her hand, patting it. "You girls were a lot of work."

"I know."

"She had patience, that one."

Carmen squeezed Papi's hand. "So did you."

He shook his head. "Not like my Mercedes." He swept his hand around. "Someone must be getting married." He frowned. "It's not one of you girls." He looked at his clothes. "I need to get changed."

"No, Papi. We rented out the place. To raise money for the winery. We're going to make sure this cru is great so we can sell it and save the business."

"Save it?"

"From the bank."

A dark shadow passed over her father's face as he remembered. "I don't know what happened."

Carmen wasn't sure exactly what the confession meant. Which part he didn't understand. She put her arms around her father, kissing his leathery cheek. The old man was still handsome, his high cheekbones and crinkled brown eyes still proud. He hadn't lost his hair like most of his friends. The black was salt and pepper now, thick and wavy. He often combed it in front of his friends as a joke, holding out his comb. "Remember what this is?"

Carmen leaned her cheek on her father's shoulder, grateful for the moment. "It doesn't matter. It's going to be fine. We're going to keep the Alvarez name alive and produce great wines. Like we always have."

Her father craned his neck to look into his daughter's eyes. "Oh no, mija, you've caught it, haven't you?"

Carmen tilted her head. "What?"

"It's in your blood. Making wine. It's not something you think about until you wake up one day and realize it's all you think about. You worry about your vines like your children. You check on the fruit more than you need to. You think about the cru like it's the only thing that matters."

Carmen's first thought was to disagree. She realized she wasn't thinking in exactly the way her father did. Hers was a more boots-on-the-ground mentality. Get through the weddings, keep Evan at bay, search into the wee hours on the computer, finding information on winemaking. She'd been slightly horrified to learn that her alma mater, Washington State University, offered a major in viticulture and enology. Had she taken that path, her life would be much simpler.

There was so much that needed doing right now, she didn't have time to walk the vines or do more than make sure the fruit was ripening on time. With that thought, her mind was off and racing.

As soon as the wedding was over, they'd need to do inventory on the barrels. Make sure the entire cave was as obsessively clean as possible. Wrangle field workers. With the immigration laws changing by the day, it was an extremely tight market. Also, maybe one of her sisters could help with their display at the First Crush Festival. Make sure Adella could be there for every wedding. Help Lola collect the last boxes from her former roommates apartment in Seattle.

So. Many. Things.

And yet.

She loved it.

That's when it hit her.

Papi was right. It was in her blood all along. Waiting.

She was a winemaker.

In the quiet beauty of the cave, with the sparkling lights, the blushing flowers and the man who had started it all when he'd crossed the border with nothing more than a backpack, Carmen felt more vibrantly alive than she had in her entire life.

She'd learned something that would change things forever.

Carmen Alvarez was a winemaker.

CHAPTER NINE

The Deal

"Oh my god, Carmen, there are sixteen little goats headbutting the flower girls. Two of them were pushed into the pool by a goat trying to get their bouquets. We kept yelling 'let go of the flowers' but the last thing those kids had been told was not to let them go. She was supposed to drop off *one* goat." Evan was frantic.

Carmen heard people yelling in the background. Her own ceremony had been flawless. It had brought tears to people's eyes. Afterwards, they'd sampled the Blue Hills wines.

People had asked if they could buy cases to take home. Carmen had plucked an impossible price from thin air. Five cases sold.

"Don't let them eat the bouquets!" Evan made a strangled noise. "They're eating the decorations!" He yelled at someone: "Don't feed it to them!" He came back on the line. "It's like an invasion. They're starving."

"Maybe the goat herder thought you needed them to eat invasive plants?" Because maybe that's what someone ordered.

"At a wedding?!"

Carmen put a hand on her phone receiver. "Shhhhhh!" she said to Adella and Lola, who were doubled over on the small stone patio outside the cave, which provided a perfect view of the mayhem they'd visited on the less fortunate Hollister Estate guests. It was like a watching the aftermath on a football field where the play called for splits and double-backs and utter chaos.

Looking down the hill, Adella lifted her wineglass. "Take that, Mr. Millionaire."

"I'm so sorry, Evan. Is there anything I can do?" The words slipped out. She couldn't help it. She was her mother's daughter.

Lola angrily mimed cutting a line across her throat.

"Do you know anything about goats?" Evan asked.

The wedding guests were eating at tables by the pool with the air of disaster survivors. Shoes were kicked off. Ties removed. There was a general consensus that after being headbutted by goats, trampled by hysterical flower girls and witnessing a formal occasion unravel into a barnyard melee, the rules went out the window. Several flower girls were splashing in the pool in borrowed T-shirts and underwear. Trays of appetizers had been taken from waiters and placed on tables where gossiping relatives caught up, gnawing with abandon on food they'd barely noticed when they'd been properly dressed.

Carmen arrived to find a shell-shocked Evan trying to shoo goats away from the patio, finding little success since the goats had moved onto the flower beds, recently planted with apparently delicious blooms. One goat stood on top of a table, munching wedding cake. The bride watched with a zombie-like stare, her face streaked with mascara. Her mother patted her hand, shaking her head. Carmen heard the mother whisper, "Well dear, no one will forget your wedding," which caused the daughter to break into fresh tears, muttering, "That goat is eating pâté imported from France."

At which point, the mother took a swig of champagne. "The goat does bear a passing resemblance to your Aunt Martha."

The bride smiled, sharing her mother's bottle.

Evan's face lit up with hope when he saw Carmen coming down the path, holding up her dress as she slid down the embankment from the Blue Hills Vineyard where the path ended. "Thank you so much for coming over. I didn't know who to call. The goat herder is out of cell phone coverage. I need to do damage control, but it's impossible without getting rid of these goats."

Carmen took out her phone. "Thank you, Google. "

"Are you kidding me?"

Carmen read what came up when she typed in "goat behavior". "We need to look for the leader. A female. Apparently, the queen."

"Why didn't I think of that?"

"Because you were in the middle of a home invasion."

Evan threw up his hands. "Did you see it?"

Carmen felt flushed with guilt, not wanting to point out that she was hosting a storybook wedding down the hill where Adella was filling orders for cases of wine to be shipped across the country, including one to a man who ran a grocery store chain. "I can imagine. Right, let's find this queen goat."

Evan looked around his patio. They both pointed at the same time to the goat on top of the table. "There she is," said Evan. "Probably."

"We need to get her to follow us."

"Okay, assuming we can get sixteen goats to follow us, where do we put them?"

"You're not going to like the answer."

"At this point they can raid my fridge and watch the NFL channel all day."

Carmen looked over her sunglasses at Evan, whose mouth opened in shock.

"You've got to be kidding me."

The goats were corralled in the expansive living room, climbing on the furniture, chasing one another around the couch, rubbing up against the long velvet curtains that looked, to Carmen, like they cost more than her car. At first, they'd tried to get the goats down the long dark hallway to the garage, but the queen kept turning around, forcing the herd to scatter throughout the house. One of the more ambitious goats scrambled upstairs and had to be enticed down with a bunch of carrots, although he fell down the last half of the stairway, causing Carmen some concern until he jumped up and started eating carrots out of her hand.

They'd turned over chairs as a barrier, but the goats easily climbed or jumped over them, heading for the kitchen. While Evan pushed larger furniture towards the two exits flanking the oversized stone fireplace, Carmen kept the queen in the living room, using blocking tactics, singing, anything she could think of to attract the goat and keep her away from the space Evan was working to fill.

Outside, the wedding planner was serving dinner while all available hands cleaned up the chaos the goats had created. Some of the wedding guests had even pitched in, saying they didn't mind, it was fun. A trio of little girls, their hair damp with pool water, had snuck around the side of the house and were peering in the windows at the goats. By the time Evan had shooed the last goat from the kitchen and into his makeshift corral, the goats seemed to have settled in, enjoying their luxurious surroundings.

The tile floor was scattered with richly patterned carpets. The tables were marble and brass. On the pale, hand-smoothed stucco walls were black and white photographs from around the world that Carmen suspected were of places Evan had actually traveled to. It was the perfect place to spend a hot summer day, or to curl up on one of the vast couches and watch the snow fall while a fire crackled in the majestic fireplace.

Carmen shook her head, clearing all thoughts of cozy winter fires. A bleating goat snapped her back into reality.

"I'm sure my, um, interior designer will love my new tenants," Evan said as he pushed aside a bookcase to enter the living room.

Carmen wondered if a former girlfriend was what he meant by "interior designer" and how far back in the past she was, before chiding herself for caring. She was here for one reason only.

"Okay, well, looks like things are under control."

Evan waved his hand around the room. "Right. This is what having things under control looks like."

Carmen sighed. "I don't know what you want from me, Evan. I came over. I am hosting my own wedding, which I left. For you. Did you ever think that maybe you're not cut out for this?"

Evan lifted his hands. "I'm sorry. What do you mean, not cut out for this?"

She waved her hands around wildly. "This. This life. I mean, how long have you been here?" Without waiting for him to answer, she kept talking. "Have you been here for a real wildfire? Spent three days in a row without sleep, spraying your vines with water so they don't catch on fire. You haven't had to burn your own vines to prevent disease from spreading. You haven't been staring at the ledgers all night like my family, hoping you have enough money to get people to pick the fruit that for once is healthy enough to produce a bumper crop."

He held up his fingers. "Five years and yes I have seen wildfires. I might not have been here running the winery day to day but I lived through it."

She blinked. "What?"

"I've owned the vineyard for five years, but someone managed it for me until I could move here full time." He pushed a goat off his sofa. It immediately scampered back up.

"You had a winery manager?" Wouldn't *that* be heaven?

"Yes! It's what people do. I wanted to be here for two long years instead of splitting my time between Seattle and Chelan, juggling a stressful job and running the winery remotely, driving six hours roundtrip to Chelan every other week, but it didn't work out that way." He flexed his fist. "Why are you so mad at me?"

She fell into the sofa. "What?" *Because you can buy your way out of anything?*

"When we first started talking in the grocery story, I thought we'd, I don't know, develop a friendship. Maybe more. That night." He shook his head. "Never mind. I thought you were different. Small town people are supposed to be salt of the earth, but you know what you are? Bigots. Look it up. Doesn't mean racist. Means you don't like people who aren't like you. No, I haven't experienced that kind of hardship, but you don't know what kind of things I've experienced, do you? You have me in a box just because I'm not from around here. Just because I come from the tech world and don't drive a beat-up old truck. Do you know what happens when I walk into the Apple Cup? People stare at me. They don't say hi. Except for your father, but I bet you've turned him against me, haven't you?"

Carmen didn't know what to say. Everything he said was true. "I didn't…" But her next words didn't come.

"Yeah, you didn't." He left, leaving her to survey the damage.

Carmen was hot, tired and ready for a glass of wine by the time she got home. After watching Evan circulate amongst his wedding guests like a seasoned pro, apologizing and offering weekends at his personal home, saying he'd ferry people around in his boat, Carmen had hiked down his rocky driveway to the lake and spent a few quiet moments throwing stones into the turquoise water, wishing she had time to swim. Watching the circles expand in the water after each stone sunk to the bottom had the same effect it had when she was young. Her mood lightened. The beauty of the lake, the surrounding hills and the soothing sounds of the water lapping at the shore were balm to her soul. She was a lake girl. A winemaker.

Who hated losing.

Evan might be ambitious, but he didn't stand to lose anything.

Carmen thought about his comment about being friends, maybe more, and shoved it to the back of her mind.

Her sisters were waiting at home. They had a plan.

She strapped on her sandals and crossed the street a few yards to the right of the Hollister Estate drive, marked by a colossal stone and marble plaque. The Blue Hills Vineyard sign was wooden, simple and elegant. Evan might be struggling today, but he could hire someone to clean up the mess and buy half of Restoration Hardware. What was a little goat poop compared to her father's life?

Carmen strolled up the driveway through their orchard, heavy with sweet-smelling pears ripening in the sun, buzzing with thousands of bees. She looked up at the fields overhead, climbing above Orchard House, stopping only when the rocks reached into the sky, deep orange against the softening blue. This place reached into the very core of Carmen's being. This place wasn't just home.

This place was part of Carmen.

She wouldn't lose it.

Not for anyone.

Carmen knew there would be a thousand things to clean up and sort out before their next wedding. The first wedding alone had been exhausting beyond belief. She knew she should have been cleaning instead of helping Evan, but she intended to get stuck in with the cleaning now. Her sisters had other ideas.

When she rounded the corner from the driveway, her sisters stood up from the patio table like angry hornets.

"Why are you helping him?" said Lola.

"¡Dios mío, Carmenita! Why go to all the trouble of messing things up if you're going to come in like the savior? What are we doing here? We need to get things straight if I'm going to spend time here instead of paying some teenager I barely trust to watch mis hijos," Adella said, arms crossed, a vivid reminder of Carmen's old boss, her old life.

A stark reminder of what she'd left behind.

Lola shook her head, pointing at the patio, where nothing remained from the wedding except some stacks of chairs and folded rental tables that would be picked up in the morning. Bags of dirty table linens hunched like goblins near the driveway. "We cleaned everything up. That wedding coordinator was next to useless. We had to tip the caterer because she ran out of checks. I suppose you stayed to clean up the mess? Because he can't afford a cleaning crew or anything."

"I helped him corral the goats."

Adella scowled. "Aye, chica, the whole point was *not* corralling them."

Carmen wanted to stomp upstairs, slam her door and escape this tribunal. But something told her they'd just chase her. She was their point person. She was also a person without a job who needed the support of her sisters. She couldn't do this alone. "Okay, habla."

Adella threw her hands up in the air, pacing. "Enough. Enough. Tell the truth, hermanita."

Carmen sat down, locating a bottle of wine and a glass that wasn't very clean, but it didn't matter. If it belonged to a sister. "I shouldn't have answered the phone."

"No, you shouldn't have," said Adella angrily, but at least she sat down.

"You have a crush on him, don't you?" asked Lola, ever the romantic. Leave it to her baby sister to focus on the drama.

Carmen lifted her hands. "No, I do not have a crush on him." She angrily pointed up at Evan's house. "There's a herd of goats in his living room right now. And a completely trashed wedding on his patio. I didn't do anything to help him other than suggest putting the goats in his house."

Adella clapped a hand over her mouth. "His house?"

Lola giggled. "And he listened to you?"

"They're in his massive living room right now, munching on velvet pillows that probably cost more than my couch."

Her older sister visibly relaxed.

"Can we talk about the First Crush Festival now? We really need an awesome booth or something."

Adella nodded. "Sure. I'll ask Bob if he can take the kids. I can't be here for next weekend's weddings, but I think you can handle it."

Lola sipped from her glass. "I'm here." She narrowed her eyes. "I have lots of ideas."

Adella grinned. "When you watch a lot of telenovelas you learn a lot about double-crossing."

"Hey!" Lola said good-naturedly. No one could accuse Lola of being a workaholic.

Adella absentmindedly texted her husband. "So, we have a booth at First Crush and do what?" Everyone knew that besides attracting sales, the goal of First Crush was to come up with clever gimmicks to get visitors. It was carnival for wine lovers.

Lola jumped up, knocking down her chair. "I've got it!" She lowered her voice to a whisper, worried that Evan might be out on his patio. The caterers could be seen in silhouette on his property, cleaning up the last of the wedding disasters. "We let people get into a vat and crush grapes with their feet." She lifted her glass. "I did see it on a telenovela. It turns out you can actually use the wine if they clean their feet first."

Adella wrinkled her nose, opening the US Fire Service app as she talked. "It sounds super unsanitary."

"Google it. People do it all the time," Lola said in a smug tone, crossing her arms.

Adella looked up from her phone. "Hey, have you guys heard about the Mile Sixty fire?"

Lola shrugged. "I heard it was contained."

"For now," Carmen said.

There was an uneasy silence as the sisters cleared the table. Two summers ago, wildfires ravaged both sides of the shore, wiping out homes and businesses, causing the town to evacuate. They'd contain one growing fire only to discover a new one spreading along the arid mountains and hills. It was a collective nightmare that caused even distant fires to seem threatening now.

As they entered the kitchen, Lola turned on the lights. "What if this doesn't work? What if Papi loses the winery?"

The sisters locked eyes in a shifting triangle across the tile island. Eventually, they turned to Adella, as they had after Mami died. Their reluctant leader in the six dark months before Papi had found his feet as a single parent.

"Por favor, don't make this any harder than it already is. We have a plan." Adella rinsed her wineglass in the sink.

Adella left for home. Lola went to her room after a halfhearted offer to help clean up. Carmen wanted time to think. She loaded dishes into the ancient Sears dishwasher, still marked with a dent where Lola had kicked it as a teen. What would happen if they failed? What was left here for her? Making wine was in her blood, this was her shot. She wouldn't start over on another winery. She wanted to make wine here, at Blue Hills. She wanted her father's journey to continue with another generation. She wanted her children to swim and play with the same freedom that she took for granted. The growth of the town could be the beginning of a whole new chapter in the Alvarez family winemaking business.

Without thinking about it, Carmen found herself climbing the hill into the vineyard, checking the fruit on the vines. She wished she'd brought the refractometer to check the brix level of the fruit to see if the sugar was rising. Too low, she'd learned from Paolo before his fit, and the wine wouldn't have enough alcohol; too high and the fruit would over-ferment, interfering with the flavor. After talking to Paolo, Carmen asked her father where he kept his refractometers. He couldn't remember. After a long search, they'd finally located one in the back of his pick-up and another stashed in his desk in the winery. Having one in her back pocket made her feel like she belonged in a winery. The fruit hung deep purple and heavy on the vine. Now they just had to get it into the shed.

Carmen had been on the phone up and down the valley trying to book crews for harvest time, which was always tricky, given the competition would all have grapes ready at the same time. Farmers helped one another by sharing crews. Carmen had gotten lots of phone calls returned based on her last name, but most of them had the same answer: immigration quotas had caused a shortage of pickers. Everyone was close to panicking.

Carmen looked back down the hill and studied the moon on the water, wavering in brilliant glittery shards, flickering as wispy clouds floated across the inky sky. Somewhere along the lake, a boat buzzed. Something splashed.

A noise startled Carmen. It came from down below.

Evan had slammed a door on his way out of his house. Carmen stayed still, her breath catching in her throat as Evan shucked his bathrobe and dove, with an elegant arc, into the pool. She watched, enraptured, as he effortlessly swam a few lengths, his lean torso catching the moonlight. His legs flipped in a kick turn that would have impressed teenaged Carmen. *He must have swum in high school,* Carmen thought.

¡Dios mío! Those shoulders. The way he owned the water. Suddenly, she was back in the pool with Evan. They'd laughed so hard. It was the most carefree she'd been since coming back home. If that night was the first time he'd been in his own pool, this must be the second. Carmen found herself wanting to go back to that night. Eating dinner on his patio. Gazing down the lake, hearing about Evan's life in Seattle. How it had been everything until—poof—it was nothing. They had more in common than she'd realized. And a deep love of Chelan. Clearly, he felt he belonged. They both wanted to start and end their days looking at this lake, walking their land, seeing the grapes grow and ripen on the vine.

Was Evan thinking about being in the pool with her?

The perfume of the grapes, lush and heavy on the vine, must be playing with her emotions.

Carmen shook her head. She needed to focus. Evan would have Paolo booking crews of pickers. He could pay more than anyone in the valley. Winning was his aim, not saving money.

Carmen needed every penny. Staring out at the lake, she thought that what she needed was people who wanted to learn about wine. What if she could find someone who cared more about wine than earning money, who would pick to be part of the process? She gasped when the idea came to her.

She could host students and people who wanted to be part of the harvest and get them to pick the grapes. She'd advertise in hospitality programs at Western Washington University and see if she could get people in Seattle, food and wine people, to come help out a local winemaker. Maybe reach out to food and wine bloggers across the mountains. Find people who wanted to experience winemaking at the root level.

Drink local and meet the winemaker. They could hire a yoga teacher to help untwist knotted muscles and sore necks.

She could offer them a case of the wine they helped make. And pay the bank.

And keep going.

This was it. Carmen knew she'd struck something that could potentially lift them from the clutches of the bank. Her vision of making wines, award-winning wines, establishing her own legacy, bringing people to Chelan for wine tasting and food experiences, maybe even opening a small restaurant that featured local cuisine like the places she'd read about in Napa. Make Blue Hills take the next step. This was the chance of a lifetime. She was going to take it and run.

Carmen was halfway down the hill before she realized she'd forgotten a bunch of grapes she needed to bring back in order to check the brix level. She scurried back up, forgetting all about Evan.

She was so busy making plans in her head that she didn't notice Evan at the edge of his patio, watching her hurrying towards Orchard House. Her mind was far from her handsome neighbor. She was busy making plans to save Blue Hills Vineyard and in doing so, create a life and a career for herself.

Everything was riding on her success.

Failure, Carmen thought, wasn't an option.

No matter how she felt about Evan Hollister.

CHAPTER TEN

Wedding Encore

Evan ended the call with the sales representative from Restoration Hardware. Replacing the pillows was out of the question. How could a single pillow cost two hundred and fifty dollars? Was it stuffed with cash?

His first wedding had been such a disaster. The goats. After the wedding, he'd waited morosely with the goats, who had finally huddled on couches and floor, bleating plaintively at the windows, like little children who didn't want to go to bed. Evan had grabbed some leftover champagne and drank a few glasses. Finally, a boy who hardly looked old enough to drive, let alone work, had chugged up the hill with a trailer. When he'd appeared at the opening to the living room, the goats had rushed towards him like teens mobbing Taylor Swift. They'd followed him meekly down the driveway, all sixteen of them pushing one another to get close to the boy, clattering up the wooden ramp.

After the boy had shoved the ramp into the trailer, talking to the goats in soothing Spanish, Evan had asked what had happened. Why had he ended up with sixteen rampaging goats instead of one well-mannered one?

The boy had turned to him with a casual shrug. "No hablo ingles."

Sure.

Evan took his coffee outside now, bringing the handwritten bill for the sixteen goats that had been shoved into his mailbox. No stamp. Hand delivered. Why should he pay for this, when they'd destroyed his house and the wedding? When he'd asked Carmen how so many goats could possibly have been delivered to his house when he'd requested one, she had said they had probably switched orders. Lots of people ordered a herd of goats to chew away unwanted blackberry bushes or invasive plants. It wasn't unusual to drive down the lake and see a herd of cloven-footed goats happily munching away. Yes, it was possible that the order had had been switched.

Evan looked at the bill. Four hundred dollars. He wasn't going to pay for a bunch of goats he'd never wanted. They'd eaten five hundred dollars' worth of pillows. He called the number on the bill. It was a landline with an answering machine. Who had answering machines? Just as he was leaving his message, a voice came over it, swearing a little as the tape played on.

"Just a minute! Hang on!" Finally, after much fumbling, a woman's voice came over the line. "This is Crystal Huttinger."

Of course, the goat herder was called Crystal.

Evan explained his predicament. He'd asked for one goat. Not sixteen.

"Most people want the entire herd."

"Why would I have ordered so many goats? And no one to look after them?"

Crystal paused. "Hang on. Oh wait. I know. Because you ordered them. Look man, I know you've got plenty of dough. And I just assume people want the goats for cleaning up their land."

Evan had a pretty good idea of what Crystal looked like. Stringy grey hair and Birkenstocks. A lifetime of smoking pot and staring out the window. He had nothing against the type, he just didn't want to pay for goats with expensive snacking habits who pooped on his Spanish tile floor. Grout and goat poop, he told her, were a bad mix.

Crystal whispered, "Hang on, Spright. I'm on the phone." A screen door slammed. Her voice returned to normal. "Listen man. If you've got a problem, it's not with me. It's with that Alvarez girl. She's the one who ordered the goats."

Evan stood up, staring down at the horseshoe-shaped Alvarez patio. Carmen was pouring her sister some water. "What? Did you accidentally deliver them to my place?" Maybe Carmen had wanted goats cleaning up the orchard near the water during the wedding.

"No. She said they were for you. You'd have someone to look after them and they'd be hanging out for the day. She said they'd have free run of the place."

Evan felt his face flush with anger. "Oh, they did all right."

"Yeah. She said they were to come hungry."

Evan paced, his grip on the phone making his fingers ache. He could see the goats leaping on tables, gobbling wedding cake, chasing the screaming flower girls into the pool. His first wedding ruined. "Oh, they ate plenty."

"So, we're good?"

Evan nodded, sitting down, feeling the urge to exact revenge before he could think straight. "We're good. I'll pay."

And so will the Alvarez sisters, Evan thought.

*

The bride was arriving by carriage. They didn't know this until the carriage driver from the Lakestream Ranch called to make sure that the driveway was accessible by carriage.

"By what?" Carmen asked, moving the centerpieces out of the driving sun. The marquees that were supposed to shelter the guests from the sweltering heat had been set up at another location, and the flowers would wilt by the time the guests arrived if they stayed out.

"Carriage. Two horses. She's not too keen on having only the two, but two of our matched set have the runs so she's not likely to love that either. I'm wearing a wool uniform, so her ladyship isn't going to suffer as much as me and the horses."

Carmen walked around to the front of Orchard House, hoping she could tell what exactly constituted a horse-safe driveway. "Yeah, I guess. My cousin used to come here on his horse occasionally. No carriage." She described Orchard House.

"Fine. Great."

Carmen hurried around to the back of the house, rushing upstairs to where her sister was still in the shower. Carmen shouted over the great clouds of steam: "The bride is arriving by horse and carriage!"

"What a snob!" yelled Lola.

Carmen came back down the stairs to find her father eating a piece of buttered toast, glancing with agitation at the tables on the back patio. "Who's a snob?"

"The bride."

"Why is the bride a snob?" said her father, who, Carmen had noticed, compensated for his memory loss by pretending to know what was happening. Tiny tables meant a wedding. A wedding meant a bride. Things his daughters clearly took care of. He could roam the fields, check on his grapes and drive into town for coffee at the Apple Cup.

"She's traveling by horse and carriage," said Carmen.

Someone cleared their throat.

It was the wedding planner, with a wry grin on her face. A middle-aged, spry woman who wore pearls with jeans and somehow got away with it. "Good morning."

Carmen's heart sunk. This was the one person in whose good graces she wanted to remain. She booked all the best weddings. And now she'd just heard Carmen calling the bride, who happened to be the wedding planner's cousin, a snob.

Carmen put her hand over her heart. "I'm sorry."

"Well," said the wedding planner. "I'm here to deliver the red carpet. It's for the bride."

Carmen held her hand over her mouth and looked at her father, whose eyes crinkled.

Luckily, they all laughed.

Carmen would look back later and think of this as the best part of the weekend.

*

It was surprising, how much fun he'd had planning it. All Evan's competitive instincts had risen to the surface as he called in favors and gleefully set about plotting the ruination of his neighbor's business. It felt wonderful to snicker to himself, imagining a wedding unraveling as thoroughly as the one he'd hosted last weekend.

It reminded him of the Microsoft days. He remembered the CEO of a smaller, very successful software company. She'd told them that a good deal might leave something on the table, but both partners left feeling good about the transaction. That, the CEO had patiently explained, was a good deal.

What she didn't understand was that their culture wasn't to leave anything on the table.

Except maybe blood.

Which was why Evan had cashed in his chips and left.

The old feeling came back in a rush. He was going to crush them. Or at least this wedding. It was so easy.

So fun.

Any guilt was swept away by what they'd done to him. Last weekend had been so stressful. Worrying what the guests were saying. Chasing after goats. Trying to think of something to make the teary-eyed little flower girls smile as their mothers rushed for towels. Explaining to the wedding coordinator that it hadn't been his fault. Did she really think that he had added sixteen goats to the mix on purpose?

When he felt the slightest twinge of guilt, all he had to do was go into his living room and imagine it full of bleating little goats. And envision a goat butting the terrified flower girl into the pool as she valiantly clutched her bouquet.

The only thing missing from his plan was someone to share it with. Someone to share the glory over a bottle of wine.

Because the one person he wanted to gloat with was the one person he couldn't.

The one person who would hopefully never know what really happened at this Blue Hills wedding.

Because Evan not only knew how to plan a perfect takedown.

He knew how to cover his tracks.

*

Weather was the problem. Unrelenting heat caused wildfires to jump barriers to the north. Chelan was sweltering before noon. By the time the horses arrived up the hill, they were in a lather, sweat glistening from their coats, tossing their heads eagerly, ready to trot down the hill to the spot where on days like today their driver allowed them a long drink from the lake. Carmen, who'd stepped outside to enjoy the spectacle, felt a flutter of anxiety. It was hotter out here than the sweltering kitchen.

The bride, nestled in the open carriage, swatted flies. Her face was flushed under her layer of tulle which mounded up like a meringue, flying into her face. Dust from the unpaved drive flew out from under the carriage wheels, coating the guests who'd gathered at the end of the garden to welcome the bride. Carmen stood behind the wedding party on the patio, praying none of the elderly guests would suffer heat stroke.

The father of the bride stepped out to greet the carriage, sweating furiously in his light woolen suit. He held out his hand to her while she gathered her voluminous skirts. A horsefly the size of a bee landed on his face. Yelping in pain as the fly chomped down, he swatted at it with the hand he'd extended to his daughter. Her hand gripped air as she leaned out of the carriage and tumbled down the folding carriage steps. Carmen watched in growing horror as a large raised welt appeared on the poor man's cheek.

Bounce. Bounce. Bounce. Like a cartoon.

She landed with a grunt. "Daddy!"

Her father, applying a handkerchief to his wound, was slow on the uptake, eyes widening when he realized that his daughter was down, and seventy-five people expected him to do something. Carmen wondered if she should do something. Offer him some antiseptic or painkiller. Didn't his daughter care that he'd just been bitten? A look of determination came over the man's face, motivated, Carmen thought, by a desire to get this spoiled creature off his hands.

Down went the handkerchief as he gripped his daughter's hand. He tugged and pulled until he realized that his daughter, in her voluminous dress, would be unable to stand until he bent in the dirt in his elegant suit and pushed his daughter up from behind.

There was a tittering in the audience. The bride glared at him as if their reaction was his fault.

"Daddy!" she hissed.

"What?" He ineffectually dusted off her dress, which seemed to push the reddish dirt deeper into the fabric. "Do you have a better idea?"

"This is a disaster."

"Don't be melodramatic!" her dad shot back.

The guests had thoughtfully drifted back to their seats. Carmen dashed inside for an antiseptic wipe. The father of the bride let her gently dab the wound before they walked down the aisle.

The bride fumed, obviously incensed that her grand entrance had been ruined but maybe there was time to make up for it. Her make-up artist ran up, offering a pep talk. "Darling, you're gorgeous, stylish, utter perfection," she whispered, while dabbing the girl's moist hairline with blotting paper.

"She's expensive," her father muttered to Carmen, who stifled a laugh.

"There's nowhere to go but up," sniffed the bride. She shot a look at her pimply teenaged cousin, slouching with her clipboard by the entrance to the patio where the guests sat on white chairs, still snickering gleefully over her cousin's misfortune.

Misters, rented at the last moment at horrendous expense, floated a fine spray of water over them, cooling them as the day grew impossibly warm.

The bride's father, his cheek visibly swollen, thanked Carmen with a nod. He approached his daughter, offering his arm. "Shall we?"

The bride took a deep breath, waved away the make-up artist and took her father's arm. "From now on, everything will be perfect," she hissed. "This wedding will be unforgettable."

As it turned out, she was right.

Carmen watched the wedding from the kitchen steps. The bride appeared serene by the time she reached her groom. The groom watched her every step down the aisle with breathless awe. Everything was back on track, which was why the buzzing in the distance made Carmen faintly nervous. Not alarmed. Not yet. The buzzing grew closer, then louder, as little insects swarmed the wedding party first, then the guests. Except they weren't insects, Carmen deduced within a minute. They were drones.

"Look out! They're drones!" The groom screamed, which didn't help the general chaos that followed. People bumped into each other, into the flower beds, swatting away at the little drones.

They kept coming.

The drones swooped, swarmed and attacked relentlessly. A young man in a goatee dashed past her, hollering something about programmed coordinates and flight patterns. Whoever had access to drones in this number and minute size was no stranger to the tech world. Carmen looked around for anyone within her line of sight, who could possibly be controlling the drones, but they suddenly lifted and disappeared just as most of the wedding party scrambled into the kitchen, shoving aside the startled caterer.

Carmen didn't have time to think about who had unleashed drones upon the wedding. She was too busy pouring champagne and reassuring the guests with forced cheer that they'd start over again. One (or two) teensy problems weren't going to get in the way of their fun. Lola had popped the champagne early, whispering to Carmen that a slight buzz would smooth things over. Carmen had to hand it to her sister: in a clinch, she rose to the occasion. Soon, the well-lubricated guests were reseated in their chairs. They'd had time to smooth their hair, sip some wine and nibble a few appetizers hastily extracted from the fridge.

The minister made light of the moment, chuckling that technology certainly invaded every area of life these days, and this couple had the distinction of hosting drones at their wedding.

"Uninvited," quipped the groom.

Everyone chuckled and sipped their champagne.

Carmen exhaled an endless sigh.

They'd recovered.

The minister had just asked the bride if she took the groom as her lawfully wedded husband, when the cooling misters increased. Instead of a gentle spritz, they began hissing water at such volume that the guests dashed from their seats, blocking one another in the aisle. The bride, standing directly in front of the misters, was instantly drenched, her hair collapsing around her shoulders in stringy strands. Her groom tried pushing down the misters, but they were tied to sand-filled bases weighing over a hundred pounds. He finally took his bride's hand to help her down the stairs. Her dress was a vast white sponge, making it hard to move. The groom tried to make light of it, spinning her in a dance move, but she stumbled. "Barry, I can't move. I'm soaking wet."

The bride's father rested comfortably in his ruined suit, sipping bourbon while holding the icepack Carmen had given him on his cheek. He raised his glass to the groom, busy mollifying his irritated bride. "Good luck, kid."

The guests were invited inside for food, but few of them stayed. They couldn't dry off well enough and went into town to change. Carmen called them back, saying they'd delay the reception, but the bride had reached a tipping point. Her husband said they'd all meet for pizza in town later at Local Myth. Seeing the bride swilling French champagne like it was water convinced Carmen that this was for the best.

"Let's call it a wrap," she said to Lola, who muttered under her breath, "Or a fiasco. Where do you suppose those drones came from?"

Carmen poured a glass from an open bottle of champagne. It hit her like a bolt of lightning. Of course. Evan could have hired all the drones, would have known exactly who to call. He could have reset the misters in the middle of the night without anyone knowing.

Carmen swallowed the rest of her champagne, handing the empty glass to Lola.

"I'm going to kill him."

CHAPTER ELEVEN

Day Drinking

He was gloating. Carmen couldn't believe it. If she'd been a cartoon, she'd have steam coming out of her ears. Not that she wanted to know what she looked like.

She'd been so furious; she didn't bother changing. By the time she'd scrambled up the hill in her sunny yellow dress and gladiator sandals, the damp dress was streaked with red dirt. Her tidy chignon sprung from her head in unruly wisps. She'd reached the top of the hill, scanned the patio for Evan and stomped toward the house. Barry had come loping towards her, tail wagging, eager to see a friendly face. He carried a drool-coated tennis ball in his mouth, dropping it at her feet.

"Oh, Barry," Carmen said, taking the sticky ball. "Why is your owner such a jerk?"

She turned to toss the disgusting ball.

She hadn't reached the back door before Barry was back, dropping the dirty ball at her feet. "I'm sorry. I have to go kill someone. Don't worry, you can live with me. We'd all be better off without him." She threw the ball again.

"So much for man's best friend." Evan spoke through the kitchen window. It was tucked under an expansive awning, opening onto an outdoor bar. He poured two glasses of wine, then came outside with a sigh, turning his face to the sun, offering Carmen a glass which she ignored.

"Here's to sunny days and award-winning wines." He took a sip, eying her over the glass rim. "How was the wedding?"

Carmen felt her pulse in her ears. This was clearly an act. This preening self-satisfaction. She decided: she wouldn't let this smug millionaire get the best of her. Or her family. If it was war, the gloves were off.

"Day drinking, I see."

"We're winemakers. Part of the job."

"Is ruining weddings part of the job, too?"

"Funny thing for you to ask."

"How *was* the wedding? Let's see. The bride fell out of her carriage. Then, mysteriously, she was attacked by drones." Carmen held her index finger and thumb together to illustrate. "Tiny little drones."

Evan raised an eyebrow. Maybe at one point she'd thought this was attractive, but today it made him look a self-satisfied jerk. "Drones?"

"Yes, and as if that wasn't enough, the misters turned into sprinklers and drenched everyone. Ruined dresses, hairdos and the wedding."

"Sounds awful." He took a measured sip.

"Oh, trust me, it was. I can imagine someone around here maybe being mean enough to mess with the sprinklers, but what I can't imagine is someone local deciding on drones. *That* sounds like someone who works in the tech world."

Evan spread his arms. "I'm in the wine world."

"Not if I have anything to do with it. I thought worrying about the bank, wildfires, soil acidity, irrigation and smoke in the wine was bad enough. Now I've got you."

"Smoke in the wine?"

Plants, Carmen had learned, were as sensitive as humans. "Google it."

Evan's eyes narrowed as he offered Carmen the glass of wine for the second time. She took it, holding it pinched between her fingers as if it smelled.

Evan set his wine down, crossing his arms. "Carmen, I agree, this thing has escalated. But you're hardly the innocent party here. We're both at fault. I talked to Crystal the goatkeeper."

"There is no comparison."

"You only saw the aftermath. The wedding was chaos."

"The goats didn't attack anyone!"

Evan sighed. "All right. We can argue all night, or we can just stop."

"By stopping, what do you mean?"

Evan studied her with a pained expression. As though he was wrestling with himself, holding back something vitally important he was determined not to share. She wondered what was going on in his mind before she stopped, chastising herself. She didn't care what Evan Hollister was thinking. Not even a little.

He broke the awkward silence. "Carmen, I have made your father a very decent offer. This is the last time. After this, it's off the table."

Carmen wiped a stray hair off her forehead. "And if you don't get my fields?" They weren't her fields but suddenly this felt personal in a way that it hadn't been before.

"If I don't get your fields, I'll get the surrounding fields. I'll buy water rights; I'll operate on all sides until I squeeze Blue Hills right out of existence. You'll be wishing you could have the deal I'm offering you right now, but your land won't be worth as much. It will be a tiny piece in the middle of my winery. And your father will lose because you let him."

Carmen's body went utterly still, her eyes narrowed in concentration.

"Carmen, this is just business."

Carmen considered what he was saying. The leather laces on her gladiator sandals were drying, cutting into her ankles. She put the wine on the table and unlaced the sandals, taking them off and dropping them in the stainless patio trash can. Evan watched her impassively.

She straightened up. She thought about losing the land and what her father had told her about wine being in her blood. This wasn't about their land. If they lost and she ended up with nothing, no career, no prospects, then she would at least have fought hard. Even if Evan stranded Blue Hills and Orchard House as an island in his empire, he still wouldn't have the mineral-rich soil that made their wines so elegant and unique. They'd won medals all over the country. Her father had built a legacy. She wouldn't let that die just because some tech millionaire refused to accept that his vineyard needed time. Papi had explained that the Hollister Estate soil needed amendments. Evan should truck in soil that had to be worked into the existing dirt, coaxed into the vines and allowed time to mature. His vines were young and required nurturing. But rather than let time work its magic, he wanted to take her father's land. Shortcuts, in a business that worked in decades.

She lifted the wineglass in her hand.

Evan's smile brightened, clearly anticipating a deal, her capitulation. He lifted his glass with a broad smile.

She held her glass aloft, enjoying the way his smile faltered when she didn't clink her glass to his. "The only people who lose are the ones who give up." Carmen poured the entire contents of her glass down the wet bar sink.

Game.

Set.

Match.

"Honestly, I think you should bury the hatchet before anyone gets hurt," said Stella, taking an enormous bite of her salad. They were on the patio of Campbell's after the lunch rush.

"Do you mean give up? He won't stop until he gets our land."

Stella looked at a leaf suspiciously. "Is this a dandelion leaf? Did someone just go pick my lunch from the cracks in the sidewalk?"

Carmen shot her friend a look. "Seriously? That's your response?"

Stella took a long drink of iced tea before responding. "I don't know how it looks from the inside, but from the outside we've got people coming into town and talking about these weddings. You know how people talk. They say you're going to keep going until you burn your businesses to the ground. Things like this don't take down the target. They take down everyone. It's a race to the bottom."

Stella shook her head. "Right. So just give up?"

"Stop trying to ruin him."

"He's trying to ruin us."

"If you want to save the winery, you've got to come up with something else."

Carmen opened her computer, turning it towards Stella. "I have."

Stella studied the screen for a long time, squinting.

Carmen smiled tentatively. "What do you think?"

"What do I think? I think you're a genius. This is exactly what I'm talking about." Stella pointed at the screen. "'Enjoy fresh air and exercise as you learn winemaking from the field. Pick grapes as part of a crew of like-minded wine lovers, picnicking in the field and sleeping under the stars. Enjoy evening concerts…'" She raised her eyebrows.

"Those guys that play at Senor Frog's."

"'Yoga classes with a view of the lake…'" Stella looked up.

"The orchard. Hopefully the skunks won't show up."

"Yoga with adorable woodland creatures…" Stella smiled. "This is wonderful. People chained to their desks might think manual labor is actually fun."

"Fresh air, swimming in the lake at night."

"Ooooh. Put that in there. Pull out that float and have towels down by the water. I love this. Now you're using your imagination instead of focusing all your anger on one person."

Carmen raised her eyebrows. "One person who deserves it."

Stella sighed. "Car, I know you don't want to hear this but whatever you two have going on…"

Carmen shook her head emphatically. "Nothing is going on."

"Hear me out. You need to stop antagonizing one another. Make nice."

"Why on earth should I try to make nice with someone who is trying to ruin me?"

"Well, for one thing, so you can keep tabs on him. Keep your friends close and your enemies closer."

Carmen took a long sip of her iced tea. "Whoever said that must have been in the wine business."

"You want pickers for free, is that it?" said Lucy Connor, manager of the Manson Villas. Carmen had inserted herself into the monthly Chelan Hotel Association luncheon to showcase her new scheme, Winemaking at the Roots. The hope was that the hotels would offer it as part of their guest programs.

"It's not winemaking really, is it? It's more picking the grapes," said Honore Sullivan, guests' programs manager at the sprawling Campbell's Resort. Honore was the big fish of hotel managers. In high school, she'd been a mean girl. Not much had changed.

Carmen steeled herself. Lola had already played the devil's advocate with such questions, grilling her for hours on how she'd convince people to do work for free that migrant laborers had done for pay. Dirty, backbreaking labor. Carmen pointed out that they'd offer short shifts, lots of refreshment, entertainment, music, canopies that moved with the pickers. She'd honed her arguments and was ready.

"Honore, what we have to remember is that I'm creating an experience. You and I both think of picking grapes as something dirty and difficult." In high school, Honore had sneered at anyone with brown skin, calling them wetbacks or pickers. "I have lots of things ready to make the experience fun and interesting. People love the farm-to-table world, and I'll not only have the harvesting experience, they'll get to taste wine, meet local cheesemakers and learn about their craft. It will be like an outdoor school for people passionate about what they eat and drink. And don't forget, these people are in good shape. They're used to CrossFit and yoga. They'll finish picking and go for a swim or yoga class, or both. It's going to be a totally immersive experience. There's nothing like it out there for your guests."

"I don't doubt that!" chortled Ike Bukasia. He'd hated everything that came out of Carmen's mouth since she'd shot him down for junior prom.

Carmen mentally thanked horrid Felicity for creating such a boot camp, competitive workplace. Her marketing skills were laser sharp. "If you understand millennials, you'll know that they crave authentic experiences. It isn't enough to have wine tastings and massages. I'm offering a day of harvesting the fruit and eating in the fields. Cheese platters made by the people serving them. This is something they'll tell their friends about, over a bottle of wine they helped create. People crave something different, and by offering this to your guests, you'll be on the cutting edge of hospitality."

Ike sat back, taking one of the brochures Carmen passed around the room.

"Any questions?"

Pale Honore sat back, crossing her bony arms. "Isn't this just an ingenious runaround to find pickers in a tight market?"

Carmen gave her a tight smile. "I wish I was that ingenious, Honore. No, this is another way we're trying to grow the Blue Hills Vineyard brand. It's not enough to make the wine anymore, it's about experiences."

Celia Diaz, hospitality director at Wapato Point Resort shook her hand, thanking her for the opportunity. The other hotel managers stretched their legs, getting water and coffee. Carmen heard herself saying that this was just the beginning of Blue Hills Vineyard experiences. "I can see us opening tasting rooms, a restaurant in the cave, classes. This is just the beginning."

Celia nodded enthusiastically. "That's amazing. I am so happy that you're back here and taking this on. Your dad must be so proud."

Carmen nodded. "Actually, he is. He always wanted one of us to keep Blue Hills going and, you know, I'm as surprised at the next person, but it looks like it's me."

Celia glanced away. "Hey, can I ask you something personal?"

Carmen followed as Celia moved to the side of the room. "Yeah, sure."

"Do you know Evan Hollister very well?"

Carmen felt suddenly alert. *What had Evan said about her?* "Yes. Not well, but yeah, I know him."

"He's single, right?"

Carmen nodded. "Yes."

Celia's face relaxed. "Okay, good. I mean, I barely know the guy, but he's been in a few times at the wine bar at work. He asked about you and I just wondered if you two were dating now."

"What did he ask?"

"Nothing very much. I think he met someone who asked if he was neighbors with you. Evan said you were nice and wanted to know if you were seeing anyone."

Carmen felt absurdly pleased before she tamped down her feelings. Whatever Evan might have felt for her at one point was now extinguished by the last few weddings. Ironic. "Well, he doesn't think I'm nice anymore."

"Oh, that's too bad." Celia looked pleased.

"No. It's fine. We have some business, um, disagreements."

"Well then, you don't mind if I…?" Celia bit her lip uncomfortably.

Carmen looked more closely at Celia, who was normally very chill. "If you what?"

"Well, since he's single…"

Carmen's eyes went wide. "Oh, right. I get it. You wanted to see if he was… I get it."

Celia blushed furiously. "Thanks. Anyway, I'm going to put the brochures in the rooms for sure. Having guests harvest the fruit, it's a cool idea." She whispered, "Don't listen to them. They're going to promote you because it's good for their guests, they just have to get their digs in, you know."

Carmen nodded. They'd both survived the same slights in high school. Wetback. Spic. Picker. Although they weren't good friends, there was a bond. "I know."

After the two women said goodbye, Carmen made her rounds, unable to rid herself of the sinking feeling in her stomach. Why should she care if Evan went out with anyone else? He was ruthless, selfish, egotistical, and mostly, he hated her. She certainly didn't want him. But she didn't want anyone else to have him either.

The idea of Evan and Celia together.

Perfectly sweet Celia, who'd gone out of her way to be nice to her today.

Why on earth should she be feeling jealous?

Because that was the word, Carmen realized, as she got into her overheated car.

She was jealous.

Carmen covered her face with her hands before placing them on the steering wheel and staring out at the lake. This was getting way too complicated.

CHAPTER TWELVE

Crushing

Paolo was FaceTiming with a woman in Italian, making furious hand gestures and sipping his wine. If he were any more hysterical, Stella thought, he'd be crying into his glass. The woman, from what Stella could see, was beautiful, seated on a patio not unlike the one at Hollister Estate. She was dressed in white, with brown curls blowing in her face. Occasionally, she'd sweep the curls out of her large green eyes with a decidedly ring-free hand. Just to be sure, Stella checked her other hand. A couple of stylish stacked bands, but nothing that smacked of matrimony.

No wonder Paolo missed his home country.

Stella was waiting for Carmen, who had taken her father to the doctor and was meeting Stella for drinks after she'd driven him home. Meanwhile, Stella was perfectly happy sipping her rosé, listening to what must be the most beautiful language in the world. The language of love.

Or was Spanish called that?

Stella couldn't remember, but whatever language this man spoke had to be the language of love. He was yummy.

And, tragically for her, missing his girlfriend.

If Stella knew anything about Italians, his girlfriend probably wouldn't pine too long for her missing boyfriend. She might have already replaced him. The idea cheered Stella, who'd taken to leaving church early, before all the eager middle-aged ladies could shove their awkward sons in her path. Boys who, years earlier, had shot spitballs into her hair and chased her with grass snakes.

Paolo closed his computer screen, gazing mournfully into his glass of Pinot Grigio. Stella took this as her opportunity, moving near his table. "Must be hard to have a girlfriend so far from home."

Paolo's black eyebrows shot up. "My girlfriend?"

She pointed at his computer.

"Oh, she. My sister."

Stella beamed, pointing at the chair across the table from the handsome Italian. "Oh, sister. Nice. Mind if I sit?"

Paolo jumped up as if electrified, darting around the table to pull the chair out for Stella, who completely lost what little chill she had around this enticing creature.

"Oh, wow, nice." Stella settled into her chair happily. "I can't remember the last time anyone did that for me."

Paolo shook his head. "The men here need some lessons in the love-making."

Stella giggled. "Well, maybe not that."

Paolo pushed his thick black hair from his eyes. "No, not like that. I mean, just the nice things. Like the chair, the pouring the wine, opening the door. You don't make love just like"—he waved his hand in the air—"one way. It's many ways. It's treating the girl like the princess. You know?"

Stella sighed. Being treated like royalty sounded right up her alley. "I wish I knew."

Paolo sipped his wine. "This wine. Not so fine. You know, if you come to my country, I could show you what the Pinot Grigio tastes like when it's got the minerals. You know?"

It was Stella's turn to shake her head. "I don't know very much about wine."

Paolo snapped his fingers. "I teach you."

Stella blinked in disbelief. Dating to Stella meant burgers at the Lakeside, listening to Bobby or Billy or Steve blather endlessly about rebuilding a Camero, or how the guys at the shop were a bunch of sticky-fingered douche bags.

A cloudy film fell off Stella's eyes. This was happening.

Paolo waited on her to respond to his offer.

"I would love that!" Stella replied breathlessly.

*

"He's single!" Stella crowed on the phone. "I could listen to him read a menu. The way he rolls his R's. My goodness Car, I never thought a man's voice would drive me nuts like this. Plus, he says he wants to cook for me. Risotto. That takes a long time to cook, so we'll be drinking wine and talking. Can you believe I said talking, instead of making out? I actually want to get to know him."

Carmen was happy for her friend. Or she wanted to be happy. She couldn't quite sum up the energy after her morning. Although people were signing up to harvest the grapes, she was having a hard time juggling the day-to-day running of the winery with the harvest and preparing to care for and feed guest harvesters. To make matters worse, they had the First Crush Festival, whose organizers had just informed them that everyone working the booths needed a food permit, for which they'd have to travel into Wenatchee. Immediately, if they wanted them in time for the festival.

The third wedding they'd hosted had gone off without a hitch, infusing the winery with enough cash to update. Plastic tubing needed replacing; deep cleaning was necessary. One wrong microbe would ruin an entire cask. Microbes, Carmen had learned, traveled in packs. And they loved the fermenting process.

Carmen checked on the grapes every night, enjoying the cool night air, the moist red dirt under her sandals, the distant glitter of the lake. She'd gotten better at measuring the brix level of the grapes. They were so close now. She needed at least twenty more harvesters. And tents, sleeping bags, food and towels. Endless lists on her phone.

Stella had been babbling on about Paolo's many charms, but Carmen was having a hard time paying attention. "Does he talk much about wine?"

"A little. He really wants to teach me about wine, which is fun. He freaked out when I told him I loved wine from a can. I really need to clean. He's coming to my place. To cook pasta and fish. Pasta Pescatore." Stella bounced the syllables off her tongue, mimicking Paolo. "Sounds much better in Italian. Cooking for me at my apartment. Isn't that sweet?"

"Very," Carmen said absently, wondering if she should place a Craigslist ad for pickers.

"He has six toes on each foot. Isn't that sexy?"

Carmen didn't hear. "Mmmm-hmmm. Yeah."

Stella laughed. "You're not listening. I said he has six toes on each foot."

"Extra toes? That's so—oh right. That was a test. I'm sorry." Carmen felt guilty. She should be happier for her friend. Stella had kissed a lot of toads. Been set up, knocked down and run away from dates gone sour. Now a handsome Italian man with an esteemed profession was interested in her.

"Stell, I'm really, really happy for you. I am. It's a bit tricky because Paolo and I didn't hit it off."

"Yeah, we need a re-do. I'll make him play nice."

"He's really not a fan."

"Tough luck. You're my best friend. We're a package deal."

Carmen winced. Stella had just met someone completely thrilling and was ready to throw him over if he didn't like her. "It's fine. It was about him teaching me the wine business. Apparently, I'm a little too American. Or something."

"He'll get over it."

"I suppose."

"Carmen, what if he taught me?"

"Taught you what?"

"What if I asked him what you need to know about the wine business, and I shared it with you?"

"Like a spy?"

"Oh yeah. Now I'm loving this idea. I'll ask him your questions and share them with you. No harm, no foul."

The idea was enormously appealing, but this was Stella. She'd met someone out of the miniscule Chelan dating pool and was smitten. "Do you really think this is a good way to start off a relationship? Spying?"

"You're my best friend in the entire world. I'm closer to your family than I am my own. I'd do anything to help. I'm not going to hurt Paolo. Let me do this. Start a list of questions and email them to me. This can work."

Carmen was quiet for a moment. "Okay."

"Yay!"

Carmen's entire body crumpled with relief. She was in so far above her head. Anything she could glean from Paolo would be a much-needed gift. "Oh, Stell. I love you."

"I have an ulterior motive, you know."

"What?"

Stella's laugh sounded like sunshine. "If you don't make some fabulous wine and keep Blue Hills open, you won't stay in town. I'm actually being completely selfish."

Stella was just making her feel better. "Thanks, Stell."

"Adiós, mi amiga. I'm off to get my nails done and my legs waxed. Then I'm going home to clean and realize I hate all my clothing."

Carmen forced herself to stop worrying about the potential fallout and enjoy her friend's happiness. "Have a wonderful time, Stella."

Carmen hung up the phone and looked at Lola, who was tallying up what it was going to cost to house and feed their guest harvesters. Carmen was driving to Wenatchee first thing to apply for food permits.

"We can't afford the tents and sleeping bags. We're going to have to put the guests in Orchard House."

"Aye. What can we tell Papi?"

Lola shook her head. "La verdad. The truth is we can't find any pickers, so we had to call it summer camp for grown-ups."

Carmen shook her head. "He's not going to believe it."

"Just tell him it will get the grapes in on time."

That was an old family joke that had suddenly become reality. You could break your leg or faint in the fields, but getting the grapes in on time was the priority.

Papi used to make them cancel dates and work if they were short of pickers. He always told them that to live on a winery was to help with the harvest. The girls would watch their friends water skiing on the lake and feel sorry for themselves. Complain that he wouldn't notice if they dropped dead from heatstroke. Now Carmen felt pride that she'd been there to help. Now she understood.

As long as the grapes get in on time.

Papi's life had become hers.

*

"Are you waiting for someone else?" asked Mandy, Evan's PR consultant, who also worked in branding.

They were having lunch in town. Evan realized he'd chosen the location because he'd seen Carmen here. Every dark-haired woman who walked in made him look up from his salad, which he'd barely touched.

He shook his head. "No, I thought I saw someone I know."

Evan wondered if Mandy had heard rumors. Chelan was a small town. A breeding ground for rumors. He hadn't helped matters by spending their first meeting complaining about Carmen. How frustrating it was having a neighbor who saw him as the competition. He'd told her that he wanted the Blue Hills vines.

"But isn't that how they make their living?" Mandy had asked.

"I'm offering them a lot of money," he'd replied.

"But sometimes people need more than money," Mandy had explained patiently.

Evan hadn't really listened. He'd wanted to vent. Mandy had bluntly stated that he was conflicted. He'd looked her in the eye and said that if he had to put the Alvarez family out of business, he would.

"Nikki at the Chamber of Commerce said their booth for First Crush is a giant barrel that people get into and crush the grapes," she said now.

Evan dropped his fork with distaste. "With their feet? Isn't that kind of gross?"

"Not really. They wash their feet first." She took a bite of her burger. "I guess people really like it. It's tactile."

Evan sighed. He didn't understand anything. Least of all Carmen. "What can we do?"

She finished another bite, glancing at Evan's salad. He'd hardly touched it.

"Technically we're only supposed to have a booth, but there's a workaround if you make a donation to the high school."

"Sounds slippery."

"Let me worry about it." She shoved a french fry in her mouth, offering him one. "I was thinking a county fair vibe. What you want is people with little kids being dragged to your booth. I'm thinking a petting zoo, a ring toss with your wines, and a dunking tank."

"That sounds like a lot of stuff."

"It is. And it won't be cheap. But people go all out on this thing. It's our biggest event for fall and people love it. I want your brand to be front and center. Go big or go home."

Evan turned his head towards the door. "Yeah. Maybe not the petting zoo. I haven't had great luck with farm animals."

"These will be baby farm animals with lots of people looking after them. I'm telling you, it's a great pull. Of course, we'll have a tasting table all set up and lots of swag. Your name will be on the best stuff." She passed him a catalog of branding items, patting it. "Pick out three to five items and I'll order them."

He left the catalog untouched. "Okay."

She ate a few more fries in the silence that followed. "I need your order by the end of the week."

Evan nodded. "Fine."

Mandy got up from the table, asking Evan if he had any more questions.

He didn't. He was too distracted. Mandy lingered for a moment as if she had something else to say. "Okay, don't forget about the order."

"Got it," Evan said with a brisk nod.

He was paying the check when he realized that he hadn't asked Mandy about social media branding. He should have. Why didn't she bring it up? He scrawled his signature, wishing he hadn't been so checked out. In a fog. He needed to focus.

But Evan had other things on his mind.

*

"Why do the pickers have to stay here? Can't they sleep in the cabins in the orchard?" Juan seemed perplexed. Carmen had done her best to explain that the people coming to help with the harvest weren't exactly pickers. They were harvesters and also guests. Juan couldn't understand why people would want to pick fruit for free. It was backbreaking work that people like him undertook as a foothold to a better life. They didn't leave their better life to pick grapes. That was backwards.

Lola had collected the last boxes of her belongings from her Seattle apartment, said goodbye to her roommate and moved back home. The sisters had been working as a team, getting closer than they'd ever been. When she was focused and motivated, Lola shed her flaky side. Carmen suspected that she adopted her little sister persona as a role because it was expected. When challenged, she blossomed.

The sisters had planned tonight's dinner hoping to explain the changes around Orchard House to their father. Cots had been ordered from Amazon. Food from Costco had arrived. The fridge contained so many eggs, they'd had to borrow space from the neighbors down the street. Not Evan's, although his kitchen was much closer. Carmen had thought about him when she'd picked up the phone. How easy it would be to use the storage issue to call him up, arrive with her hands full and needing help. *No. No. No.* Even with her days filled to the minute, overflowing with tasks, the one thing she couldn't do was kick Evan Hollister out of her head.

"Pero mi corazón, it makes no sense," Juan Alvarez said. Carmen sighed. It was so hard to make Papi understand. He'd seen a lot of change in the valley in the past decade. Rich men who'd never walked in dirt drove fancy trucks. People took photographs of their tiny little glasses of wine, called them flights, artfully arranged them on rustic wooden platters. Restaurants grew a few rows of vines, called themselves wineries and bought wine, slapped on their own label and fooled everyone. The price of a pizza was what used to be a day's pay.

When Juan had started in the fields, the wine growers had dirt under their nails. They pitched in during the harvest. They put out planks on sawhorses to feed the pickers before they slept in the little cabins at the edge of the orchard. Some people didn't feed their pickers, but the Alvarez family always had.

But allowing the pickers into his home? Carmen knew Juan thought this was too much.

"What's wrong with the cabins?" Papi asked.

Did he remember how old and broken down the tiny shacks had become? They'd gone up like tinder two years ago during the wildfire. "They're gone. But Papi, even if they were there, we can't put these people in tiny little unheated cabins."

"Si. Mami was always the one to remind me not to get conceited. 'Tú es principalmente mexicano,' she'd say, when I tried to play the big shot."

"Papi, these people who want to see what it's like to live on a vineyard and work in the field. We'll rotate them in and out of Orchard House. They'll get their meals, but we won't pay them." Lola looked at her sister for help.

"Mija, who would want to do that? Don't people go to Disneyland anymore?"

"Sí Papi, they go to Disneyland. These are people without kids. People who want to learn about wine. They work in offices all day and want to know what it's like to be a winemaker. We'll have winemaking classes and yoga. Mrs. Huttinger is bringing her goat cheese and teaching people how to make it."

"If they work in offices, why do they want to make wine?"

Carmen looked up from her lists, putting her hand on her father's. "They don't want to make wine. They want to learn more about it. For fun."

Lola gave her sister a look. "Papi, would you be part of the lecture? Tell people your story. How you came here and got your first job. How you worked your way up. How you became a winemaker."

Juan looked pleased. "You think people want to hear all that?"

Carmen could see they'd gotten to him. "Papi, this is exactly what people want. They want to know where all this"—she swept her arms around the land, green and bursting with life—"came from. They want the story behind what they are drinking. And you are the story. You are Blue Hills Vineyard."

Her father studied the hill behind them, fragrant with ripening fruit that hung deep purple on the emerald vines. The garden burst with hot pink and white impatiens, marigolds, coral roses and lavender, intercut by lacy maidenhair. It hadn't looked so good since before Mami died. The remains of Papi's favorite meal, carne asada, was on the table.

One of the few sit-down dinners they'd enjoyed in the last few weeks of hard, seemingly endless toil. Carmen had sensed they needed to spend more time with their father, explain more of their plans.

Juan lifted his wine to the sun, swirling it. "See how the color is slow to return to the bottom? That's a good sign. If the side of the glass was instantly clean, we'd be drinking a light red wine, which is fine for a Pinot Noir, but this isn't a noir. It's a Cab Sauvignon."

"I have so much to learn," Carmen said, fortifying herself with a deep breath. The air smelled of roses, fresh soil and an undercurrent of smoke.

"We have time," said her father, patting her hand.

They raised their glasses together, clinking.

"To the harvest," said Lola.

"To getting the gringos to work for free," said Juan.

Her father was a quick study.

CHAPTER THIRTEEN

Celia

Carmen's arms were full of food from Bear Foods Natural Market. Turned out, feeding foodies wasn't cheap. They could get pickers for less than feeding and housing the tourists, but then again, where to find them? With the grapes within picking range, Carmen didn't have any choice. She and Adella were maxing out their credit cards, hoping this would be the bumper crop it appeared to be. Lola, already in debt, wasn't allowed to help. If they could only get the fruit in the winery.

This was the third provisioning trip Carmen had made into town in the last two days. The first crew of harvesters was due on Saturday morning. She'd hired some high schoolers as cooks, convinced a friend to teach a yoga class and found guitar players for a concert in the orchard. Her press release had promised all this and more.

She just needed to find the more.

Leaving the store, Carmen noticed two things: Stella waving at her, and Evan sitting at small table on a café patio across from a pretty dark-haired woman. Her throat clenched, heart pounding. Reminding herself that he was an entitled jerk, she clutched her groceries tighter, squeezing the packages until they fell from her arms, scattering on the sidewalk. A cloud of gluten-free pancake mix puffed up in the dry air, covering her black T-shirt and shorts. Bear Foods didn't offer bags.

Now this.

Stella came rushing out of the restaurant. Before she arrived, Carmen heard a familiar voice. "Hey, need some help, neighbor?"

Carmen looked up, shielding her eyes from the sun. Fatigue filed down her anger, leaving her vulnerable. Evan was heartbreakingly handsome in a denim shirt and white shorts, sunglasses pushed up on his head, pulling back his short curls. He'd gotten a haircut. It suited him. Everything suited him. In another life, she would have thrown herself at him. Hard. She bit her lip to stop from crying. She was so tired. "Oh, hi."

He gathered packages of organic baking mixes. "Having some hippies over?"

She smiled halfheartedly. "Something like that."

His sleeves were sprinkled with flour from the leaking packages. "Where's your car?"

She pointed down the street. "Shouldn't you be getting to your date?"

He bit his lip. "Yeah, I guess. I told her I had to help my neighbor."

The woman at the table was Celia Diaz. She moved fast, Carmen thought, wishing she didn't care. "Right."

"Oh hey, hi, Evan. It's Evan, right?"

They both turned to Stella, who was appraising Evan. He offered a hand then retracted it. "Sorry my hand is covered with…" He read the label. "Organic spelt flour. Mmmm. Delicious."

Stella gathered the remaining groceries off the ground. "I know your wine master. Paolo."

Evan nodded enthusiastically. "Yes! Okay, you're the reason he's no longer walking around like his dog just died. He's actually okay to be around. So, thank you."

Stella beamed. "I'm showing him more of the valley."

They walked to Carmen's car, where she loaded the groceries. Evan peered in her car, which was loaded with supplies from a Costco run to Wenatchee. "Wow, you're expecting a crowd."

"She's—" Stella started to talk, then snapped her mouth shut when Carmen gave her a look.

"I'm stocking up. You know. That time of year. I'm a squirrel. Burying nuts." Carmen couldn't stop. "Winter." She faked burying things in the ground with her hands. "That's me. Ready Eddie. Winter is coming."

Stella grabbed her friend's hands. "He's got it, Car."

Carmen flushed brilliant red, wondering why Evan always brought out her inner middle schooler, ready to humiliate herself rather than expose her true feelings. Of which, she immediately reminded herself, there were none. Zero. "Okay, I'll get back to my winter supplies and you get back to your date."

Stella forced a fake grin on her face. "Yes, the date. Evan, you are on a date." She took Carmen's arm, dragging her away. "I'm sure Celia has gotten over that little kleptomaniac issue. Have fun!"

Evan stood rooted to the pavement with a puzzled look on his face.

Carmen let herself be pulled down the sidewalk. "He's dating Celia Diaz?"

Stella rolled her eyes. "Oh please. The man's trying to make you jealous."

Blue Hills was under siege. Everywhere you looked, someone was cleaning, fluffing, unloading, polishing, shoveling or sorting in anticipation of twenty to thirty guests. Carmen had drilled it into her family's head that they had to live up to the vine-to-table experience she'd sold. In exchange for their labor, these people expected to be well-fed and given unique experiences tailored to their interests. These were fastidious millennials, who craved authenticity above all else. They wanted to meet the wine master, walk the fields and know the origin of their food and wine.

"We're selling them the story of Blue Hills wine," Carmen had said last night. Before everyone had collapsed into bed, Carmen had held a meeting with the staff, her sisters and Juan, explaining next week's schedule.

"Blood, sweat and Pinot Grigio," her father had said, amused at the entire endeavor.

Carmen had pointed at her father. "Exactly, Papi!"

"Carmencita, bonita. These gringos aren't used to picking. What happens when they start cayendo como moscas?" Papi said. "Those gringos aren't used to working in the hot sun."

Lola put her arm around him. "Papi, let us worry about that. You just be your charming self. ¿Bueno?"

Juan had settled back into his chair, seemingly satisfied. Carmen could tell that he loved having all these people around. He must have been lonely, rattling around Orchard House, worrying that the place was getting rundown but unable to do anything about it.

Now, three teenage cooks were in the kitchen, possibly googling "how to feed a crowd" while surveying their supplies and hopefully, Carmen thought, making a list of anything else they'd need. It wasn't very reassuring when from upstairs, she could hear one of them ask, "What's this?" and heard another reply, "Eggplant." A shiver ran down her spine when she thought of them cooking vegetarian and gluten-free meals, but she had to let it go. You got what you paid for. Carmen had promised them credit for volunteering, which they needed for graduation. She made a note to call the high school principal to make sure the work credits would count on their transcripts.

In the meantime, her harvesters would be fed.

But not with eggplant, apparently.

Carmen was making the beds on the second floor. Her back ached from bending over. Juan appeared in the doorway with a load of sheets in his arms.

"¿Mija, dónde van estos?" he asked.

"On any bed that doesn't have a sheet yet. That includes cots and air mattresses." Carmen rubbed her back. Standing up felt good. The lake looked so inviting. At the very least, she could offer lake views. She made a note to have Lola drag out the float and put towels down at the beach.

"Sí. What time do the pickers arrive?" asked her father.

"Papi, call them harvesters. Por favor."

"But they're picking?"

"Sí."

He nodded, lifting his finger, teaching her. "Then, they're pickers."

Carmen shook her head. "No. They're teachers, journalists, office workers, dentists."

"¿Dentistas?"

"Sí."

"Who want to vacation by picking?"

Carmen sighed. "Sí. Harvesting. It sounds better."

"Bueno. I call them harvesters and they pick for free."

Her father was halfway down the hall when he heard his daughter yelling, "They harvest!"

"I'll call them the King of England if they help us get the grapes in."

Carmen put her hands together in prayer, rolling her eyes. "Gracias, Papi."

*

He couldn't stay away. He'd gone on another date with Celia last night and found himself glancing discreetly around the Campbell's bar, hoping Carmen was there to see him with another woman. What if Carmen didn't care? That would crush him more than he'd admit. Even to himself. Mostly he worried about not being fair to Celia, who'd looked lovely last night. She'd seen Stella, had reminded him that Stella was dating Paolo, which meant she'd gotten her hair done. He'd complimented it, saying it looked nice.

"It's shorter, right?" Evan had asked, trying to engage.

She'd laughed. It was a different color. Or was that what she said? He couldn't remember. He'd tapped his glass, signaling to the waiter that he needed another. A nagging voice in the back of his mind said he was drinking to get through this date. Even when he was fighting with Carmen—and if he was honest with himself, that's what they did—there were sparks. He felt so brilliantly alive around her. Fascinated.

The date stretched on. When Celia had suggested a walk by the lake, he'd wracked his brain for excuses. It was too early for bed. He had pickers coming in the morning, but Paolo took care of that. What he'd really wanted to do was go home and swim. Because Carmen would be checking on the grapes, walking the fields. In a weird way, it felt like they were communicating because they always went out at the same time. The humid dark, the sound of the lake, distant voices on the water coming from Wapato Point.

It felt intimate. Shared.

He knew it wasn't rational, but it felt like they had some kind of agreement. A ceasefire every night.

Did she feel the same way?

All these thoughts ran through his brain as Celia told him about growing up in Chelan. The only time he could focus was when he wondered if Carmen had had the same experiences. He needed to end it with Celia. She was a nice woman. She deserved better.

Earlier today, he'd walked down his driveway and back up Orchard House drive carrying a box of eggplants. They were left over from a wedding. Maybe the Alvarez household could use them. That was the excuse he made to himself. It was a flimsy pretext to see her again, even though nothing between them had changed. The kitchen hands had taken the box from him, staring at it like he'd offered them coal. One of them thanked him and went back to their lists, which seemed to perplex them.

"We've got like, twenty-three for dinner tonight?" asked the girl.

"Twenty-three people?!" the boy screeched. "Dude, my cooking experience is like, opening a can of Pringles."

The girl crossed her arms. "That's not what you told Ms. Alvarez."

He shrugged. "I thought she was hot. And I needed credit."

The girl pushed her hair off her sweaty face. "Great."

"So, is this for a wedding?"

Both teenagers stared at Evan, surprised that he was still there.

The girl shook her head. "No, this is for like, people who are picking grapes."

Evan nodded. "She found a crew?"

"No, they're volunteers. It's camp for people who like wine."

Evan was astonished. Audacious didn't begin to describe Carmen Alvarez. "And manual labor in the blazing sun?"

The girl shrugged. "I guess. They're going to have like, lectures and stuff in the orchard. Yoga classes, I think. I know my aunt is coming to talk about making goat cheese. I don't know. I just hope they don't have to eat Pringles for dinner."

Evan smiled. "Yeah, well good luck with that."

*

Carmen, who'd heard Evan's voice, hurried down the stairs just as the screen door shut.

"Did you talk to him?" she asked the confused cooks.

"Yeah. Why?" asked the girl.

"Don't talk to him. Okay?" Carmen said.

The boy turned to the girl. "I thought he was kind of sketch."

The girl rolled her eyes as Carmen headed outside.

"Hey! What are you doing here?" Carmen yelled at Evan, hating herself for thinking that even his back, in a damp polo shirt, was sexy.

He lifted his hands, slowly turning around like an outlaw. "Don't shoot!"

"Very funny. What's up?" She stood on the patio, arms crossed, trying to keep her tone light.

He pointed to the kitchen, where the crack of breaking dishes was followed by yelling. Carmen tried not to be distracted by the chaos. Worryingly, there were no signs of dinner.

"I brought food. To feed your crew," Evan said.

Oh no. He knew. "My guests."

He lifted his sunglasses on his head. "It's not a wedding, Carmen. The cat's out of the bag."

Carmen sighed, looking up at the hill to the Hollister Estate. "I don't know where you found pickers." She was so tired of feeling like the underdog.

"I can send them over here when they're done."

She lifted her eyebrows. "Nice. You'd like that, wouldn't you?"

Evan shook his head, glancing at the canopies being installed in the orchard. "What are you talking about?"

She rolled her eyes, wishing she wasn't wearing old shorts and a faded T-shirt. "You get your grapes in while we wait, depending on you."

He cocked his head. "Would that be the worst thing in the world?"

"Do you know what happens to wine made of high sugar fruit?" She'd been doing her research and emailing Stella her questions.

She wasn't the girl who'd driven in from Seattle. She was serious. They'd started watering at night, instead of morning, which is what she knew Paolo had told him to do. "Too much alcohol."

"Two days isn't going to make much difference."

She looked shocked. "Two days! How many pickers do you have?"

He grinned. "Enough."

That was it. He'd come to gloat. To see how she was slaving away just to get enough people to harvest. As if it wasn't bad enough that he'd screwed up their wedding—the bride was still posting nasty comments on their Facebook page—he was looking for ways to rub this in Carmen's face. Money might not buy happiness, but it sure could get around the visa situation at the border. He was bringing in truckloads of pickers while everyone in the valley scrambled.

She hated him.

Hated how he brought her back to high school. Crushing on a rich boy who kissed her, but smiled when someone said, "greasy wetbacks".

Never sure if she wanted to slap him or kiss him.

She waited until he was halfway down the driveway. She took deep breaths, clenching and unclenching her fists until her breathing slowed. By the time she'd calmed down, Evan had reached his own property. He briskly walked the length of his house, head resolutely forward, pointedly avoiding looking in her direction.

She rushed back into the kitchen and grabbed the box of eggplants off the counter. The girl cook opened her mouth but saw Carmen's face and changed her mind. Carmen dumped the entire box of eggplants, purple and shining, into the garbage.

CHAPTER FOURTEEN

Not Pickers

Evan Hollister paced the length of his patio while Mandy proceeded to devour her lunch. The woman, thin as a straw, ate constantly. He found her appetite slightly nauseating, given the heat and her apparent lack of sensitivity. She squeezed a packet of ketchup over her fries, licking her fingers with gusto.

Evan looked away.

She studied her fingers for more ketchup. "I don't see what the problem is. She's your competitor. You need her land. Let nature, literally, take its course."

Evan ran a hand through his hair, looking down at the crowds milling on the patio, clutching plates of what looked like hamburgers. He bet the girl cook had come through. The boy had looked terrified. He found himself missing that war room mentality, where you were the underdog and it was up to your little team to snatch victory from the mouth of defeat. Carmen's anger at him had gotten to him. Since he'd known her, he'd become a different, more sensitive person. It was like walking around with his skin inside out. "Do you think it's fair to let people get terrified just because we're in the middle of a land dispute?"

Mandy finally stopped eating. She wiped her mouth with a paper napkin, blotting it daintily. "Okay, wait. Let me take this apart for you. They're mice. As far as I know, mice have never killed anyone, at least not directly. A few mice at an outdoor yoga class aren't going to cause any lasting trauma. They're going to freak some people out. Which is what we need. Secondly, a land dispute? Evan, it's her land."

"It's her father's land."

Mandy gave him a closer look. She pushed her lunch away, wiping her hands with a napkin. "Her father's land, which will be hers someday, which is how these things work."

Evan stopped pacing, not liking her change in tone. He hired people who were strong enough to call him out, but it didn't make it any easier to hear. "I know how things work, Mandy. However, before she arrived on the scene, I was about to buy the land from her father."

Mandy shut her lunch box as a fly approached. "Let me ask you something, Evan. Do you really want this land, or do you want to make nice with Carmen Alvarez?"

Evan smiled. "You don't mess around, do you?"

She gave him a sly grin. "That's why you hired me. I get you from point A to point B. Point B is the winery with national sales, awards and big numbers. It's running with the big dogs in California. You have it within your capability, but from what you've told me, it can't happen without additional land and grapes. You can buy the grapes or buy the land. The land next door is very high in minerals, which makes great grapes, which makes great wine. Or you could have your agents go look for grapes and have them shipped here.

Which has its own set of problems. But to me, it looks like you have an issue here."

Had he gotten soft? Had he let his attraction to Carmen muddy the issue? Maybe the old days weren't so far behind him. Carmen was putting together an army down there. What was he doing? Making excuses. "I don't have the land."

She shook her head and pointed over at Blue Hills. "Maybe you like the old man, maybe you like the daughter. But you to need think very clearly now. The bank was well on its way to seizing the property. Blue Hills refused your generous offer. I don't think you're doing anything that wasn't already going to happen on its own."

"Until Carmen showed up."

Mandy shrugged. "From what I heard, until very recently, she worked in marketing. I doubt she can run an operation like Blue Hills Vineyard."

Evan stood at the edge of his patio, looking down at the people mingling on the Alvarez patio. They were young, fit-looking and apparently ready to spend hours in the sun for the privilege of getting in touch with their agricultural roots. Carmen had her pieces lined up. She wasn't wasting any time worrying what Evan thought or felt. She was going to win if he didn't focus. He'd hired Mandy for a reason. It would pay off. Unless he wasted this opportunity.

Let the chips fall where they may.

Evan turned around, taking the chair across from Mandy. He lifted his sunglasses to reveal a burning intensity. "Okay, tell me what you've got."

Mandy's smile was that of a wolf entering a pasture. This was going to be fun.

*

Carmen raced down the stairs, dodging a question from a guest asking about extra toothbrushes. Feeling guilty, she doubled back up into her own bathroom, extracting a new toothbrush from the countless dentist trips she'd taken as a child. All those shrunken boxes of dental floss, mini mouthwashes and travel-sized toothpastes. Funny how she'd never cleaned them out. Although when she thought about it, she realized why. They represented time with Mami.

Now part of her stash was being handed to a goateed PE teacher who held the future of Blue Hills in his tattooed arms.

Carmen ran back down the stairs, through the kitchen where the two cooks were arguing about breakfast, and into the cool night air before anyone could ask her another question.

How many more endless days would it take?

She still had to plan the First Crush Festival booth location and staff. Once she breathed in the night air, she felt invigorated. This ritual of visiting the crops had become vital to her nighttime routine.

If she was honest, seeing Evan was a huge part of going outside each night. It was almost like they had a relationship based on distant nightly visits, like some wartime romance where they could only gaze at one another through a fence. Every time she buried the notion of a crush on Evan, he showed up in navy blue swimming trunks patterned with sharks, his torso lean and muscular like a soccer player. He'd bend over, throwing his arms above his head to stretch. Barry would lope over to nuzzle him. Evan would talk to him, murmuring affectionately, rubbing him behind his ears until the dog flopped on the patio, begging for a belly scratch. Evan often delayed his swim to indulge Barry, grinning as the dog reflexively churned his rear leg. Papi used to say you can tell a lot about a man by the way he treats animals. She was learning things that made her want to cram her feelings into a little box, bury them somewhere.

Evan Hollister was a situation.

By the time Carmen had walked out into the vines, she was relaxed enough to imagine a post-harvest world. Once they'd paid the bank, would Evan admit defeat?

Did guys like Evan ever lose?

The crates for the harvest sat ready at the end of the vine rows, making it hard to reach the spot where she normally looked over the valley. She went diagonally down the field until she reached the cave, standing on the wall that bordered the patio to the winery. It was close to Evan's house, the tiny slice of land above his hilltop property. She'd have to be careful that she didn't make any noise. The night was completely still. She'd learned as a kid, hiding in the vines past dinner time, that any sound ricocheted across the lake.

Carmen peered down the hill and couldn't see the pool. A warm glow from inside Evan's house lit the patio, but she couldn't see him. Maybe he wasn't swimming tonight. Perhaps he was inside, plotting her demise. Or was he floating on his back, admiring the moon? She climbed on the stone wall to get a better look.

The moon danced on the lake. An owl called in the distance. There was a flutter of wings. One of Blue Hills' resident great horned owls, returning with food for its babies. Conjuring Evan's presence was silly. Adolescent. Absurd.

And yet.

Seeing him was reassuring.

Carmen turned to jump off the wall. A patio door slammed. She turned her head, lost her footing, spinning her arms like a windmill trying to regain her balance. This went on for what felt like eternity.

Please don't let this be happening. No. Please. No.

She could not be falling right now.

He could not find out.

Not now.

Of course, she fell. Because that was the universe in which she lived. She tumbled off the stone wall, down the hill and through scrubby bushes that should have, if the pitch wasn't so steep, stopped her. But she was sliding, trying desperately to grab prickly sage, rocks, anything to stop.

She landed within feet of Evan. He'd dashed to the edge of his property to see what was making its way through the bushes towards him. He looked as though he was expecting a deer or bear when he parted the bushes, keeping his head back to avoid startling the wild creature.

His expression changed when he saw it was Carmen. He jumped into the bushes barefoot, immediately puncturing his tender insole on a sharp rock. "Carmen! Ow! Ouch!" He hopped around for a moment, blood streaming from his foot. "Are you okay?" He crouched down, putting a hand on her shoulder.

"Yes. No. I don't know." Everything hurt.

He pulled her out of the bushes, squeezing her by the shoulders, asking her to bend her arms, turn her head. Count backward by sevens from a hundred.

She frowned. "I'm a hospitality major. I can't do that."

"Fair enough." He looked up the hill. "That was quite a fall."

Carmen peered at her elbow, embedded with gravel and blood. "I think my pride took the hardest hit."

"What were you doing up there?" He led her to the table, getting her settled, watching her hobble.

She scratched her head. "Checking the vines?" She didn't seem to believe her own answer.

Wiping his foot with a towel, Evan disappeared into kitchen, returning with a sturdy first aid kit and an ice pack, handing both to Carmen.

She found it comforting that he was the kind of man who kept a first aid kit substantial enough for an entire summer camp, let alone one adult with a thoroughly bruised ego.

"There are no vines on that part of your property." He surveyed the tiered contents of his multi-level kit, selecting band-aids, ointment, wipes.

She ripped open a tiny packet containing an antiseptic wipe, dabbing it on her wounds. "Checking the wines."

"The night before the harvest?" Evan tended to his foot, looking up at her with one raised eyebrow.

Carmen sighed. It was, after all, the nightly truce. A perfectly valid explanation of why, by daylight, she felt differently. "I might have been watching you swim."

"I wasn't swimming."

She spoke before thinking. "But you normally…"

He smiled. "I normally swim. And you walk the fields. Except tonight, you went to the winery."

"Yes. Look, I'm sorry I got upset when you brought the eggplants over. This harvest is getting on my last nerve. And don't get me wrong, I'm still mad at you about the wedding..."

He nodded. "Likewise."

"But..."

His face grew serious. "But..."

They studied each other, their faces shifting from somber to grinning, acknowledging their complicity. As if they'd discovered a pocket of air inside the seething current of their hostilities.

Tonight.

Tomorrow would be different. Daylight would bring new realities. The harvest. The need to keep the winery.

To win.

As the pool reflected the moon and an owl lifted off from the Alvarez winery, swooping low over their heads, they threw back their heads, laughing. Silently agreeing to a grace period. Evan limped into the house, returning with a bottle of wine and two globe glasses.

He poured the special vintage without asking. "We're quite a pair. My foot."

She lifted her glass. "My everything."

"Your everything seems fine." He raised an eyebrow. "Very fine."

She let herself enjoy the compliment.

They clinked glasses. "To accidental meetings."

They drank, enjoying the quiet and each other's company. Coyotes howled through the inky darkness. The lake's mineral tang mixed with the sweet grape-scented air. It was a heady combination that, when combined with the velvety wine, was intoxicating.

Evan put his glass down on the metal table. "Maybe we should stop relying on accidents. Maybe we can work around…" He waved his hand at the fields, the land. "All this."

She played along. Why not? It was night. The rules seemed suspended. "Maybe."

Evan stood up, wincing as his foot bore his weight. "Let's go for a swim."

She looked at the pool. "Now?"

He nodded. "In the lake!"

She put down her wine. "You're crazy."

Evan nodded. "This whole night is crazy. And it may never happen again, but why not? If this is the one night we get to do this, then let's do it right."

Carmen took a deep breath. "One night."

His smile lit up the dark. "One night."

He wore his swim trunks and she found a suit left in the family shack by the lake. As she pulled on the bikini in the dark shack, she heard the distant plop of rocks he was throwing into the dark lake, one after another, echoing off the hillside.

She found Evan perched on a boulder on the shore, eyeing the black water, looking worried. "Wow, it's dark."

Carmen's father had situated the shack on a space free from rocks near the shore. She laughed, diving headfirst into the lake. End-of-summer warm water embraced her. She surfaced, twisting toward Evan, waving. "Come on, it's nice!"

She started to swim, which was, she thought, a change. Him watching her swim. The water was the perfect temperature. "Excellent idea, Evan." She liked saying his name.

"Thank you. I'm full of them. Most of them aren't so scary."

Carmen could tell that he wanted to join her in the worst way but unlike her he didn't know the shallows. He couldn't map out the boulders, the sandy spots where it was safe to dive, in his mind. Evan wasn't a man accustomed to venturing places where he had less control. Where measuring obstacles was impossible. Carmen had been swimming here since she could walk. He should take her word for it. She was, after all, leading the way.

Carmen reached the rock where she had contemplated much of life as a child and young adult. Her thinking rock. She pulled herself out of the water onto its rough surface, finding the smooth spot that folded over like a chair, providing the ideal seat for one. Or two, provided they were friendly. She settled in, turning to the shore. Evan paced, limping on his bandaged foot.

"Hey!" Her voice carried over the water. "Wasn't this your idea?"

He stopped. "That was before I saw this water. It's like ink."

"Do you want me to swim back and get you?"

"No, thanks. I'll just stand here and feel like an idiot."

She stood up. "I'm going to."

"No, I'm fine. I just need a little more—"

She dove into the lake, leaving a white ring on the surface, swimming half the distance to him underwater.

Her head rose, sleek as a seal. "Ready?"

He shook his head, teeth white in the dark. "Show off."

"We used to have underwater swimming contests."

"And you won."

"Bingo."

"I've never swum in the lake at night."

"Evan Hollister, I can't believe it."

"A great many people have never gone night swimming in a lake."

"A great many people don't know how to live."

"And I suppose you are going to show me how to live?"

She was quiet for a moment, ducking her head under the water, slicking it back with her hands as she surfaced. "I am."

CHAPTER FIFTEEN

Breaking Eggs

Evan peered over the side of the shore. Carmen was quite close now. Her sleek hair accentuated the fine bones of her cheeks, the arch of her forehead. She was beautiful. His throat constricted at the thought. The night wasn't long enough. He needed to get over his fear. Who was it who said do one thing every day that scares you? This scary thing was keeping him from being close to the amazing creature backstroking through the water. She would show him how to live. How to feel instead of think. Maybe this was love. Plunging in, despite your fear.

Evan took the leap.

It was darker than anything he'd known. He should have kept his eyes shut. Should have stayed on the shore. His heart seized into a tight underwater knot. He kicked for what he hoped was the surface, panicked that he might mistakenly be swimming to the bottom. He'd read stories. Knew it was possible. Then Carmen swam towards him. He felt her presence. A couple of kicks and he broke the surface. Around him were the hills, the lights of Wapato Point, shimmering. The moon.

Carmen's face glistened with water.

"Hey, you made it. Isn't the water nice?" She trod water without effort, completely unaware that he'd been having an underwater crisis that now receded further into the distance with every breath.

"Beautiful." More than that. It was breathtakingly gorgeous. The night. The air. The carpet of stars spreading above their heads. The Milky Way stretched out like watercolor across the shimmering sky. He wanted to hold onto this moment, access it for the rest of his life.

"Come on!" Carmen kicked towards the rock.

He followed, suddenly as comfortable in the water as if it had been broad daylight. But it wasn't. It was a gorgeous, silky night dropped like a gift into his lap. He was breathless with gratitude. If there was a perfect moment, this was it.

For once, he was completely aware.

In awe.

Carmen scrambled up the rock, turning to help him up, her hand cold, slick and firm. They sat with their arms and legs touching on the rock. Evan was acutely, blissfully aware of every inch of contact with her skin. Her glowing skin.

Carmen shivered.

"Are you cold?"

She turned to look at him. "No. Just happy."

Their faces were so close. Kissing would have been the most natural thing in the world, but he didn't want to ruin it.

"Me too." He turned his face to the water. He was so happy it was ruinous.

They both allowed the silence to fill the space. It was comfortable. The quiet allowed the beauty of the night to take hold. Water lapped softly at the rock. Voices rose from a campfire across the lake. Bats flitted erratically across the sky. The moon peeked from a cloud, tracing a path of silver water.

Carmen's arm felt cold against his. She tucked her legs inside her arms, hugging them tightly. After a while, she said she had to get back.

"Yeah," Evan reluctantly agreed.

"This rock…" Carmen began slowly, taking a deep breath. "It was the place I'd escape to as a kid."

"Every kid needs one."

She nodded. "After my mom was diagnosed with breast cancer, her friends invaded the house. Cleaning, cooking, bringing food, gossiping. I'd swim out here and just, you know, breathe. Does that make sense?"

He nodded. "Completely." His brain couldn't pluck words to express his feelings. *Thanks for bringing me here* felt inadequate.

They swam back slowly, scrambled out at the shore. Evan waited while she wrapped herself with a towel and shook out her hair, feeling like a coward for not kissing her.

Across the street from the water, where both their driveways met the road, they turned to each other.

Carmen realized she'd been holding her breath. "That was…"

Evan laughed. "Yeah, it was."

"Pretty incredible." She twisted her hair, letting the droplets hit the dust.

Evan nodded. "Thanks for introducing me to night-swimming."

"One of the perks of living here."

"Good luck with your harvest."

"Good luck with yours." Her response was perfunctory.

"Good night, Carmen." His voice was soft.

"Good night." Her voice, Evan thought, already had an edge to it.

*

"Miss Alvarez?" A voice whispered in the dark. Carmen groaned, rolling over. Didn't she just go to bed? "What time is it?"

"It's five-fifteen," said the girl.

"Who is it?"

"It's Nathalie. The cook."

Carmen rolled over, letting her eyes adjust long enough to look at her phone. "Okay. Why are you waking me up?"

"Chip bailed, Miss Alvarez. He texted me last night that he up and quit, and I can't do this. I can't make breakfast for this many people on my own. I couldn't even make waffles for my mom on Mother's Day."

Carmen sat up, feeling for her shorts on the bed. "You said you liked cooking breakfast."

"I do, but I'm not very good at it. I thought Chip could help. You know. Make pancakes or something. But we've got people who don't eat gluten and vegetarians and I don't what else, and then Chip goes AWOL on me. I didn't know what else to do."

Carmen pulled her shorts on under her sleep T-shirt, whipping her hair into a ponytail. She shimmied her bra under the shirt. "Where did he go? Can't we just call him?"

"He's working at another winery."

Carmen poked her head out from the closet, where she was clawing her way through sweatshirts. "What winery?"

"Hollister. He said it was right next door. The guy paid more."

Carmen growled. "Of course, he did. Probably didn't even need a cook."

Nathalie shook her head, still in the hallway. "No, he needed cooks. He wanted to hire me too, but I made you a deal. I didn't want to leave you without anyone to cook breakfast."

Carmen padded to the hallway, facing the girl. "Please tell me you're not leaving after breakfast."

"I, um." Nathalie nervously nibbled a nail before stopping herself. "No. I'm not. I wouldn't. No way."

Carmen hurried into the kitchen, realized she needed to ask Nathalie a question and doubled back. Nathalie was furiously texting. Carmen caught a glimpse of the message. *Tell Mr. Hollister that I can't make it. I'm staying here.*

Cracking eggs was therapeutic, if you put some muscle into it. They were cracking dozens. Carmen spoke tersely with Nathalie, who'd been so completely focused on her message, she hadn't noticed Carmen's return. Afraid of her own anger and worried about losing her remaining cook, Carmen had quickly ducked out the hallway.

Carmen couldn't believe that Evan was such a liar. A two-faced skunk. It made her look stupid, and worse, humiliated. She'd thought last night had been one of the best, if not *the* best, of her life. She'd shared the thinking rock with him. Brought him to the place where she'd faced growing up, the death of her mother, the harshness of life. She'd been stupid enough to think the rock had become a place to find beauty. Love.

It had all been a lie.

The pain was sharp and breathtaking.

Carmen chopped a cantaloupe as if it had broken into Orchard House.

After a quick survey of the refrigerator, Carmen had planned a hasty menu: migas (Mami's specialty: eggs with fried tortillas, peppers, smashed pinto beans and cotija cheese), fruit salad and vegetarian sausages. Gallons of hot coffee from the dispensers she'd rented in Wenatchee. She'd told the harvesters that they'd need to be down for breakfast at six to avoid the heat of the day.

There wasn't much time for talking while she and Nathalie worked steadily, getting breakfast outside on the long table set up on the patio.

At six o'clock, Carmen wondered if she should go rouse the harvesters. Then she heard her father's guitar. Carmen bent over laughing. A second later Lola came downstairs and poured herself a cup of coffee. "Traen de vuelta nuestra infancia." *Brings back our childhood.* She pointed upstairs. "Padre loco."

Nathalie's mouth gaped open as she heard Alvarez senior strolling the hallway, strumming on his guitar, singing the classic mariachi song "México Lindo y Querido" at the top of his strong baritone voice. He belted out the song as if roaming an outdoor fiesta.

When they'd stopped laughing, Lola explained to Nathalie, "When we were kids, we always used to complain when my dad played his mariachi records. He'd come home from work and walk around Orchard House in his undershirt, singing these songs. He'd dance with my mom. It was so corny. We'd just plug our ears and moan. One day, Mami woke us up and nobody came down to breakfast. Papi got his guitar and started playing the mariachi songs."

Carmen snorted. "And singing."

Lola smiled. "So loud. Just like…" She pointed upstairs.

Nathalie grinned. "That's kind of sweet."

Lola took another sip of coffee. "Yeah, you know, I'd give anything to see him and Mama dancing to those mariachi songs again."

A bleary-eyed math teacher in yoga pants came downstairs. "Man, that's so authentic."

Lola offered him a cup of coffee. "What's authentic?"

"Hiring a mariachi singer to wake us up."

Lola and Carmen burst out laughing.

"Yeah, that's our dad. Senior auténtico."

Nathalie proudly opened the door to the patio, where the long table groaned with breakfast foods heaped onto platters.

"That looks amazing!" the math teacher enthused.

Carmen slung an arm around Nathalie. "It does."

Nathalie gave her a grateful look. "Thank you."

"Eat up," said Carmen. "Lunch will be here before you know it."

While she sat at the table with her enthusiastic crew, Carmen forgot, for a moment, about her renewed hatred for Evan Hollister.

Once all the harvesters were seated, Carmen saw her father pushing his chair back with a solemnity she recognized. She felt an urge to stop him, to make sure he wasn't going to embarrass himself or her. His memory loss was at fault, she thought, forcing herself to sit down. He was entitled. This was his winery.

He clinked his glass until the assembled group, most of them half his age or less, settled, listening with rapt attention.

"Buenos días. This is early for you city people, and the middle of the day for farmers," he began. "I'm not just the mariachi singer from earlier..." There was a smattering of laughter and clapping. "I am Juan Alvarez and I came here fifty years ago from Mexico, over the Rio Grande." His audience was spellbound. "I worked first in the fields, for many years, always staying late, asking questions, learning. I know many of you are interested in how we do things." He raised a hand thick with calluses. "We do them by hand. Thank you for being here." His eyes grew moist as he looked at Lola and Carmen. He put his hand over his heart. "Mis hijas. My daughters. They have gathered you here to help with a thing we can't do alone. Muchas gracias from the bottom of my heart. I hope that you learn what I learned many years ago. When you give to the land, it gives back to you. It heals you. Makes you whole."

As the sun rose over the eastern hills, spreading across the lake, there wasn't a dry eye at the table. The young people took his message to heart, standing to give the old man an ovation.

Juan raised his hands. "Stop, or you'll get more singing."

They clapped harder.

Juan shook his head, clearly pleased.

Carmen wiped her mouth, taking a last swig of coffee. "Okay Papi, now we work."

Juan nodded. "Trabajamos."

Lola put her hand on her father's shoulder. "Papi, you don't have to come."

Juan patted her back. "Lola, por favor. I'm not dead yet."

He was the first person in the rows with his clippers.

Breakfast had gone well, despite Evan's latest move. But a steady stream of meals? That was going to be problematic.

Fury drove Carmen through a morning of organizing the harvesters, delivering water, and eying the steady rows of identically straw-hatted workers who moved like an army through Hollister Estate vineyards. She trudged back to the Orchard House, ignoring the tightness in the pit of her stomach and the thought that these people, these lovely, sweet, good-intentioned people, weren't going to last. By ten o'clock they were gulping water, going pink in the heat, wincing at cuts on their fingers.

And the comments.

"Wow, this is so much harder than I thought!"

"My arms feel like they're going to fall off."

"Do you think we could take a break and swim?"

Carmen would have loved to take a break to drown Evan Hollister in his own pool. She'd march over there and ask him how he could have looked into her eyes, pressed his legs against hers and had what she'd thought was a real, meaningful connection, all while he was plotting to steal her cooks. Everyone knew that a crew ran on its stomach. He wanted to cut them off—her off—at the knees.

By the time she reached the kitchen she'd fortified herself with rage. "Thank you for staying!"

Nathalie looked up at her from a chopping board. She was crying.

"What? What is it? I'll pay you more. I'll double what I'm paying you."

Nathalie shook her head.

"I can't offer more than double."

Nathalie wiped her eyes. "It's the onions."

Carmen could have kicked herself. Of course, it was the onions. How could she have not noticed the smell? She was too busy hating Evan. Better to funnel her anger into something creative.

"What are you making?"

"Spaghetti."

"You do that for dinner. If I can have some of these onions, I'll make the famous Alvarez enchiladas. This crew needs something to get them going." She didn't want to hurt Nathalie's feelings, so she added. "That'll give the marinara time to cook, okay?"

Nathalie nodded eagerly. "That would be awesome. I've been staring down the clock all morning, worried that I couldn't get it done. I keep thinking about all those people working in the fields all morning. They'll be starving by lunch. I really didn't want to make them wait."

Carmen swept the onions into the huge pot her mother had once used to make her green enchilada sauce. Before she went out to pick tomatillos from the kitchen garden, she turned to Nathalie, hunched over a recipe on her phone. The girl looked exhausted.

"Why don't you get that sauce simmering and take a siesta?"

Nathalie shook her head. "Oh, no. I couldn't."

"Yes, you could. Have some lunch and go upstairs. I'll do the clean-up. Okay?"

Nathalie looked relieved. "That would be amazing."

Carmen wondered how she was going to pay the girl double now that she'd offered it. She decided to worry about it later. Cooking her mother's recipe always brought back sweet memories. Picking the sweet oregano, papery tomatillos and tiny orange peppers made her happy. Her crew would enjoy a taste of home. Her home. Fragrant Mexico, grown in Chelan.

Outside in the garden, Carmen heard a high humming noise coming from the lake.

A large military green helicopter. A familiar sight in the summertime. She lifted her basket of herbs, shielding her eyes from the sun. The helicopter flew north, diving towards the lake in a low arc. Hanging from four thick cables was a large canvas carrier that the crew carefully lowered into the water as the helicopter hovered. Carmen could see the pilot signaling with his fist. The helicopter waited until the canvas was filled before lifting off, heading up-lake. Carmen watched until the helicopter and its load of water disappeared around a sloping hill.

Gathering the tomatillos warming in the growing heat, she noticed her harvesters looking up at the lake, talking amongst each other. Walking into the house, Carmen's worry spiked.

Forest fires.

CHAPTER SIXTEEN

Bunking Down

The group coming out of the fields for dinner was different from the jovial troupe who'd gone into the vineyard that morning. After work, they went straight to the lake, dove in, then trudged back up the dusty driveway, marginally refreshed, and sat down to dinner with little conversation. Carmen had tried to make the scene as picturesque as possible, with lights strung between trees, mason jars of flowers and potted succulents scattered across the long table. But the conversations ended. Cutlery clattered.

The change made Carmen nervous. One day had woken her guests up to the reality of agricultural work. It wasn't tourism. It was backbreaking labor that only undocumented workers would undertake. There was a reason for the shortage of workers.

Carmen hoped she hadn't misled them, but then again, who could really know how hard it was until they'd spent hours hunched over in the blazing heat? Her father had always told them that he'd worked so hard all his life so his children wouldn't have to labor in the fields.

When the yoga teacher appeared, asking how many people would make it for yoga, only six raised their hands. Sheila, the teacher, who had hired a babysitter for the night, raised an eyebrow at Carmen before clapping her hands. Her day job was as a teacher at the high school and she wouldn't let people out of class without a fight. "Come on now. You've just knotted up all kinds of muscles. Who wants to stretch them out?"

The math teacher raised his hand. "I don't know if I can last another day if I don't do something. I'll give it a shot."

Carmen saw nods of agreement in the group. She and Lola exchanged alarmed looks.

Lola jumped up from her chair. "Look, I know it's hard work. We really appreciate that you're doing this. We've got all kinds of cool things planned, and I hope you stay around for them. Not just for the harvest—getting to know you guys is fun. I'm hoping you'll be the charter members of Friends of Blue Hills Vineyard."

She looked at Carmen, who raised both eyebrows as her baby sis went off-script, curious to see where this was heading. "We're hoping to build a community of people who care about making wine by hand, in a family and community-based setting. This our kickoff event. I know this is hard, but it's getting us off the ground. If you stay, the rewards will be huge. We'll have annual tastings for our members. Enchilada bake offs, where we send you home with our homemade sauce made with vegetables grown right here on the property." Lola moved over to Carmen, slinging an arm around her sister as if they'd hatched this together.

"We want Blue Hills Vineyard to become a place where you feel ownership. Taste wines that you've had a part of making. We want you to get married here. Celebrate here and join us in making some of the best wines in the world. I know it's tough and right now you're exhausted, but this is a chance to be part of a community of people like yourselves. And honestly, you guys are amazing."

There was an exhausted silence. Carmen and Lola stood on the patio, waiting to see the reaction. Lola reached over and took her sister's hand, squeezing it in a gesture that brought tears to Carmen's eyes. Both had dirt under their nails and aching muscles. They'd come this far together using creativity, sweat and grit. If this was all they accomplished, they'd done well. Together. That was the important part. Carmen thought of Mami, never happier than when the family was united over a meal.

The math teacher, quickly emerging as group spokesman, stood up. "You know what? This isn't what I envisioned when I first came here. It's hot. My back is killing me. I'm pretty sure I kept everyone awake snoring."

Carmen felt herself sinking into despair.

"But…" The math teacher raised his glass. "I'm in. I tell kids in school every day not to give up. It's so easy to say no. How often are we asked as adults to stretch ourselves? What would I be saying to my students if I gave up? 'Yeah, I tried this really cool thing but it was too hard, so I quit.' Everything is rough in the beginning. But you gotta start somewhere, right?"

One by one, people stood, stretching their arms and legs. One woman joked she was in if she could get the enchilada recipe.

"It's yours!" Carmen said with a giddy laugh. It would have made Mami so happy. A Blue Hills cookbook had been Mami's dream, showing people how to pair wine, not beer, with Mexican food.

Everyone drifted off to their rooms to get ready for yoga in the orchard. Now their complaints about aches and pains sounded like badges of honor. Lola had shifted their outlook. They were part of something bigger. Their pain had meaning.

Carmen leaned into her sister, whispering. "When did you come up with that?"

Lola winked. "On the spot."

"Pretty inspired."

Lola started clearing the table. "Desperate times and all that."

"But it's a really good idea."

Lola stacked plates like a seasoned waitress, nodding at the leafy vineyard. "We can't do this alone."

As the group of harvesters assembled on the patio in their yoga gear, Carmen nodded. "Agreed, but we can't keep offering them stuff."

Lola moved towards the kitchen with her arms full of dishes, turning around to her sister. "No. We just have to keep them happy."

Carmen studied the neat rows of vines and full crates of deep purple fruit. Keeping people happy was complicated. Then again, nothing about saving Blue Hills Vineyard was simple.

*

The sun had set on the orchard. Deep grasses and leafy trees offered ample shade and cooling ground cover. Twenty-eight harvesters settled on their mats for the last third of their workout, cooling down by deep breathing, legs crossed, eyes closed.

"Oh! What's that?!" a girl in bright purple leggings and a lime green crisscrossed top cried out.

Everyone opened their eyes. The long grass was alive with hopping creatures. A woman screamed as a fluffy brown mouse jumped onto her mat. The tiny creature looked equally horrified. Mice leaped out of the grass and onto the mats at alarming frequent intervals.

"What do we do?"

"They're everywhere!"

"What are they doing?"

The math teacher was the only one who remained calm. "They're mating."

"Right now?" asked the first woman to scream.

The math teacher nodded, calmly observing. "Not mid-air. It's more like they're, um, enthusiastic."

"Why do they have to do it now?" said a panicked girl with a bun that had unraveled into her face.

The math teacher shrugged. "They're mice."

Sheila took stock of her panicked yoga students, feeling responsible and yet unsure what to do. Everywhere she looked, the field was alive with mice. It was unbelievable how high they could jump. It was funny, unless of course you were stuck with two dozen terrified city folk who liked their mice in children's books.

Sheila clapped her hands. Surprisingly, it got their attention. "Here's what we're going to do. Roll up your mats and make a line. We'll go single file and hopefully the mice will leave us alone."

"And what if they don't?" said a girl who spoke in short gasps, possibly experiencing a panic attack.

"You'll bump into a mouse," said the math teacher.

The girl turned an alarming shade of grey.

Then she fainted.

Landing on a mouse.

*

By the time the ambulance arrived, the young girl was alert, drinking juice and mortified that an ambulance had been called.

"We had to call them," Lola explained, making a face at Carmen that said, *back me up, I'm winging it again.*

"Protocol," Carmen said, nodding sagely, as if there was some rodent winery health protocol.

Sheila had made everyone promise not to tell the girl that she'd landed on a mouse. Most people were more concerned about the mouse, who had been fine, thanks to the soft covering of the tall grass. Everyone but the girl saw the mouse scamper off when she sat up. A few people had gasped, but Sheila had immediately launched into a loud speech about drinking enough water. It distracted the girl, avoiding a second fainting spell. They'd all agreed, she didn't need to know she'd came into direct contact with an amorous mouse.

By the time the medics had finished, Carmen had talked them into a plate of enchiladas to go, and returned to the girl.

"I'm so sorry." Her name was Ellie. She was a diabetic who, it turned out, shouldn't have gone without snacks during the day and needed to up her water intake. Also, she was terrified of rodents.

Carmen patted her shoulder. "Don't be sorry. You worked so hard today. Thank you."

Ellie sniffed, tearing up. "I should just go home."

Carmen sat down with her, offering a refill of water. "For one thing, you shouldn't drive. But if you want to go home tomorrow, then what you've already done is wonderful. You know we don't expect people to take yoga with mice."

"I've always been like this. The idea of touching one scares me to death."

Carmen prayed that nobody would tell her the truth. "I don't imagine it's something you have to worry about in Seattle."

Ellie shook her head. "No. But listen, if I rest tomorrow, can I stay and help?"

Carmen broke into a wide grin. "Oh. Wow. If you're sure, we'd be honored."

Ellie looked relieved. "I like it here. What Lola said at dinner was amazing. Also, I love your dad. He's really cool."

Carmen couldn't wait to tell Lola and Adella. A twenty-three-year-old hipster with a food blog called *Graze* thought their craggy old father was cool. "Yeah, I never thought about it before, but I guess he is."

The nice thing about the emergencies, Carmen thought as she tidied up the kitchen, was that they kept Evan Hollister out of her mind. She shut off the lights, wondering if not thinking about someone was just a way of keeping them in mind. Oh well. It didn't matter. She'd be down here in eight hours making waffles for twenty-eight either way. Right now, Evan Hollister was the least of her problems.

CHAPTER SEVENTEEN

The Italian Next Door

"Everything is going to be so perfect!" Paolo touched his fingers to his lips, moving like a dancer through Stella's kitchen.

The man could cook. He could dance. He'd swivel his hips like Shakira while singing random pop songs with a kitchen towel thrown over his shoulder. He liked hiking and kayaking, but could also spend an entire Sunday on a dock putting sunscreen on Stella's back.

In other words, he was perfect.

Which was a problem.

Stella did not want to fall in love with a man who lived on another continent. As sexy as she found him, with his irresistible accent, his attentiveness and his skills in the kitchen—and the bedroom—she knew this was a dead-end romance. She knew her place. Right here, on the southern tip of the most beautiful lake in the world. Chelan was home and Dorothy had gotten it right.

There is no place like home.

Paolo had shopped at the Manson Farmers' Market for the food for tonight's dinner, collecting admiring glances and free samples with each stop. Nobody got more free ripe cherries, pie wedges or flirtatious glances than him. Stella felt like she had to insert herself into every transaction until Paolo took her aside, kissed her and told her that in Italy, flirting was like breathing.

"You don't need to breathe all over everyone," she'd grumbled.

He'd lifted her chin, looked into her eyes and promised that if it was bothering her, he'd stop.

He couldn't stop, she thought. He'd changed. Her sunny smile had melted the grumpy expatriate routine. He'd started appreciating the good things about Chelan.

To be fair, he flirted with everyone: from the old woman selling pastry from her truck, to the little girls in braces who turned bright red when he bought some of their braided bracelets.

He was a man meant to be adored.

As her apartment filled with the smell of roasting tomatoes, fresh herbs and garlic, Stella set the table on the back porch, calling into the kitchen, "How's the harvest going? I tried calling Carmen but she's not answering. I guess she's rushed off her feet."

Paolo brought her a glass of red wine, enjoying the sun setting behind the hills bordering town. It promised to be another spectacular sunset, thanks to the forest fires nearby. Her clients had been talking about the fires nonstop. It made Stella slightly nauseous, thinking of the chaos two summers ago when the entire town had been evacuated. She'd rounded up pets from people unable to shelter them, driving them to homes and schools where volunteers had taken care of the scared little animals.

Paolo wiped the sweat from his forehead. Stella's apartment was old and spacious but didn't come with air conditioning. "Your friend next door? You know she tried the experiment but is not going so good. Her tourists? They're getting tired. They don't know speed, you know? They waste time dumping the baskets at the end of every row. They need to take their slower pickers and have them be runners. And they should already be crushing the fruit they picked. Not letting it ripen."

Stella's forehead wrinkled. "Oh no."

"Sí. I wish I could tell her something, but Evan, he watches me. He wants that land. He wants that land more than he wants the air. You know? To breathe. It's crazy."

Stella took a sip of the wine. She didn't know much about wine, but this tasted of summer, of long warm nights, of boat rides on the lake. How silly was that? If she was a wine critic, nobody would understand what she was talking about. "But does it matter that much? Can't he just buy someone else's vineyards or grapes?"

Paolo nodded enthusiastically as if he'd already given it thought. "Yes and no. If he buys fruit, it is always different. The grapes next door, they are right. And they have the soil, the acid, from the minerals. It's like the lovers. The chemistry has to be perfect for the blend to work. Winemakers want to grow their own grapes. And Evan? He wants those good Blue Hills grapes."

"He's trying to put the Alvarez family out of business."

Paolo nodded. "Sí. But they were already having problems. I see the father walk up the hill to talk to the pickers, but he goes back down."

"He has memory problems."

Paolo nodded. "Sí, which is very sad, but the wine business is tough, bella." His voice grew softer. "You can't save a business like that unless you know very, very much."

"But you know very much, right?"

Paolo shook his head. "No."

Stella moved towards him, batting her eyes. "Yes."

Paolo shook his head. "No."

Stella moved her face so close to his until their lips almost met. "Paolo Ricardo Gentillo. You *can* help me."

Paolo's brown eyes met her blue ones. "I cannot."

"He can't, but I can," Stella said, pulling Carmen aside. She'd shown up after dinner, waltzing into the kitchen looking enviably fresh and well-rested.

Carmen looked up from spooning leftovers into a Tupperware container. "Okay, let me finish in here and then we can talk."

Nathalie was doing the dishes, loading the washer as fast as she could. Stella pitched in, rolling up her sleeves and donning a canvas apron. Carmen stopped working for a moment, massaging a tight knot in her neck. "Thank you so much, Stell, but you don't have to do this. This is my mess."

Stella dried the larger mixing bowls, stacking them up on the stone-topped island. "Remember when I borrowed my dad's speedboat and we ran out of gas?"

Sophomore year of high school, Carmen thought, smiling at the memory. "My feet had blisters for days."

Stella nodded. "Yeah, because you walked into town and back with the gas can."

Carmen nodded. "Yeah, back when our biggest problem was running out of gas, right?"

Stella stopped drying. She grabbed her friend and hugged her. "Look, amiga. We're gonna get through this. You gotta believe it. Nothing a little girl power can't handle."

Carmen noticed Nathalie looking at them. "Come on over here."

They gathered the girl into their hug. She seemed grateful for the contact.

Lola came into the kitchen with a stack of dishes. "Lemme get in on this!"

The four girls hugged and smiled. When they drew apart, Stella made each one of them take off their aprons. "Listen. Here's the deal. No arguments, okay? You are going into the living room and putting up your feet. I'm gonna finish up these dishes, and then I'm going to tell you what a certain person who knows a lot about wine told me."

"The elusive Paolo!" Lola said, eyes round. "I've heard about him. I've heard his accent is just like, boom," she swept her hand across the counter. "Knocks women flat."

Stella grinned. "Don't even get me started. It's like nobody in this town has ever heard an Italian accent." She herded them into the living room. "Go."

They'd all chosen a soft chair and put up their feet on the stone coffee table when Stella returned with a tray. "My mother always said that there is nothing ice cream can't handle."

Nathalie perked up as she surveyed the bowls heaped with ice cream. On the side were toppings Stella had found in the pantry and fridge. Fran's Ephemere Sauce, salted caramel, pecans, peanuts, M&M's. It was, Carmen thought, so like Stella to provide spontaneous cheer, whip up something fabulous by opening a few cupboards.

Stella pointed a finger at each one of them. "Eat your ice cream and I'll be back with the good news."

"Thank you so much," said Carmen with teary eyes. Was there a single part of her body that didn't hurt?

"Nuh-uh. Nobody can cry while they eat ice cream. Those are the rules. You got it?" Stella waited with raised brows until Carmen gave her a weak smile.

Carmen licked the frozen spoon, swirling dark chocolate into her ice cream. How could she have ever forgotten what a fabulous best friend she'd chosen for herself when she was thirteen? Who knew that a decision she'd made that young could work out so well?

Now if she could just get the crop in on time.

She tried to concentrate on the icy sweetness melting in her mouth, trying, for the hundredth time that day, to not think of Evan.

*

"You need to think strategically," Stella said, perched on one end of the living room couch. Carmen was slumped on the other end, fighting to concentrate through a fog of exhaustion. Lola sat across from them, filing her nails. Nathalie had gone home. The guests were in the orchard, getting a lecture on making goat cheese. Those who were awake. The bulk of them were lying in bed, reading or on their phones, exhausted. A massage therapist had come out last night and had been swamped. She'd promised to come back with some friends from her massage school who were vacationing in Chelan.

"My friend said that you need to take the slower pickers and have them run the fruit to the totes. He also said we should be crushing the fruit. I told him about the brix levels and he said you can't mess around."

Lola looked up from her nails, rolling her eyes. "Why don't you just say Paolo? We all know it's Paolo."

Stella shook her head. "He could lose his job."

Lola flung her hands around the cavernous living room. "Who is going to tell? Me? The harvesters? They don't even know him."

Stella stubbornly shook her head. "I don't want to get him in trouble."

Carmen gave Lola a sharp look.

Lola opened her mouth, annoyed. "What? I don't see what the big deal is. Nobody is going to find out about him telling us anything."

"¡Es su trabajo estúpida!" Carmen snapped at her sister.

Stella nodded. It was more than his work; it was his career. "Should I keep going?"

Carmen nodded, giving her sister a warning glance. "Yes. Thank you. Lola will stop being an idiot. Right, Lola?"

"Touchy," Lola grumbled.

"She cares about him!" Carmen said, with a little too much force. "What's so hard to understand about that? Sometimes we have these feelings and they become impossible. They eat us up from the inside and become too hard to manage. It feels like we're going to explode from…" Carmen's voice trailed off as she realized she'd lost the thread. She stared out the window, chewing on a nail.

Both women looked at Carmen with alarm.

"Okaaaay," Lola said.

"Car?" Stella asked gently. "Everything okay?"

Carmen snapped her mouth shut. "Fine. I'm fine. Back to the harvest, right?"

There was a long awkward silence. Stella and Lola exchanging pointed looks before Stella spoke. "Right. Fine. Okay, where was I?"

*

It was midnight by the time they got their strategy set. Without being asked, Stella had canceled all her hair appointments for the next day. Carmen tried to talk her out of it, knowing the financial hit would be significant, but Stella cut her short. "Stop it. You'd do the same for me."

"By giving people horrific haircuts?" Carmen asked.

"Right. You'd ruin my business. That makes me the better friend."

Stella helped them come up with a list of plans they'd implement in the morning before they moved to the kitchen to prep for breakfast. Carmen was emptying the dishwasher and Stella and Lola were mixing up pancake batter when Stella asked to spend the night.

Carmen turned, her hands full of coffee mugs. "I'd love that."

Stella covered the pancake batter with plastic wrap. "In the last few days, I've thought about this a lot. You guys aren't just important to me, you're important to Chelan. You're one of the oldest wineries in the valley. We can't let that go. I'm team Alvarez, all the way."

After the breakfast prep, Papi joined them, listening to Stella's suggestions before leading them up to the vineyard, marking the spots where the crates should be stationed so the forklifts could move them in the morning. Papi showed them how the harvesters could work as a team, each with a runner sending the fruit back.

They'd take turns, although if someone couldn't handle picking, serving as runner would provide a change in pace. They'd take water breaks together and eat in the fields, which they'd tried to avoid until now.

The brix levels were too high. The fruit was dangerously close to producing wine that was high in alcohol that would distort the full-bodied flavor.

Juan agreed that he would work with Lola in the winery, supervising the juice extraction from the fruit. They would get the juice into the casks as quickly as possible to allow the next crate into the press. They had to strain the juice several times through increasingly smaller sieves and ensure that all the casks had been rigorously cleaned. Juan would carefully check each batch, verifying that it was funneled into the right casks. It was a fast-paced, delicate operation requiring careful monitoring at every step. Carmen worried that her father might not be up to it. But it didn't matter. He was all they had.

They trooped back into Orchard House to snatch a few hours of sleep.

Carmen stopped her friend at the bottom of the stairs. "I don't know how to thank you."

Stella rested her head on Carmen's shoulder. "I do. Let me get some sleep."

*

Evan watched from his patio as the Blue Hills pickers held a meeting. He sipped his coffee as the sun rose over the eastern hills, painting the lake with swaths of dusty pink. Lola divided the harvesters into teams, handing each of them a water bottle, pointing to different parts of the fields. Totes were driven to stations by a harvester who drove the forklift. There were a few misses. At one point, the lowered forklift went into the dirt, lifting the vehicle's rear wheels off the ground with the abrupt stop, nearly flinging the driver from the cage.

It was a good system, Evan thought, and new to Blue Hills. The totes were at the foot of the hill instead of up the sides of the hill. People would run the fruit down rather than having the forklift drive up and down. The runner would ferry the fruit down the hill, freeing the forklift up to make warehouse runs. Very clever, Evan thought, wondering if it was Carmen's idea.

Evan had almost finished his coffee when Paolo joined him, gazing down the hill with his own cup, which he stared into mournfully, as if deeply disappointed with its contents. Evan studied the Italian. He was much happier these days, arriving on time, eager to work instead of dragging his feet and complaining endlessly about rural America. *Thank you, Stella,* Evan thought, before giving Paolo a double-take.

Stella, who was Carmen's best friend.

"They're getting organized." Evan said, gauging his employee to see if he'd react. Evan had been explicit about Paolo not sharing harvest methods. Paolo hadn't seemed to mind or push back. He'd even joked about not confusing work and romance, like an American. But what if he was? What if a chain of communication ran through Evan's master vintner to Carmen? What if Paolo was helping the competition?

"Yeah," Paolo said, glancing at his phone while sipping his coffee. Two weeks ago, he would have been lamenting the brew, saying it was coffee-flavored water. Followed by complaints about the bland bread, the antiseptic grocery stores and the revolting restaurants. Now, he just showed up and went to work.

Evan didn't turn around as he spoke. "Why do you think they changed things up?"

Paolo looked up from his phone, frowning. "Maybe they saw what we were doing?" He scratched his curls. "I don't know." Paolo finished his coffee in two gulps. "Have you been up to see how the press is doing since they changed the gears? I don't want them running without one of us checking in."

Evan shook his head. Before he could respond, Paolo was headed up the hill, telling Evan to join when he could. There were some things he wanted to discuss.

That was another thing: Paolo seemed to be taking on more and more work, experimenting with different varietals in his workshop in the cave, taking copious notes without explanation. He'd assumed that the grapes had been sourced for Hollister Estates.

Had it been for Carmen's benefit?

What if Evan was contributing to his own demise?

Evan eyed the Blue Hills workers as they hiked up to the vineyard.

Carmen was walking back to the house, wearing an apron over her shorts. She paused for a moment on the steps. He could have sworn she glanced in his direction. He finished his coffee, wondering if it was just wishful thinking. He went into the kitchen to put his coffee mug away before joining Paolo in the winery. Had she been looking for him? Probably not. But it didn't stop Evan from thinking about Carmen Alvarez for the rest of the day.

*

Carmen paused on the steps before going inside to face the mountain of breakfast dishes. Evan was there, on his patio, peering down. She stopped herself from waving. Not to be friendly, but just to let him know that she saw him. She'd skipped watching him swim since the harvest had begun. She was furious about him stealing her cook and simply too tired, dropping into bed, conking out immediately. The alarm felt like it went off seconds later.

The sunrise this morning was beautiful. Blush pink spreading across the sky like an unfurling rose. "Get up and enjoy this gift," Mami would say, opening the curtains before kissing her daughter's sleepy head, hidden in the covers. A gentle breeze ruffled Carmen's hair now. She shut her eyes for a moment before opening them wide.

Was the beautiful sunrise simply a result of dawn, or was it refracted ash from the up-lake fires? Would this be a replay of two summers ago, when she'd called her father hourly to make sure he'd been evacuated? Would her efforts be for nothing, as wildfires suffocated the fruit and stopped the harvesting? Carmen looked up again at Evan, but he seemed to be looking at the sky too. She went inside.

Maybe they were worried about the same thing.

They were both farmers battling the elements.

Maybe, thought Carmen as she adjusted her apron, burying her hands in the soapy water, they had more in common than she thought.

Carmen dried her hands when the phone rang. She picked it up without looking at the caller ID.

"Hi, Carmen. It's Evan."

She stayed quiet, worrying that, impossibly, he could tell what she'd been thinking.

"Evan Hollister."

"I know. Hi, Evan." She thought about sitting next to him on the rock. Their arms touching. His cold skin warming against hers. The deep breath she'd taken before bringing Mami into it. Moonlight, and the soft lap of the waves on the rock. She'd never sit on that rock again without thinking of him.

"Hi," his voice was softer. "How's the harvest going?"

She sighed. "We've got fainting pickers and jumping mice and we're all exhausted, and you know what, Evan?"

"What?"

"The thing is, I'm just tired. Tired of going back and forth with you. I mean, the whole time we went for that swim it was… nice. That's what it was—nice. Maybe more than nice."

"It was more, Carmen. You know it was."

"I do. What am I supposed to think then, when I find out that you've hired my cook right out from under me? That I've got twenty-eight people to feed and one sixteen-year-old kid to do the cooking? You do the math. Thousands of bushels on that hill that are going to rot because we can't do this. We're losing the battle. That's how it's going, Evan."

"I didn't know…"

"Of course not. You don't know, because you have the best pickers money can buy. Theoretically, my pickers should be up to the job, but they aren't. They aren't pickers. They're great people that we've basically tricked. We told them that we were going to give them this amazing experience and they're so wiped out they can barely function. But they're still here. They can be part of the end." She was crying. "You're happy, right?"

"Carmen, I wish I was there."

She wiped her eyes. "Just… don't. You want to gloat."

"I didn't hire the cook away from you. My housekeeper did. I didn't even know where he came from until now. If you want, I'll send him back over. And yes, I did get pickers because I could pay more. I think you're giving those people a great experience. I'm sorry you are having such a hard time. I don't want to be part of it."

"Spare me. You are the cause of it."

"Carmen, please. You can't blame me for wanting the same things you do."

"Did you grow up here? Do you have a father who worked his entire life to build up this land and these vines?" She sighed. "Why did you call? To tell me that your grapes are in?"

"I'm doing the set-up for the First Crush Festival."

She threw up her hand. "Of course you are. Because that's how my life works. What now?"

He was apologetic. "You were supposed to have your booth set up by today."

"That's next week."

He paused for a long moment. "It starts Monday."

Carmen shrieked. "Oh no! You can't be serious."

"Do you need help? I can come over or help build it, or whatever you need."

The last thing Carmen wanted was to be anywhere near Evan Hollister. "Oh, no. We're good. Yes, um, we've just come back from Wenatchee with everything we need."

"Okay then, I'll be at the fairgrounds. I can help you set up."

"Don't bother."

"Our display is the one with the corral."

"Okay, I'll bite. A corral?"

Evan sounded embarrassed. "It's a petting zoo."

"Right. Because small farm animals and wine go together so well."

"It wasn't my idea."

"That seems to be a theme of yours."

"Carmen. Can't we talk? I need to clear the air."

Carmen shook her head. "The air around here isn't going to be clear until the end of summer. You've been living here long enough to know, Evan. Things are just starting to get heated up."

Carmen hung up, rushing upstairs. She hated to wake up Nathalie, who'd just gone to sleep after getting up at four to cook breakfast. The poor girl was running on fumes. But there was no way to avoid it. She'd have to do the dishes and get the lunch out by herself.

Carmen had to drive into Wenatchee to pick up a custom-made barrel that had cost a small fortune. It was basically an oversized open cask with a door. Adella had paid for it.

Thank God for her sister. For both sisters.

By the time Carmen came downstairs with Nathalie, Stella was doing the dishes.

"Go back to sleep," Stella ordered Nathalie, who blinked at Carmen, looking for directions. "Seriously. I can make grilled cheese and tomato sandwiches. Everyone will be happy." Stella pointed at Nathalie. "You. Sleep."

The two friends stared at each other. "I owe you big time," Carmen said.

Stella shook her head. "What you owe me is an explanation. What's going on with you and Evan Hollister?"

Carmen rolled her eyes. "It's complicated."

"Don't you give me the old 'it's complicated' runaround." She pointed at herself. "I invented that one, sister."

Carmen nodded. "You did."

Stella folded her arms. "So."

Carmen pushed her hair off her face with both hands, breathing deeply. "Ever since I met him, we've been at each other's throats. He wants the winery. I want to pay off the bank and stay here. So. You know. Nothing can happen. Ever."

Carmen nodded. "But?"

Carmen clenched her fists. "But we have this chemistry. I mean, look at him. It's like, at any other time..."

"At any other time, you might not have had this chemistry. I mean, I get it. You both want the same thing. You're both fighting hard. You both find each other's passion very appealing. But Car, what is going on? I heard you on the phone. You went swimming?"

Carmen wrinkled her nose. "Yes. We swam out to my rock."

Stella's eyes went huge. "Wait, you took him out to your rock? That's *huge*."

"Right? There's barely enough room for one person. Things got cozy."

"Very cozy!"

"We were chatting and it was fun. And I felt like things were, I don't know, headed somewhere. I honestly thought he was going to kiss me."

"And?"

Carmen shook her head. "No. Worse than that, I found out the next morning that he'd hired my cook away from me. Except now he says he didn't. And he seems to blame other people who work for him for almost everything, but the bottom line is, nothing can happen between us."

Stella cocked her head. "You don't know that."

"Yes, I do."

"No, you don't. Carmen, you're putting everyone ahead of yourself."

"The stakes are too high."

"This isn't an either/or thing. Maybe you should see him, face to face."

"We fight every time we talk."

"Make it different."

Carmen tilted her head. "There isn't time."

"Make time." Stella patted her friend's arm. "Think about it."

Carmen grabbed her car keys. "I'll be back to make dinner."

"Take some time to think," Stella smiled.

"Okay," Carmen said as she pulled her purse over her shoulder. "I owe you for all this, you know?"

"Name your first child Sunshine Unit and we're even."

Carmen smiled. "Sunshine Unit is going to love you."

Stella gave her a soapy wave. "Don't count yourself out, Car."

Carmen was rushing out the door when she saw her father returning from visiting the fields. "That old pressing machine still works, mija," Papi said, looking tired.

Now that the place was overrun with strangers, Carmen wondered if he felt out of place in his own winery. She put a hand on

Papi's shoulder. "Hey, would you come keep me company on a ride to get something in Wenatchee?"

Papi raised his eyebrows, looking enthusiastic. "What're you getting?"

"Papi, you're not even going to believe it."

She found herself looking up the hill for Evan. He wasn't in his garden or near the pool, but she looked to the left, at the lake's vanishing point, where it curved into the blue hills. The foggy haze of smoke was getting thicker.

CHAPTER EIGHTEEN

First Crush

"With their feet? People are going to step on the grapes?" Her father had decided to drive to Wenatchee. She'd take the wheel on the return, carrying the tub in the back – hopefully disassembled in a box, since the whole tub wouldn't fit into her father's truck bed. There were a couple of deep scrapes on the side of the car, Carmen noted before she got in. Her father never would have allowed scrapes on his beloved F210 before. The girls called the fancy truck his favorite child. Another sign that the Papi she knew was changing. Carmen felt a twinge of guilt as they drove down the steep incline on highway 971 and through the mountain tunnel. Why had it taken a crisis to get her here?

"Sí, Papi. People get to crush grapes."

Her father peered down at the Columbia River, wide and muddy jade, bordered by lawns and orchards. He shook his head. "They want their feet dirty and stained?"

Carmen looked up at the steep red cliffs, hoping to see the tiny mountain goats stuck to their sides like magnets. "Yes. Some people think it's fun."

"And this will sell wine?" He sounded doubtful.

"Yes," Carmen said firmly. Never underestimate a marketing gimmick.

Her father drummed his thumbs on the steering wheel. "Carmenita, I know you and your sisters have big plans for the winery. But the pickers, I mean harvesters, you have hired and the stepping on the grapes and you quitting your job in Seattle. It's a little confusing. I thought you liked your job?"

Carmen was quiet for a moment. She'd never thought to ask her father if keeping the winery was what he wanted. What if he wanted to retire, maybe even move into someplace easier to maintain? A less remote location where he could walk to the Apple Cup, or a senior center. What if he wanted something entirely different?

"Papi, I did like my job. Well, most of it."

"So why did you leave?"

Carmen glanced over at him. The sleeves of his plaid shirt were rolled back. He wore the watch her mother had given him the day they got married. The band was scratched and nicked. Aged and worn to perfection. Like her father. "Papi, I came here because I thought you needed me."

"Carmenita, I want you to have your own life. That's why I worked so hard. Have it easier."

"Let me finish, Papi."

"Sí." He nodded.

"I *thought* I was coming here to help you. That I'd help you get the harvest out and go back to Seattle. Now I want to stay for me. To learn the wine business, like I told you. It's in my blood."

Her father nodded. “Sí. Yo sé. But all these things like”—he gestured ahead—“the stepping on the grapes. What does this have to do with making wine?”

Carmen sighed. “Papi, you can have the best wine in the world. If nobody knows about it, it doesn’t do us any good. These things get people talking. It’s social media. You give people something to talk about.”

Papi chewed it over. “I’m glad to have you here. I know how to make wine. But that’s it.”

“I love the marketing side of it. Lola’s been very creative. She came up with a whole friends of Bluehills Winery thing. It’s brilliant, really.”

Her father nodded, then wiped his eyes.

“Papi, what’s wrong?”

“Oh nothing. I just like having you girls here so much. I’m happy that you want to be here.”

Carmen reached over and squeezed Papi’s arm. Orchard House, Blue Hills, their way of life could blow away so easily, red dust off a cliff. Suddenly it became more important than ever that she save it.

For all of them.

The tub barely fit on the truck bed. Although the guy at the fabricating warehouse had strapped it down, Carmen worried about freeway driving. “Take the back roads,” an older worker suggested. Juan insisted on driving. Carmen caved, not wanting to embarrass him.

Juan tugged at the nylon cinches holding the load, satisfied. “Bueno. Gracias.”

The workers opened the gates, waving them off onto the gritty road lined with fruit packing plants and RV sales lots. They turned and the truck wobbled in the brisk wind. Carmen kept looking in the back window, worried. Juan drove the truck over the river towards the southern shore. They'd have to slow down when they drove through the small communities peppering the road. Some of them were no more than a fistful of houses, but the signs posted said to drive at twenty-five.

It was a pretty drive with the wide sage river on their left, the rolling green orchards and large houses with weeping willows spreading across their improbably bright lawns, lush with access to river water. Flickering silver ribbons on fruit trees kept the birds at bay, glinting in the morning sun. The large barrel was wedged sideways, fighting the wind like a sail, rattling the truck as the wind blew down the river canyon. Canyons on either side made it seem that the world was just this: green water and red stone.

"We're falling behind with the harvest, Carmencita," Juan broke the silence. "The sugar can't get too high. The fruit will spoil."

Carmen let the wind ruffle her hair through the open window. "I know."

"Maybe you ought to ask our neighbor for help."

Carmen frowned. "What makes you suggest that?"

Her father kept his eyes on the road. "His crew is almost done. It's what we do. Remember when we lent our crews to the Sundersons? They didn't have to ask. We knew."

Carmen shook her head. "We can do it, Papi."

A blast of wind shook the car. Juan kept a firm grip on the steering wheel, holding the truck steady. It had been this way her whole life. Papi kept things steady. Even after Mami died. When the freezer was empty of casseroles, Papi had shopped at Safeway, the place where he'd met his wife, filling the cart with food he recognized, hoping he'd get it right.

"And what if we can't, mija? You girls have been working so hard. What if all your work is for nothing?"

"We can do it." She wasn't sure. She might be too stubborn. What if her pride let this all crash down on her shoulders? Could she live with that? But could she live with asking Evan for help? And what if he said no? Maybe that would be the worst outcome. Knowing he put greed before everything. She didn't want to know that about him.

Juan was silent as the truck ate up another mile of river road. "I trust you."

Carmen's eyes filled with tears. She sniffed. Her father reached over and squeezed her hand.

Just when she needed it.

Carmen looked up at the top of the canyon. There was a faint haze in the sky. Smoke or clouds? Juan turned on the radio and found a song in Spanish on KOZI, his and Mami's favorite public radio station. Every Sunday, KOZI broadcast in Spanish all day. When the girls were little, the Alvarez family went to church in Manson, across the lake. After the service they'd eat donuts in the community room, balancing paper plates while hugging friends. Afterwards at Orchard House, when it was warm enough, the girls would race to the lake while their parents took a siesta with the radio on, falling asleep to language of their homeland.

Father and daughter both sang along, enjoying the ride, forgetting everything in the simple pleasure of togetherness.

*

"Hey Mr. Alvarez! Nice to see you." Evan shook Juan's hand with genuine enthusiasm. Carmen hung back by the truck on the fairgrounds. It was a beautiful site, with views of the canyon and the river winding to the north. Winemakers from all over Central and Eastern Washington were driving onto the grounds with large trucks, setting up their booths and trailers. There was an air of easy camaraderie between the winemakers, catching up during the busy harvest.

Carmen watched her father and Evan talk, envying their easy rapport. Her father seemed to forget that Evan was the one who wanted to take their winery in the first place. He didn't even seem to hold anything against the bank. When she'd pointed out that he'd been doing business with Mr. Wilfrey for decades and maybe the man could have done more to help, Papi had shook his head. "Mija, it's business. The man's done everything he could." Maybe it was his memory or maybe it was hard-won wisdom, but her father didn't seem to hold grudges.

Maybe she should learn something from him.

As he walked over with Evan, Carmen felt flushed with anger. Evan's smile was the same one he'd offered her the night of their swim. Which had led to nothing. Which, to him, had meant nothing.

He seemed to be searching her eyes as he approached.

She didn't give anything away.

"Carmen, it's great to see you." He squeezed her arm warmly.

She pulled away quickly. "Just show us where to set up." She added a terse, "Thanks."

Her father looked between them, curious. Carmen knew what he was thinking. His daughter wasn't normally so curt. This was their neighbor after all. "No podemos hacerlo solos," he told her. We can't do it alone.

Carmen shook her head slightly, hoping her father would take her lead. "We've got people coming."

Evan looked shocked. "Carmen, you don't have to. I mean, I've got people. Shouldn't you be keeping people on the harvest?"

Carmen threw her hands up. "That's rich, Evan. You of all people, giving me advice on what to do about the harvest. How about if you didn't mess up our weddings? Or steal our cooks?" She turned to her father, pointing at Evan. "He's been sabotaging us every step of the way."

Her father put his hand on her shoulder. People passing by were giving them looks. "Carmen, por favor."

"No. No. Papi, I came here because I was worried that he would buy the land right out from under you. That he would just take everything, and for what? His ego? He doesn't need the money. He can buy grapes from anywhere in the world. But he wants our land. And you know why? Because he can't have it!" She turned to Evan. "Isn't that right? It's a measly eighty-seven acres. Do you know what we're called now? A boutique winery. It's not the grapes, Evan. It's that someone finally said no to you. Isn't that it?"

Evan was shaking his head. He lifted his hands. "Okay, you win. You can figure out how to set up on your own." He nodded at Juan. "Mr. Alvarez, if you change your mind, let me know. I can send people over."

Juan nodded. "Yes, I'm sorry."

Evan shook hands with him. “Don’t be. I haven’t—”

Juan lifted a hand to stop him. “I think I understand.”

Both men exchanged a glance.

*

Evan wondered if Carmen’s father truly understood. He didn’t want the older man to think badly of him. Evan admired Carmen’s father more than either of them would ever know. Alvarez senior was truly a self-made man. He’d not only built up a great business, he’d done everything Evan aspired to do. Make award-winning wines, marry well, raise a family and establish roots. While Evan’s wealthy parents played golf and traveled around the world, Evan planted vines. What he really wanted was roots.

As he walked away across the trampled grass through the clusters of chatting winemakers and workers, Evan wondered if Carmen was right. Had he just wanted to own those vines because they weren’t on the market? Had he wanted to buy Juan’s dream as a shortcut? Carmen’s words made him feel like an impostor.

But it didn’t matter. Tomorrow the festival would begin, and the world of wine lovers would be at his door.

He had to be ready.

He looked across the windy fairgrounds, hoping that everything would come together.

Carmen and her father were at the truck, talking. He’d messed things up with her. Maybe it was too high a price to pay. Maybe sometimes success wasn’t worth it.

*

"Car, we can't spare anyone," Lola said. To Carmen's surprise, Lola had become the crew boss, along with Marcus, the math teacher who was used to talking people into things they didn't want to do. The two of them led trivia games, brought in ice cream and went the extra mile to make life sustainable in hot, windy weather. "We're doing everything we can."

Carmen looked around the fairgrounds. Everyone had big signs and concessions. She didn't know she was supposed to sell food. Or that this was such a big deal. She should have known there would be food because it was at the fairgrounds, but she didn't know they were going to take up the entire place. Someone was assembling a tasting room in a huge circus tent. An electrician was testing the lighting. Why hadn't she thought of that? Who would willingly stain their feet when they could sip free wine under strands of Pinterest-worthy lights?

"This barrel is huge. I can't do this by myself. Even with Papi. You should see this thing. I hope it works, because we almost got lifted off the highway by the wind."

"Listen, you've got to find someone else," Lola said. "Everyone here is dragging. We have more than a third of the field left and people are slowing down. Come back."

Carmen heard panic in her sister's voice. She was at her limit. "Bueno. I'll get this figured out and come back. Don't worry. It's all going to work out." Hearing the words come out of her mouth felt like a lie. The harvest wasn't going to be enough to save Blue Hills. They'd lose everything, including her childhood home. It would all be her fault.

Carmen slipped her phone in her jeans, desperate for someone to reassure her that she was doing the right thing. Evan was across the fairgrounds on the scrubby grass, talking to a man with a dog, bending to scratch the dog's ears. She didn't need a man to encourage her. Nobody had told her migrant father to keep going before he'd met her mother. He'd survived on sheer grit. Carmen took a deep breath, letting the movement settle her nerves. Survival was in her DNA.

"It's fine," she told herself.

CHAPTER NINETEEN

Where There's Smoke

Evan nodded, talking to Hank Freeburg, indicating he'd be there in a minute. It gave Carmen a chance to catch her breath. Evan chatted easily with Hank, who Carmen knew from around town. The older man smoked a cigarette, but rather than wave the smoke away from his face, Evan nodded as Hank politely blew the smoke in the other direction.

"I couldn't get some of the crop in. Sold it to Saint Michelle, see? Wasn't my first choice, but it saved my bacon. Nothing sadder than a load of grapes rotting in your fields." Hank ground the cigarette under his boot to a fine pulp, placing the remains in a tin that went into his jacket pocket. A typical sight in a land racked by wildfires.

"Hope they gave you a good price," Evan said, nodding at Carmen.

She had to admit that it was nice to see Evan giving Hank his attention. He could have brushed Hank off. Could have truthfully said he had any number of duties to attend to. But he listened.

"Aye," Hank said. "Hard to see strangers working in my field and trucking away my crop, but it was a swift deal. They knew they had me, what with the heat and all. Fair enough, given what they could have done."

Evan nodded. "Good to know."

"Get yours in?" Hank asked.

"Yes. I was lucky," Evan said.

Carmen knew that Evan could have told him more. That he'd had a record harvest. Paolo had told Stella. He could have also said that the grapes were exceptional, too. Maybe from the new irrigation drip system he'd had installed at great cost that infused liquid fertilizer into the soil. But he hadn't. Carmen begrudgingly admired his sensitivity.

Hank nodded at Carmen. "I'll leave you to it. See you during all the hoopla." He waved his arm around the fairgrounds. "Well done, son."

Evan gave him a two-fingered salute. "Thank you, sir."

Carmen and Evan watched Hank and his dog make their way slowly across the fairground. "Nice man," said Evan.

"You were very decent."

Evan did a double-take. "Excuse me, do I know you?"

Carmen's lips twisted. "Very funny."

Evan tilted his head, studying her evenly. "I am decent, in general, you know."

Carmen sighed. "I have evidence to the contrary."

Evan put his palms up. "Okay, I'm not getting into this again. I think we already traumatized your father. What can I do for you?"

Carmen turned to her truck, where her father waited, impatiently grinding the heels of his beloved cowboy boots into the dust. "Turns out, we don't have help coming."

Evan broke into a huge grin. "You need help." It was a statement.

"You're going to make me say it, aren't you?"

Evan scratched his chin. "Don't tempt me."

Carmen shrugged, heading back to her truck.

"Hey, wait. I'll help you."

She kept walking, waving.

"I said I'd help you!" Evan yelled, attracting unwanted attention.

She didn't stop, but she did say, "Thank you."

*

Evan shook his head the entire time it took to walk to the fairground office. She deserved to be stranded with that oversized hot tub wedged like a sausage into the truck's narrow bed. He would assist Juan, he decided. He liked the man, despite his hot-tempered daughter. Every time he thought he'd found a way to talk to Carmen, it blew up. A relationship with her wouldn't be work. It would be a full-time job. She was saving him, really. The last thing he needed was a difficult woman. She was the most difficult of them all.

If someone asked him what he saw in Carmen Alvarez, he'd be stumped.

She was impossible.

The sooner Carmen realized that her father would be happy as a wealthy retiree, the better.

*

Five men tilted the massive tub off the side of the truck while the waiting crew stopped it from crashing to the ground.

"Stop! Hold up!" The ground crew hollered, but one of the men in the truck lost his footing. The tub slipped, landing in the dust with a thud, rocking back and forth.

Carmen's nerves bunched up her spine. Now what? She circled the tub, locating a crack running down one side. This thing had cost a fortune. But she couldn't take it out on these men. They'd volunteered to help. A few apologized. Carmen patted their shoulders while her father knelt on the ground, examining the crack, running his fingers down the breech. "No problema. We can fix it. Gracias. It's going to be fine."

She knelt down beside her father. "Can it be fixed?"

Her father looked up. "Sí." He sighed. "Carmen…"

"Yes Papi?"

He looked up at her, his warm brown eyes concerned. "Did you and that Evan fella work out things? You're awfully hard on him."

Carmen nodded. "Sí, Papi. Es bueno." He didn't need to know. Papi would never understand the roller coaster of conflicting feelings that Evan evoked.

Juan stood up, patting her shoulder, his face relaxed. "Bueno. This is nothing. I'll come back and work on it. Nothing a trip to the hardware store can't fix." He walked to the truck. "Come on. Mami will have lunch ready."

Carmen followed him back to the car, wondering what to say to her father. It was so hard. One minute he was fine, and the next he thought Mami was alive. Should she tell him that Mami was dead? That he'd learned to plait hair, dry tears and sometimes call his sisters in Mexico when he didn't know what to say? Could she bear to tell him that everything had changed forever when cancer had taken away the love of his life? Would it help if he knew that he'd managed beautifully? Raised his daughters and done a fantastic job?

As they drove off the fairgrounds, Carmen sighed. She needed to go with him to the doctor. There were so many, many things that needed taking care of.

Her father patted her hand. "Don't worry, mi amor. I'll fix it."

Carmen wished she lived in a world where her father could still fix everything.

Carmen joined the picking crew after lunch. Six people had left that morning. The remaining harvesters were quiet, doggedly picking with swollen fingers and aching backs. The only people the pickers wanted to see at the end of the day were the massage therapists. Carmen had called a massage school in Wenatchee. She'd found students willing to work on the harvesters in the evening for the practice, and to help with the harvest. They lined up their tables on the patio. If they had expected Mexican pickers, they didn't say anything, welcoming the tired people onto their tables. Waiting harvesters sat in the shade, drinking lemonade.

Carmen had decided to serve dinner by the lake tomorrow night. She'd talked to Lola about making the recreational activities easier. If the harvesters would rather rest in their beds or read, she'd make dinner more interesting.

In the field, the crew was noticeably quieter. Three days ago, they'd chatted, getting to know their fellow harvesters. Now they bent at their tasks, looking up only to wipe their faces or get drinks of water. When Carmen shared that they'd be eating at the lake the following night, most people just said, "Okay."

Carmen felt an obligation to make this experience what she'd advertised. "Tonight, we're making ice cream."

That got a better response. Carmen picked up her phone and called Nathalie. "Can you go into town and get about three gallons of heavy cream?"

Nathalie laughed. "Right. What're we doing, bathing in it?"

"No, I'm serious. We're making ice cream."

"Cool. Okay, I'll go buy a few gallons of cream."

"At Walmart," Carmen told her.

"Thank you."

"Just leave dinner. I'll finish it."

"Cool," Nathalie said.

Poor kid. Grocery shopping was now a huge treat.

"Okay, fill the inner jar with two cups of cream, some sugar and whatever you want to flavor it. We've got blueberries, raspberries and good old vanilla." Carmen turned to Nathalie, clapping. "Thank you, Nathalie, for finding all the delicious fixings."

The harvesters cheered for Nathalie, who beamed under the attention.

Harvesters spread out on yoga mats on the patio, gathering around the tables to fill their jars while Carmen continued. The sun hung low on the smoke-blurred horizon, behind the craggy plateau over the fields. Overhead, the sky shifted from pinky orange to purple. The lake reflected the colors over a haze of dark blue.

Carmen felt relieved seeing everyone so relaxed. Most of the people had gotten a second wind after she'd talked up the ice cream making, saying they could sit on the patio and make the ice cream themselves like she had when she was a Girl Scout. Several of the women had shared their happy memories of doing the same thing. Carmen went over to the tables that Nathalie had organized.

"Once you get your fillings on the inside, you place the tightly closed jar inside the Yuban can in the middle, and surround it with layers of rock salt and ice. Nathalie, can you bring them out?"

Nathalie disappeared into the kitchen, returning with large boxes of rock salt. A few moments later she had bowls of ice. The Yuban cans were stacked at one end, a result of Carmen's father's coffee drinking and a belief that a Yuban can had multiple purposes in life. The cans had waited decades in the garage for just such a moment. Carmen thought of her mother rolling her eyes at the stacks of rusting cans every time she got into the car. She sent a message to her mother. "Mami, Papi was right on this one."

Once they'd finished the layering of the salt and ice, the teams sat on their mats and rolled, as instructed, the Yuban jar between teams, mixing the ice cream and chilling the cream. It was, as Carmen had hoped, a good team-building activity. As the first few little bats flapped overhead, swooping erratically in their hunt for insects, the teams chatted and laughed, jumping up when the Yuban cans went sideways. When the cans bumped, they joked about sabotaging one another.

"It's going to take a while!" Carmen said. She couldn't help but notice Evan on the edge of his property, looking down with a drink in his hand. For once, he didn't wave. He just turned from her. It was surprising, how much it hurt. Every time she thought she'd shaken him off, something happened to remind her that there was still a vulnerable part of her that craved his attention.

Whatever.

"It's fun!" said Nathalie, who had been paired with a boy her own age. They chatted amiably as they rolled the Yuban can, laughing when it rattled off the yoga mat onto the stone patio. Carmen's mother's tropicana roses glowed in the twilight. Their buds started as pink or tangerine before exploding into tropical hues, some tipped with hot pink and some a hot orange, like the lipstick their mother had favored. Mami would take her single glass of wine out onto the patio at night, inhaling the perfume from the roses, comparing their color to a fiesta.

Laughter floated up into the night as the lights strung over the patio lit the ice cream makers, sitting legs splayed, rolling the cans back and forth.

This was, Carmen thought, what she'd hoped the harvesters would experience. Not just the sunburns, blistered fingers and aching backs, but the feeling of summer camp. Of getting away from their regular life and making friends. Trying new things.

She wanted this week to be something they'd remember fondly.

Tonight felt like a win.

Tomorrow, they'd drag all the tables down to the beach and have a barbecue. She'd try to forget the last time she'd been at the beach. She had to make new memories. Get over her irrational feelings.

It was time to move on.

*

"Car, get up!"

There was a gorgeous red pink sunset on the wrong side of the lake. Carmen sat on what they now called "our rock" with Evan, so close she could feel the dampness of his bathing suit. What were they talking about? Everything. Nothing. It didn't matter. They were getting along. And happy.

"Car! You've got to get up!"

It was Lola, intruding into Carmen's dream. She cracked open one eye, studying her sister's outline in the doorway against the light.

"Go away."

"Get up. I'm going downstairs. It's an emergency. Please!"

She was gone before Carmen could ask what kind of emergency. There were people in the hallway, the murmur of voices. What were they all doing up? Her phone said three in the morning.

Oh no.

Why wasn't everyone sleeping?

She entered the hallway, fiddling with her robe belt.

"Get out! I need to..." It was Marcus, the math teacher, weaving down the hallway like he was drunk.

Did they all get drunk?

Marcus pushed her aside, trying to reach another bathroom. He didn't make it. Threw up in the linen closet.

Carmen stopped, trying to get her bearings. Was this what rude awakening meant? One minute with a handsome man watching the sunset, the next watching a stranger upchuck in your linen closet.

A pack of zombies lurched her way. Zombies in adorable summer PJs. The zombies moaned, pleading to use her bathroom. There wasn't another option. Carmen pointed into her bedroom. It was the only en suite bedroom, besides the master. She'd pay heavily for this luxury.

Both ends of the hallway were blocked by sick people. She dashed downstairs, hoping to find Lola, who was in the kitchen hunched desperately over her phone, her eyes huge. "Oh, my goodness, Car. They've got food poisoning."

Carmen found a barstool before she fell. "You're kidding me?"

"No. The raspberries." Her finger traced a triangle between the three of them. "We ate plain vanilla ice cream. It's only the people who ate the berries."

Nathalie was teary-eyed. "I didn't know."

Lola patted her back. "How were you supposed to know?"

Carmen glanced between them, perplexed. "Know what?"

Nathalie shook her head. "Raspberries cause a lot of food poisoning."

Lola looked up from her phone. "They *can*." She gave Nathalie a pointed glance. "Look, it could have been any one of us who bought those berries. You just did the shopping. Please. Let it go. You did exactly what we asked."

Lola faced Carmen, who felt like a bomb had just gone off in her face. "I let you sleep for as long as I could." Carmen waved her off. "I called the nurse hotline. She said to keep them hydrated and if anyone seems to be dehydrated to bring them in. Or if they have fevers"—she looked at her phone—"or profuse sweating, tremors or delusions."

Carmen rubbed her forehead, growing increasingly horrified. "I can't believe this."

"I know. I called Mami's friends from the prayer group to see if they could help us."

Carmen nodded. “That was a great idea.”

“Thanks.” Lola leaned into her sister. “But what about the grapes?”

Carmen jumped up. She’d better get dressed. “We can’t worry about that now.”

But as she dashed up the stairs two at a time, that’s exactly what Carmen worried about.

What would happen to the harvest?

More importantly, what would happen to the winery?

CHAPTER TWENTY

Juan

By six o'clock, they'd used every towel in Orchard House. The washing machine ran nonstop. Lola, Nathalie, Carmen and a couple of the harvesters who'd forgone the ice cream gathered in the kitchen, drinking strong coffee. After a sip or two, most of the harvesters begged off, heading upstairs to find a clean bed to grab some sleep.

A young barista from Yakima put her mug in the sink. "We're not picking today, are we?"

Carmen shook her head. "No. Thanks for asking."

The girl gave her a weak smile before climbing the stairs.

"I keep waiting for the locusts," Lola said, staring bleakly into her coffee.

"Don't say that," Carmen countered. It seemed conceivable, after the night they'd had. After two hours, the harvesters had finally stopped running to the bathroom. Carmen, Lola, Nathalie and the healthy harvesters had changed beds as fast as they could, cleaning frantically, wiping every surface with Lysol.

When the last sick harvester had finally flopped down into bed in an instant sleep, they'd slumped in the hallway, staring at the walls like survivors of an alien attack.

"I've never seen anything like that in my entire life," Nathalie said.

"Hopefully you never will again," Carmen sighed.

"I'll never eat another raspberry," said Lola.

"Lots of things carry listeria. Grapes, lettuce, meat, shellfish. You can get it from almost anything. Literally," said a harvester, who wanted to keep talking but noticed the glares coming her way and wisely shut up.

"Is this it, or could they keep, you know, doing more?" asked Nathalie.

"When I was a kid at camp these kids got it from some lunch meat. It went on for days. Seriously, it can last a whole week," said the doom-seeking harvester.

Lola threw a washcloth at her. "That's enough out of you."

"But probably not," said the harvester. By this time nobody was listening to her anyway.

Morning light filtered into the kitchen. Carmen looked out the window over the sink. The morning dew dried on the fields, so fresh and green. Full of life. *Ha!*

Lola wrapped an arm around her sister. "Who wants to go swimming?"

"Seriously?" asked Carmen.

"Um, yeah. Look, it's a beautiful day." She pointed up the stairs. "They'll be fine for a little while. "Let's go swimming."

Nathalie stared at the sisters, raising her eyebrows. Suddenly, she smiled. "What the heck? I'm in."

Lola squeezed her sister. "Vámonos, Carmenita. We've got the rest of the day to face this mess. Let's go to the beach."

It sounded like something her sister would have said years ago, when she'd dented her father's truck or forgotten to water her mother's garden.

Carmen sighed, her body slumped to fake out her sister, before she hopped off the barstool, racing upstairs as fast as she could. "Last one in is a rotten egg."

Lola squealed, dashing after her sister, grabbing the back of her T-shirt. "You lousy cheater!"

Nathalie followed, smiling for the first time in four very long hours.

Chelan, it seemed, was asleep. Except for the drifting fisherman in the middle of the lake. Sunrise lingered in the buttery light warming the water. The sisters dove into the crystalline blue. Carmen first. She'd beat Lola, who'd lost her flip-flop in the race down the gravel driveway, shouting at Carmen to wait up. They'd tossed their towels on the shore. Nathalie gingerly waded in, but didn't last long. The water made her gasp and shiver. She ran back to the house to warm up.

Carmen felt the shock of cold for a second, opening her eyes to the turquoise blue underwater, her face breaking the surface. She trod water, spinning slowly, soaking in the beauty of the lake, the purplish green hills, the sun creeping over the hills above the vineyard. As her sister swam underwater to join her, she realized how deeply connected she was to the lake. How she felt most alive wrapped in its presence. Coming home had been the best thing she could have ever done. It had taken a disaster, or what was shaping into one, to bring her here.

She felt very small, realizing how a slight turn in events had brought her life to this point. *Maybe that's all of life,* she thought. *Maybe we don't have much choice.*

In another life, maybe Evan and she could have fallen in love. Got married.

She winced, chastising herself for thinking of Evan. She gazed across the water at the rock. Her rock. For a short while, it had felt like their personal island. She shook her head, as if to knock out the memory.

Lola gasped as she broke the surface a few yards away. She studied the towering shale cliffs bordering the lake, deep blue in the smoky light. "It's gorgeous."

"It is." Carmen swam over to join her sister. They moved to the rock by unspoken agreement. "I'm so glad I came back."

"Wasn't it hard, leaving your job?"

Carmen shook her head, her chin dipping in and out of the water. The temperature was perfect. A lonely truck traveled the road at the foot of the cliffs towards town. The engine noise carried across the water. "No. I've told you about my boss. My best day at work was the day she was trapped for the three hours in the elevator. We ordered in lunch and had a little party. Isn't that sad?"

Lola grinned. "No, it's funny. But you had a real career. People in town ask me what I'm up to and it's awkward because the truth is that I'm an art school dropout living at home."

Carmen was the first one on the rock. She leaned down to offer her sister a hand while making a game show buzzer noise. "Uh, no.

Wrong answer. The correct answer is you left school to help the family. You have an important job at the winery."

"I know it shouldn't matter but can we give it a name?"

"You're um, hospitality manager. You oversee our special guest programs."

"Thank you." Lola stood on the rock, wiping water from her face. "Super awkward question. Do you think we'll ever get paid?"

"Honestly? I don't know. Don't quit on me now. You know I can't do this without you."

"Thanks." She shielded her eyes with her hands, looking back toward the winery. "What a disaster."

Carmen shrugged. Strangely, her feelings about Evan seemed to put it into perspective. She'd been fighting this battle since the moment she arrived. It was a relief to put down her arms, if only for a moment. "I don't know. We tried. We brought all these great people here. Got in half the harvest. We learned a lot."

Lola had tears in her eyes. "We can't pay the bank, can we?" She was quiet as a duck landed with a splash, slicing the calm water with a neat wake.

Carmen hadn't realized until this moment that Lola—sweet, carefree Lola—was as heavily invested, as deeply entrenched, as passionate as she was. Carmen had been so consumed by the daily minutia of running the winery, consuming every bit of information she could on viticulture, she'd never considered that Lola was right there beside her, putting in the hours, sharing the burden.

She'd never been in this alone. Maybe that was the point of this whole journey. Rediscovering her sister. They'd drifted into adulthood, stranding their father on the shores of old age. Maybe the loss of the vineyard wouldn't be the worst thing if it had let her reunite with Lola.

She put her arm around her sister. "No matter what, Lola, we still have each other."

Lola rested her head on Carmen's shoulder. They watched the day begin on the lake. A lanky teen on the Wapato dock checked the rental boats. A water skier threw up a lacy spray. The Lady of the Lake, the passenger ferry heading to Stehekin, near the North Cascades National Park, passed by on its daily commute carrying tourists and hikers. The thrum of the motor echoed off the cliffs. As the boat neared, Carmen and Lola grinned.

It was an old tradition from their childhood. Morning and night, the Lady of the Lake threw a wake of premium waves on an otherwise still lake. As kids, they'd timed their summer swims with the boat schedule. Now, they waited for the waves to grow closer, then jumped into the water as they had as children, bobbing like otters in the turbulence.

When the lake quieted, Lola swam closer, pointed her chin at the shore. "Shall we?"

It was a loaded question. It would be so much easier to float here, staring up at the cloudless sky.

The sisters swam back and climbed out of the water, wrapping themselves with towels. With one last shared smile, they crossed the street to whatever awaited in Orchard House. Carmen decided she'd take Lola to the bank with her to admit defeat. She didn't need to do this alone.

There was a car they recognized in the driveway of Orchard House: Adella's. Lola had called her, knowing she was an early riser, pleading for help. But the gravel drive was also lined with a dozen unfamiliar cars. Who on earth would show up this early in the morning? Carmen and Lola were so busy speculating about the cars, they didn't notice Evan in his living room window, his eyes switching between the two towel-clad sisters and the sky.

The prayer group had arrived. Their old mini vans and sedans, purchased for hauling around children that had long since grown up, clogged the driveway. It was, both sisters thought, reminiscent of their high school days when their mother had hosted the prayer group.

Walking into their kitchen was like entering a warm bath of love. The kitchen counter was covered in baked goods and casseroles. Sixteen ladies spoke Spanish, hugging the sisters so tightly they gasped for air.

"Aye, Carmencita, Lolita, we heard about the food poisoning. What bad luck. Me personally, I never eat fruit. Bad for the digestion." Martina Runes dyed her graying hair a black that seemed to absorb light.

"Sí, we heard about you girls running the harvest. Helping your Papi. We should have come sooner," said Nece, a short woman with a single gold tooth. "But when we heard, we spread the word."

Growing up, the sisters had called it the Mexican Party Line, back from when the phones had been on shared trunk lines. All you had to do was tell one Mexican mama and it was as good as it would be nowadays posting on Lake Chelan Now, the community Facebook page.

The women were clustered into the kitchen like a brood of hens, all talking at once in a mixture of Spanish and English. On and on it went. The harder Carmen and Lola tried thanking them for the food and show of support, the more the ladies apologized for not showing up sooner.

It went around in circles until Carmen was exhausted.

"Well, you're here now and thank you all so much. It's so nice to see you." Carmen's face hurt from smiling so much.

After another eruption of Spanish, Lola managed to quiet them down. "Mami would be so happy."

"She'd be so proud of you girls. Look at you. Taking care of your Papi. Getting the harvest in," said Lenore Fretter, serving everyone coffee.

"How are the pickers? I heard terrible things," Adella said.

"The doctor said that when the people upstairs wake up, we should make sure they are hydrated and eat soft food." Carmen looked at the offerings covering the counter doubtfully. "So, thank you so much for coming to help take care of them. Hopefully the worst is over."

Patrizia, a plump woman in her seventies with a bubble of curls pulled into a bun that never seemed to contain the mass, stepped to the front, shaking her head. "No mija, we're not here to take care of the people."

Lola nodded. "Okay, well, thanks for the food."

Patrizia shook her head rapidly. "No. We're here for the harvest." She pointed up at the hill.

For the first time, Carmen noticed that the women were dressed rather casually. Most of them favored summer dresses and sandals this time of year. The sisters exchanged glances.

"What?" Carmen frowned. "But it's—"

Patrizia shook her head. "Listen, mija. Your mami was a sister to all of us. We all…" she motioned around the room. "When we first came from Mexico we all worked in the fields. Your mami was one of us and she would do the same thing for us. We know the harvest has to be in and the workers are…" She fluttered her fingers in the air. "So, we do it." She flicked her wrist at girls. "You get some sleep and we go."

"I can't let you…" said Carmen.

Patrizia pushed Carmen towards the stairs. "You don't got no say. Get some sleep and maybe you feel better. Don't want you getting sick."

The kitchen was immediately filled with chattering Spanish once more. There was a festive atmosphere as the women showed each other their gloves and clippers, comparing notes and what their husbands and children were up to.

Carmen and Lola looked at one another. The chill of the lake and the swim had made them relaxed and sleepy.

"What should we do?" asked Carmen.

"Sleep," said Lola, shrugging.

"Maybe you fix us lunch," said Patrizia, once again pushing them towards the stairs. "Later. Okay? Rest now. Sleep."

The two sisters watched the kitchen empty as the older ladies marched in a steady stream of pastels up the hill, chatting the entire way as if they were heading to a picnic.

"This feels like the weirdest dream," Carmen said.

Lola shook her head. "Maybe Mami sent them."

"Maybe she did."

Their father came barreling down the stairs, clutching his hat to his head. "Did you see them? Mami's friends. They came to help!"

It was the most elated they'd seen their father in years. He grabbed a piece of cinnamon pull apart, shoving it in his mouth as he opened the kitchen door, racing to join the women, checking to make sure his gloves were in his pocket.

Lola went to the window. "He's running. He's actually running to catch up to them."

Carmen laughed. "I don't think any of them have picked grapes in like, thirty years."

Lola shook her head. "What if a bunch of seventy-year-olds end up saving the vineyard?"

Carmen tilted her head, watching the older people disperse into neat rows like a professional crew. "Then it will be a miracle."

CHAPTER TWENTY-ONE

Prayer Ladies

Carmen hated leaving the prayer group behind, but when she went up the hill to tell her father that she had to go to the First Crush booth, he happily waved her off. "¡Es como los tiempos viejos!"

It did feel like the old times. As if her mother was in the kitchen, getting lunch ready. But Lola was fixing the food. Carmen had to rush off to pick up Stella and hurry to the booth at First Crush. With her father and the women picking with greater speed than the guest harvesters had ever managed, it was beginning to seem like they might get the harvest in on time. The brix was at the tipping point. The heat of the day could send it over the edge, but if they could cool the grapes with the shade inside the winery, they might be able to slow it down.

Carmen went down the hill with a lightness she hadn't felt since she'd first arrived in Chelan. Lola was hard at work in the kitchen, chopping vegetables. There was no sign of the stricken harvesters.

"How's it going up there?" Lola wiped away tears from the onions.

Carmen shook her head. "It's the craziest thing. Those old ladies can pick like monsters. I've never seen anything like it."

"Car, think about it. They're first generation immigrants. They raised their families in a totally foreign environment. They've faced racism, poverty and hard physical labor. They're fierce."

Carmen looked up on the hill. Already, they'd progressed up the hill to rows closer to the top. They were working at warp speed while keeping up a steady patter of Spanish and English. "They are."

Lola went back to chopping. "We could learn a thing or two from them."

Carmen nodded. "We already have."

Stella got out of the car and shouldered her bag, gazing around at the First Crush Festival with wide eyes. There were close to fifty vendors with impressive displays. Five Horses Vineyard had planted rows of grapevines, forming a mini vineyard with beautiful watercolor painted boards highlighting different types of grapes and wines. Rustic white tents featured bars in every corner, offering wine and cheese tasting. There were giant wine bottle balloons and a Dunk-the-Winemaker fundraiser to raise money for wineries affected by the wildfires.

"Wow, this is amazing. Why didn't we ever go to this before?" Stella asked, as they headed for the trailer that served as an office.

"I don't know why you didn't, but I didn't live here. The wine merchants association started it about five years ago," Carmen said as they passed a six-foot-tall wineglass overflowing with flowers.

"Who knew it was such a big deal?"

Carmen kept an eye out for Evan. She had to talk to him about finding someone to help fix the broken vat. In the rush of helping the sick harvesters, she'd forgotten to remind Papi and take him to the hardware store. They had enough grapes in the back of the truck to fill the bottom of the vat but the juice would all run out if they didn't fill the crack. What if they were still mending it when the festival started?

Stella poked Carmen's shoulder. "Hey, look."

Up ahead, situated between a tent and a thirty-foot inflated wine bottle, was the vat, all set up on a platform. Beside it was the sign she'd ordered and had sent directly to the fairgrounds. It was mounted on a rustic wooden stand. In front of it was a long table with a linen tablecloth, bearing wooden crates with the Blue Hills Vineyard logo stamped on the side. Neat rows of Blue Hills Vineyards wines were grouped in front of tasting glasses. Someone had worked hard to organize the entire booth, even going so far as to put out ropes to control the lines.

"Wow. This is..."

Stella turned to her as they walked towards the booth. "You told me we had to fix it all up. It looks amazing, Car. Someone's got your back."

Carmen climbed the platform, opened the door to the vat. She searched for the crack. Someone had filled the gap with wood glue and sanded it down. She stood up, dusting her hands. "Maybe one of Papi's friends?"

Stella shrugged, looking around at the clusters of people carrying things from trucks, readying their displays. Curious onlookers were already walking past, reading the sign: *Crush your own grapes!* "Should we go get the grapes?"

Carmen nodded. "Yeah. They cleaned out the tub and everything. I guess that's it."

And it really was.

Carmen would have to find whoever had done this and make sure to send them a case of wine. It looked a lot of work. The tablecloth was a rustic burlap-colored linen that worked perfectly with their deep blue and gold logo. The tasting glasses were stacked into miniature wooden crates so the wind wouldn't blow them over. The napkins, stamped with the Blue Hills logo, were weighted with potted mini roses. They'd thought of everything.

Standing on the back of the truck bed, Carmen and Stella dumped bushels of grapes into the tub until the bottom was a foot deep. By the time Carmen came back from parking the truck, two little girls were dragging their mothers towards the giant vat. Stella winked at Carmen while she told them that's how the ancient Greeks made their wine, shrugging at Carmen as she winged it.

"After you're done, we have a wine tasting area over here," said Carmen to the two mothers.

"And grape juice for you guys," said Stella to the children.

Carmen raised her eyebrows at Stella, who pointed to the table.

"What? I brought grape juice."

"What would I do without you?"

"You'd have bad hair, bad advice and a loser best friend."

They watched the children stomping gleefully in the grapes as their mothers laughed. Nobody seemed to care that the children were getting covered in juice. The sun shone as Carmen brought Stella a small glass of wine. They clinked glasses.

"To friendship," Carmen said.

"To love," Stella replied, keeping an eye out for Paolo.

They both drank and enjoyed the moment.

*

Six hours later, the last people wiped their feet after exiting the barrel, laughing and giggling. Carmen closed the barrel. Slipping on their shoes, the group perused the bottles set up on a table, artistically spilling out of a wooden crate. They purchased three bottles of last year's vintage, saying that stomping grapes had been entirely therapeutic.

As the sun touched the top of the canyon wall, making long shadows on the crushed grass, a cluster of teens came up, wanting a turn. Carmen decided to let them. "But no wine!"

The teens thanked her profusely, shoving one another in their haste to enter the barrel, shouting in glee. "I have grape skin between my toes!" a girl hollered.

"It feels so weird, right?" another kid said.

One boy leaned down to paint stripes of juice on his cheek.

Carmen shook her head. "So many people's feet have been in there."

Stella tucked her chin into her neck. "I wish I could unsee that."

Carmen laughed. "Right?"

"At least they're having fun." Stella began putting wine in the cases they'd stored under the tables. They'd sold close to a hundred bottles. *Not bad,* Carmen thought. Except, was it good? How much profit was it? She had so much to learn.

Evan strolled over from a wine garden, sporting a baseball hat and aviator sunglasses. "Ladies," he doffed his cap in greeting. "Everything going okay?"

Carmen felt her entire body flush. "Yep." If she said one more word, she wasn't sure what would come out. He caused such a strong reaction; it was better just to keep her mouth shut. Pretend that he was any other person.

"It's been epic. Really great. Thanks for organizing the festival" said Stella, elbowing Carmen. "Right, Carmen?"

"Yes." Carmen stood woodenly, wishing she had a glass of wine in her hand. Or something to do.

"What Carmen means is… Do you know who set up the booth and fixed the crack in the barrel?" Stella strained her head confidentially toward Evan. "Was it perhaps you?"

Evan shifted a little, seemingly uncomfortable. "No. Carmen has been very clear that she doesn't want anything to do with me. That would be breaking the rules, right Carmen? And one thing I've learned is that Carmen doesn't like people who break the rules."

Three deep breaths, Carmen told herself. That's all it took. She wouldn't take the bait, although her delivery was stiff and formal. "Thank you for fixing the barrel, Evan. We really appreciate it."

Evan tilted his head. "You're welcome."

An awkward silence followed as a farmer drifted past talking about the smoke. Stella conjured words to break the tension. "That barrel would make a wicked hot tub."

Evan laughed. "Do you need help loading it?"

Carmen's response was lightning quick. "Nope. Thanks."

Evan took off his cap, gazing at the sky. "Look, it's not a problem. I've got five guys here to help and honestly…" He took off his sunglasses to look at Carmen. "We're neighbors, right?"

Carmen gritted her teeth. "That's rich, coming from you."

Evan rubbed the bridge of his nose. "I'm not the one who unleashed sixteen goats during a wedding."

"What's worse? That, or attacking innocent people with drones or soaking their clothes with misters?"

"Well, isn't this nice?" Stella said. "World War III at a wine festival."

Carmen lifted her chin. "Which is perfect, because it started at a winery."

Evan flung his hand at her. "It's called progress! It's what people do if they want to be a success. Even the seasons change, Carmen. Blue Hills will evolve. You can't make me the bad guy."

Carmen couldn't believe that a few days ago they'd been night swimming, blissfully gazing at the moon. That seemed impossible now.

And yet.

Was this passion?

Was this one of those heated relationships that thrived on conflict? Stella's time with Paolo sounded like one blissful moment after another. Delicious food, fascinating talks, walking down the street holding hands. Stella said they constantly laughed over the silliest things.

Stella stepped in front of Carmen before punches were thrown. "Look, Evan, you've done a fantastic job. Thank you. We're going to clean this out and have someone come get it tomorrow, okay?"

Evan seemed to have calmed down. "Thank you. Your display was great. Big success." He didn't seem to mean it. "I've, uh, well… See you later."

He walked off quickly.

Stella shook her head. "That was awkward. Thanks for that."

Carmen thumped her chest. "Me?"

"Yes, you. It's like you're a bomb and he lit the fuse."

"Oh, come on!"

"That wasn't you?"

"That was me and Evan Hollister." Carmen opened the door to the tub, eying the purple muck clinging to the bottom. She handed her friend a bucket, preparing to wade in with a shovel.

"Then stay away," said Stella, disappointed. "I thought it would have been fun to double date. But after that? Thank you, no."

Carmen slid the first shovelful of grape gunk into the bucket, wiping her hair off her face with the back of her hand. "Trust me, I'd love to keep my distance from Evan Hollister."

When Carmen got back to her car there were six voice messages on her phone, which she'd accidentally left hooked up to the charger. They were from Lola, growing increasingly worried.

"Hi, it's me. We just had a ranger stop by who said we should put water on the roof and water the vines."

"Hey, me again. Call me."

"Hey Carmen, please call me. We're working like crazy to get everything wet."

"Hey Carmen, there's smoke blowing in here thick and fast. Does Papi have asthma? I don't know if we should evacuate or not. Call me."

Carmen dialed Lola's number, but there wasn't enough strength in the signal.

Stella had barely climbed into the truck when Carmen put it in drive, rattling out of the fairground dirt parking lot, leaving a wake of dust.

"Hey, slow down," Stella said, trying to fasten her seat belt with difficult on the bumpy unpaved road.

Carmen looked over at her, then up at the sky. They'd come around the corner of the hill with a view up lake. Towards the northwest, a layer of smoke clung to the lake by Wapato Point. "That looks like it's near the winery." Stella had her phone out. "Would you look at the Forestry Service site?"

Stella shook her head in frustration. "No reception."

Stella turned on the radio, searching through the AM stations to see if she could get an update. When she finally found one, Carmen wished she'd never heard it.

If the wind didn't change, all of Chelan would burn.

CHAPTER TWENTY-TWO

Evacuate

It was like driving onto a movie set. A disaster movie. Smoke loomed over Chelan at the head of the lake. Visibility had dropped to half a mile. Tiny white flakes settled onto cars and pavements, speckling the grass as if it was snowing. As they drove down Lake Street towards the heart of town, Carmen and Stella were traveling upstream. Cars loaded with families, barking dogs and luggage were pouring out of town. The owner of the Black Dog boutique was taping a sign to her window as they passed: *CLOSED FOR EVACUATION. SEE YOU SOON.*

Carmen gulped, staring at Stella with wide eyes. "Are you sure you want to go to the winery with me? Maybe you want to go check on your cat and pack up."

Stella nodded. "It's fine. Mrs. Hartner texted me. She's taking Misha to her sister's in Twisp, so I don't have to worry about him."

"Poor kitty."

"He'll be fine. He loves Mrs. Hartner, and I don't want him running off with all this smoke."

Carmen nodded. "Okay." After a moment she added, "Thanks, Stell. I'm really glad you're here."

"It's going to be fine. Seriously. Just a little smoke."

It was strange to see the sidewalks empty. The business doors closed and locked. Stranger still to drive down Lake Street and only see a quarter mile of lake, dim and sluggish in the eerie half-light. They drove slowly before taking a left onto the old bridge across the canal. Families crowded the parking lots of the lakefront hotels, packing their cars.

Stella leaned her head on the window, gazing outside. "This is like last time."

Carmen shook her head. She'd been in Seattle during the bad fires two summers ago. It had been a close call. The wind had changed, sparing the town. "Let's hope not."

"Yeah. Let's." Her somber tone made Carmen glance over. Stella's face was clouded with worry.

At Pat and Mike's Store there was a slight back-up where the road turned up the hill to leave Chelan. Carmen and Stella sat in the right turn lane, watching the line of cars drive up the hill, fleeing town. Cars pulling onto the road from their lakeside cabins were causing the delay, along with people filling up with gas at Pat and Mike's. The closer they got to the thick smoke, the more frantic people appeared. At the gas station, a man stood red-faced and yelling at a woman with a baby in her arms. The baby was crying as the woman pointed to a car that was blocked by another car.

Stella turned to watch them as Carmen drove past. "Wow. That was intense."

"So much for emergencies bringing out the best in people. Makes me wonder what's happening at the winery."

Stella patted her arm. "Everything's going to be okay. You know that, right?"

Carmen nodded, offering her friend a tight smile that was more of a grimace. "I'm sorry things were a bit awkward with Evan."

Stella waved a hand. "No worries. Maybe I needed to see it to get over that whole hot millionaire thing."

"He's complicated."

Stella shook her head. "I think actually, he's quite simple. He wants to be successful."

Carmen gave her friend a sideways glance. "Whose side are you on, anyway?"

"Yours, obvs. I just mean maybe down the line when he's figured out his deal, you guys can date."

"Yeah, because it's going swimmingly well as friends."

Stella looked out the window at a boatful of teens pulling a water skier, oblivious of the smoke. Or maybe they just didn't care. "Let me ask you something."

"Sure." Carmen glanced at the lone boat in the water.

"If Evan wasn't trying to buy your vineyard, would you go out with him?" Stella studied her friend's face, but it was unreadable.

Carmen drummed her fingers on the wheel, thinking for a moment. "Hard to say. Competition is all we know."

"With each other."

Carmen gave a little smile. "Right."

"You're both very competitive?"

Carmen nodded. "Yeeees."

"So, let's say that you just met him in town and say, I introduced you. Wouldn't you find him the least bit attractive?"

Carmen shook her head. "If you take the competitive nature out of Evan Hollister, there is no Evan Hollister."

Stella's eyes went theatrically wide. "Oh. Hmmm. Let's see. Who does that remind me of?"

Carmen rolled her eyes. "Nice, Stella. Real nice. You could have just out and said it."

"Wouldn't be half as fun." Stella twisted a bracelet on her wrist. "Besides, I didn't say it. You did."

Cars rolling down the driveway blocked their entrance to the winery. One right after the other. The driveway was only wide enough to accommodate one car, so Carmen pulled to the side of the road, watching the recovered guest harvesters drive off. Some of them saw her and waved, others were talking to each other, seemingly stressed, as they headed back to their homes.

"At least they're well enough to drive," Stella commented.

"It's too bad it had to end like this." Carmen watched the cars leave one by one. A couple of women from Mami's prayer group followed the guest harvesters, driving through the dust kicked up by the stream of cars. "We were going to do dinner down here. By the lake."

Stella nodded, looking to her left at the water. "That would have been cool. You know, maybe you can do it again but without having people do the actual harvesting. A food and wine series. Have people come here and learn about how wine is made. You could totally do a blog about it."

"In all my spare time." Carmen tapped her lip, thinking. "I did like hosting. I'd much rather do a thing where we take people out in the field, clip a few grapes, show them how we read the brix level."

"Maybe have Paolo talk to them in his super sexy accent."

Carmen laughed. "That too. Yeah. It could be fun. But first, we need to solve the business. There goes Tia Joaquina. In the minivan." The chubby lady waved. Carmen blew a kiss.

Finally, there was a break in the traffic.

Carmen turned up the driveway.

"We made it!" Carmen said, eager to seeing her family and make a plan for the encroaching fires.

When Carmen walked into the kitchen, the assembled ladies hugged her. "Carmencita," one of them said. "We picked a lot of grapes."

"It was like the good old days!" Jovita said.

"The best thing is we don't have to do it mañana!" laughed Consuela. She patted Carmen. "Don't worry bonita, it was fun. If grapes could talk, we wouldn't have a friend left in town."

Which led to bunch of chattering in Spanglish.

One by one the ladies proffered hugs, explaining they had to get home. Although they were lavish with their goodbyes, there was an air of urgency. A casual onlooker might think they lingered, but Carmen knew these ladies usually took an hour to say goodbye.

There was always one more child to discuss, one more nephew who had gotten into a fancy college or was getting married.

"Are you going to evacuate?" Carmen asked.

Frieda put her hands on her hips. "When the fire hits the town, that's when I leave. Not a moment before." She waved her hands around. "The whole time I was picking, I prayed to St. Jude for the wind to change."

Jovita put her hands together in prayer. "Oh sí, with all that praying you didn't gossip at all."

Frieda laughed, waving her hand good-naturedly. "Me, gossip? Aye Jovita, yo soy una santa!" She drew an imaginary halo atop her thick black hair.

"Isn't Saint Jude patron saint of lost causes?" Stella asked, tasting the sauce simmering on the stove.

The older lady wagged her finger. "Stella, you would know if you weren't chattering like a monkey during Sunday school. Saint Jude is for lost and *desperate* causes."

"Asking the wind to change direction is a pretty desperate request," said another old lady.

"Exactly!" said Frieda.

Carmen got another round of kisses as the ladies departed in a group, showing her the fridge full of food. She walked them outside, where the daylight was being swallowed by an early dusk, thanks to the smoke.

Carmen shivered despite the heat. Something about the eerie light, the bird swooping in frantic, worried loops above. It was all very unsettling. "Ladies, I don't know what we would have done without you."

Jovita hugged her, pulling back to admire the girl's beauty, to pinch her cheeks. "Darling, you are our daughters. Juan would have done the same thing for us in our hour of need." Jovita hiked the same cavernous purse she'd carried since Carmen had noticed such things.

"Where is Papi?" Carmen asked Honora, as the older lady waved from the door.

"No sé."

Lola came into the kitchen with a load of laundry. "Probably sleeping. He picked for eight hours."

"Well, thank you so much." Carmen said to Honora. "We'll have you all out to dinner after this nonsense dies down."

"Don't you worry!" said the older lady. "The wind is going to change!"

Except, it didn't.

CHAPTER TWENTY-THREE

Papi

Carmen decided to stay up late and keep an eye on the sky. She made coffee, cupping it in her hands, sitting on the patio on the west side of Orchard House, looking up the lake. Over her shoulder, she was aware of Evan doing the same thing, although if he wanted the best view of the approaching fire, he'd be on the other side of his house. From time to time she got the sense that he'd shifted, but she didn't keep track. Her mind was on other things. For once, the complicated windstorm of emotions Evan brought out in her didn't appear.

The approaching fire changed everything.

Once, when she was a child, they'd evacuated the vineyard. Mami had been very firm: she would drive the kids to Wenatchee and stay with her sister, shouting at her husband that a bunch of grapes wasn't worth his life.

"It's everything and you know it!" Juan had calmly replied in Spanish.

His wife had called him a stubborn pig and continued loading their van. He'd told her that they'd be back before sunrise. His wife had stayed two days with her sister just to spite him.

When they'd come back, their father had had breakfast waiting. When Juan had asked his wife in a teasing tone if they'd had a nice little vacation, she'd smiled. "You're lucky the wind changed."

He'd kissed her and said, "You're lucky. Where else would you find such a handsome man?"

She'd rolled her eyes. "Girls, listen to him. So full of himself."

Their father had turned, displaying his profile. "Such a nose. Such a forehead, full of deep thoughts."

"Full of beans!" Mami had laughed.

They'd all started giggling. Carmen remembered feeling safe, sitting around the kitchen island, knowing her parents would always watch out for them. Would keep them safe.

Now it was her turn. The wind showed no sign of changing. The lake glittered dangerously in the dark. In one day, it had changed from an inviting blue oasis into a vast betrayal. All that water so close, and yet, except for the infrequent planes and helicopters flying low to collect it, useless. The water dumped on fires left damp spots around which the fire traveled, relentless.

Carmen finished a second cup of coffee outside on the front patio, facing the direction of the fire. She stood, realizing she was sore and hungry. She went inside to get some dinner.

After dinner, she decided to get some rest. After checking the Forest Service website to make sure that evacuation wasn't mandatory and that the fire was still fifty miles away, she set an alarm for four o'clock. You couldn't spend a childhood in Chelan and not know that wildfires traveled faster than cars. Fifty miles wasn't much of a barrier. Tomorrow she'd set the sprinklers around the house to dampen the roof and talk to Lola and Papi about evacuation. Changing her mind, she set the alarm for three and went to sleep.

Something woke Carmen from a dead sleep. *What is that noise?* Her room was dark. She glanced outside through the curtains. Complete darkness.

Someone was yelling, pounding on the door. She sat up in bed just as Lola rushed inside. "Someone's at the door."

"So, answer it!" Carmen snapped, crabby from lack of sleep. She opened the window, leaning out to get a look at the back door. The view was blocked by her father's upstairs balcony.

Lola was already running down the stairs.

"Make sure you know who it is first!" Carmen yelled, scrambling into a robe.

By the time she got downstairs, Evan was in the kitchen talking to Lola. He glanced at her and continued. "Paolo is bringing the car so you don't have to drive. I think it's better if we all go in one car."

Carmen, still groggy with sleep, tried to make sense of the strange scene. It was twenty after two in the morning. The air felt thick and heavy. It was strangely quiet.

Evan looked at Carmen as he talked, trying to bring her up to speed. "The wind picked up. There's an advisory for seniors and anyone with respiratory issues to evacuate this part of the lake. The fire's now on both sides and the Forest Service is worried about smoke inhalation. They'll notify us if it becomes mandatory but to me it looks like it's headed that way. The fire jumped the lake south of here. We're going to go up to Twenty-Five Mile Creek and pass over there."

"Wake up Papi," said Lola. "I'll pack some food."

"Paolo is coming over with the van now. Don't worry about food. We need to go."

Carmen shook her head. "Evan…"

Evan lifted his hands. "Carmen, we don't have time for this. We've got to have a truce. I don't care about anything but getting everyone out of here as quickly as possible."

She nodded. She'd intended to ask him if there was time to turn on the irrigation system. She looked outside. She'd dart up to the winery shed and turn everything on. They probably didn't have time to wet Orchard House again. Hopefully, what they'd done yesterday would be enough. For a split-second, Carmen felt tears choking her throat. Evan watched her carefully, as if gauging how well she was functioning.

She nodded at him, throttling her emotions by breaking down what she needed to do. First, get dressed. That was all she'd let herself think about right now. Putting on clothes. Then she'd wake up her father.

In her room, Carmen quickly put on jeans and tennis shoes. Normally she'd be wearing sandals, but if they were stranded, they might have to walk. She'd driven past enough tiny start-up fires on the side of the road to know that they could crop up anywhere. After she pulled a sweatshirt over her head, she went to the door, saying goodbye to her childhood room, praying it would be there when she returned. On her shelf was a beloved stuffed rabbit from her childhood, worn nearly to pieces. She made a move to bring him with her, then superstitiously put him down. That would be asking for her home to burn down. He'd be fine. She left him sitting on a shelf, next to her collection of *Anne of Green Gables* books. Everything would be exactly the same when she came back.

Papi wasn't in his bed, which didn't alarm her. He'd probably heard the commotion and had gone downstairs. His bed was made, but then, Mami had beaten it into them all—if you leave the bed, you make it. It was the way a civilized person started their day.

He'd be making coffee. Papi couldn't start a journey or a day without coffee. It would just like him to be calmly measuring Yuban into his trusty Mr. Coffee while Chelan County was on fire. But when Carmen went downstairs, he wasn't there. There was no coffee in the pot. No reassuring aroma.

The little hairs on the back of her neck stood up. Lola was still upstairs, so she ran up to the winery, turning on all the irrigation spigots before entering the building. She turned on the lights. "Papi? ¿Papi, estás aquí?"

There was no answer. The winery felt frighteningly huge and still. A bat had somehow gotten in and swooped around frantically. Carmen left the doors open for the bat, running back down the hill to the Orchard House as fast as she could. By the time she entered the kitchen, her phone was ringing. It would be Papi, calling to tell her he'd gone to check on something. But when she answered, it was Evan. "I saw you running down the hill. Is everything okay?"

"It's Papi. I can't find him anywhere." She heard the panic in her voice.

Evan's tone was smooth and reassuring. "I'm sure he's nearby. Paolo and I are getting into the van right now. Stay there. Don't worry. We'll find him."

Carmen felt her throat squeeze into a tight knot. The only thing that stopped her mind from traveling down dark paths was remembering what Evan had said. Her father would be fine. There would be an easy explanation.

But still.

Where could he be?

It wasn't like Papi to leave his family.

*

"You've looked in the winery, the fields, the beach, the barn?" Evan asked the assembled group. Juan had invited him into the weathered old barn once. It was a long shot but worth pursuing. Paolo, Lola and Carmen looked at one another.

"We haven't looked in the barn," said Carmen. "The only thing he keeps in the barn is that old truck of his."

"Does it run?" asked Paolo.

Carmen frowned. "I don't know."

Lola shrugged. "Maybe? I don't know either."

Evan pointed to the van. "You guys load the van and I'll go check the barn." Before anyone could respond, Evan was out the door, running.

The barn was an old structure built with the original home, and had long been left to decay. It was halfway down the orchard, on a side of the vineyard rarely used except as storage. Unlike a lot of growers, Juan was pretty good about getting rid of equipment he'd outgrown or didn't use. The barn was used for seasonal machinery, like his snowplow, and tools that might come in handy. The truck was the sentimental exception. An old Chevy held together by rust and love; Evan saw him tooling around in it a couple times of year. He said his daughters had badgered him about selling it, but he said one day he'd fix it up and then they'd be begging him for rides.

Evan hurried down the driveway as fast as he could, stopping a few times, staring into the wooded copse to look for the barn, slightly hidden in the trees. He remembered Juan's delight, talking about his old truck, how it brought back memories of family excursion to the mountains for picnics and hiking. It should have been the first place they looked. Juan clearly loved that hunk of metal.

The doors of the barn swung open with surprising ease. Someone took care of the place. After his eyes adjusted, Evan entered the gloom, carefully stepping around some old irrigation piping. No truck. The place where it had been parked stood empty. Evan crouched down. Fresh tracks. Outside, he turned on his phone's flashlight feature, following the tracks into the orchard. From there, they turned left onto the driveway.

Wherever Juan was, he wasn't on the vineyard.

Evan marched back up the orchard, dreading telling the sisters that their father was definitely missing.

*

Lola's hand was shaking on the countertop. They all noticed it, but nobody said anything. Lola looked down, staring at her hand as if it belonged to someone else.

Carmen was on the phone, talking to the Chelan County sheriff. To their surprise, the emergency operator had patched her through. He told her that with his dementia, her father would go to the top of the list for missing persons. "Either way, a fella his age shouldn't be running around on his own right now."

Carmen wanted to correct him. Her papi wasn't "running around". And dementia wasn't the defining thing about her father. She wanted to explain: her father was a responsible man. A loving father. A business owner and maker of fine wines. She wanted the sheriff to see the whole person. Papi wasn't some crazy old man. There would be a logical explanation for wherever her father had traveled. But then again, did she really know? How much did she really know about his life during the five years she'd been in Seattle? He could have been taking long drives all over the county, visiting people she'd never met. For the past few weeks, he'd only been accounted for during the harvest, working with them.

What if he had a secret life they knew nothing about?

Maybe if she hadn't been so busy trying to save the winery and fighting with Evan Hollister, she would have noticed that Papi needed more attention. Maybe they could have gone to Seattle to see specialists.

Had she been in denial about her father's worsening condition? A wave of guilt and anxiety clamped down. She reminded herself to breathe, stop imagining the worst and focus on the sheriff.

At the end of the phone call, the sheriff gave her the option of filing a missing person's report in Wenatchee or Chelan. Although Wenatchee would have been the safer option, Carmen said she'd come into Chelan. The sheriff advised her to avoid the direct route into town down the side of the lake on the 971, heading north instead to the Twenty-Five Mile pass, avoiding the fires that had jumped the lake. That would be the safer path. "Check the update on the Forest Service app before you leave," he said.

"The app?" She'd been checking the website.

"You do have the app, don't you?"

"Yes," she'd said, even though she didn't. She'd already lost her father. She didn't want to sound like a complete idiot.

Carmen hung up, stunned. How had this happened? Stella wrapped an arm around her, squeezing gently, whispering: "Car, I know you're over-analyzing this. Just stop. Okay?"

Carmen nodded, then explained the choices to Evan, Paolo, Stella and Lola, who had listened to her side of the conversation, glancing at one another with worried expressions.

Evan was already checking the Forest Service app which he, of course, had.

"We have to make a report in person. We can do it Wenatchee or Chelan. He recommends going around the fires by Twenty-Five Mile pass and then looping back if we're going to Chelan." She studied their faces. "What do you think?"

Lola spoke first. "I vote for heading directly into town. I can't see Papi going anywhere other than Chelan. He wouldn't leave us."

Carmen nodded. "He wouldn't."

"If he went into town on the 971 and his truck broke down, he could be in serious trouble," said Evan.

Paolo shrugged. "I do whatever you want."

Evan grabbed his car keys. "Okay. We'll head into town."

They filed out of the kitchen. Carmen stopped to lock the door, then decided to leave it. Maybe her father would come home without a key.

Maybe that was a silly thought, but one thing Carmen knew for sure was that Lola was right. No matter what, her father would never leave them.

The last thing Carmen grabbed was the kitchen fire extinguisher. When she climbed into the car gripping it, Evan grinned.

"Don't make fun of me," Carmen snapped.

"I'm not," said Evan, buckling his seat belt. "You're optimistic. I like it."

As they rattled down the driveway, facing the thick pocket of smoke trapped over the lake, Carmen thought that they'd all need to be optimistic. Otherwise they'd lose hope.

Right now, optimism was all they had.

CHAPTER TWENTY-FOUR

Prayers

How quickly things can change, Carmen thought. The morning sky was a permanent dusk. Smoke hung low on the lake. The sun burned faintly overhead as they drove into town on the lakeside road. The normally busy road felt desolate, with few other cars. Carmen sat in the front seat next to Evan, watching his hands on the steering wheel. He scanned the side of the road, glancing occasionally at Carmen, who nervously chewed the side of her lip.

It was quiet as they slowly drove along the road, hedged between a row of lakeside houses and a steep shale cliff.

"Won't he go to the Apple Cup when they open?" said Evan. "Isn't that his hang out?"

Carmen nodded. "They open at six."

"All right, we'll look then," Evan said. "And you're sure you searched the entire house?"

Carmen twisted in her seat to look at Lola. "You checked the basement, right?"

"You said you were going to."

"No, I didn't. I said I'd look upstairs and asked you to do the lower floors. That included the basement." The basement was small, mostly filled by a large furnace. An old couch occasionally provided a quiet place for cool afternoon naps in the summer heat. The stairs were narrow and tight; Papi avoided them.

"The basement isn't the lower floor, it's the basement."

Carmen's voice was tight with exasperation. "I can't believe you forgot."

"Me? You can't blame this one me!"

"I went up to the winery. I looked in every shed. You had loads more time to look around the house."

"You could have asked me, 'Hey Lola, did you look in the basement?' and I would have said, 'No, great idea Carmen' but you didn't, so get off my back."

Evan had pulled over to the side of the road, trying to interject but the sisters ignored him with their squabbling. Paolo clapped his hands. "Please, enough with this. You both worry too much and you both don't go to the basement." He turned to Lola. "What is the basement?"

"A room my sister forgot." Lola swooped one hand under the other to demonstrate. "Under the house."

Carmen shook her head. "We both forgot."

"How about if I drop someone off back at the winery to do a thorough search, and if they find him, call us?" Evan said. They still weren't far from the winery.

Carmen shook her head. "I think it's too dangerous to leave someone behind. What if the road becomes impassible?"

Evan glanced at her, nodding. "Good point." He executed an immediate U-turn in the middle of the road, driving back to the winery.

Carmen felt a momentary shock. Was Evan Hollister actually saying she was right? Part of her wanted to memorialize this moment. *Dear Diary, today, while we were running from a wildfire, Evan Hollister said I had a point. Or was it Evan? Is it possible that Evan is now being inhabited by a new and improved entity? Someone reasonable?*

She didn't say anything. There was no fun in needling Evan. Nothing was fun. There was just the big, open, scary question of where her father was and how could they locate him.

"Chelan seems like such a small town until you have to find someone," said Lola.

Carmen set her jaw. "He's at home. He went down to the basement to take a nap and forgot to tell us. We're idiots for not checking."

"That's the most likely explanation," said Lola.

Nobody said another word until they got back to Orchard House.

Juan wasn't in the basement. Carmen ran downstairs, twisting her ankle in the process. She fell the last two steps, landing on the cool cement floor facing the ratty old couch. Her mother had wanted to get rid of the couch, but Papi had said with a houseful of women, he needed someplace to hide. He hadn't hid very often, but occasionally, when they were teenagers, he'd emerge refreshed and yawning from the basement.

When she stood up, Carmen couldn't take much weight on her ankle. She made it halfway up the steep stairs, wincing and sweating in pain.

"What happened?" Evan stood at the top of the stairs. His frown said everything. He'd been worried.

"I twisted my ankle. He's not here. Obviously."

Evan hurried down the stairs. "Here, let me get on the same step."

She moved over. The stairway was so narrow, they were shoulder to shoulder. Evan put his arm around her, lifting from under her armpits. The pain was sharp.

Evan stopped her after one step. "Maybe we should get more people."

Carmen shook her head, gritting her teeth. "I'm not that heavy."

"That's not what I meant."

"Afraid to be alone with me?"

"Somewhat. You have a habit of biting my head off every time I open my mouth."

"And you have a habit of, ouch, of sabotaging my business."

"We're back to this, are we?"

"Ouch! Apparently."

They'd only made it up five stairs. Evan asked, "Are you okay?"

Carmen's face was damp with sweat. "Do you think I'm going to give you a different answer?"

"There's the girl I know."

Carmen rolled her eyes. "Exactly. I was thinking it was weird, that whole getting-along thing."

"I was quite enjoying it."

One more stair. Five from the top.

Carmen inhaled sharply. She hadn't sprained her ankle since fifth grade, ice skating in Wenatchee. It. Hurt. So. Much. "Yes, but it's not what we do."

Evan lifted her.

Three more.

"Maybe we should try something new? You do know that some people actually communicate without sarcasm. It is possible."

"You don't say?" she smirked.

"Now that's…" He grinned. "Oh, I get it. You were being intentionally sarcastic. Okay. Well played, Carmen."

"I always hated my name." *One more*, Carmen thought. *One more.*

"This is the part where I say Carmen is a great name, but you won't believe me."

"It's the 'Sarah' of Mexico. Very common."

"Evan has about as much flavor as a cheese stick."

Carmen sighed. They'd reached the top. "I miss cheese sticks."

"I'll get you one when this is all over."

Evan pulled his arm away. Carmen found herself missing the steadying influence. Also, the warmth and closeness. The basement, in a weird way, had made things easier. They had been hiding from reality. As soon as they left Orchard House, there would be the smoke and the terror of Papi out there, on his own.

As she steadied herself on the wall, Evan reached over to help her.

"Thank you."

He nodded, opening the door to the kitchen. "We're going to find your dad. You know that, right?"

Carmen stopped for a moment, wanting to believe him more than anything in the world. “Yes. I do.”

Evan nodded, holding the door to the kitchen open. For good measure, Carmen called upstairs. “Papi? Papi? ¿Estás aquí?”

There was no answer.

The drive into town was like something out of a science fiction movie. The visibility was so poor that Evan inched along, catching glimpses of the lake between the houses. Smoke swirled on the water’s surface. On the side of the road, little fires burned like on a movie set. Homeowners had stretched their hoses across the road, attempting to halt the fire’s progress. Everyone had left their sprinklers running, some on the rooftops. Boats were tied in clusters to buoys in the middle of the lake in case the docks burned. Nobody was on the lake.

Although it was early in the morning, Pat and Mike’s was open, although nobody was inside. Evan filled up with gas and came back with bottles of cold water. Carmen rolled the sweating bottle over her cheeks before gulping it down. She was thirsty. They finished the waters in grateful silence. Nobody said they were hungry, although they’d been up for hours. Nobody had eaten breakfast. Another thing they’d need to take care of.

Carmen had two baggies of ice wrapped around her ankle, fashioned by Evan, who insisted on tying them to her leg with a kitchen towel. She’d wanted to hurry into town to file the missing person’s report. “You need to walk slowly, Carmen,” he’d said, tugging the towel a bit too tightly as he spoke. The intimacy they’d shared inside Orchard House had now evaporated into the smoky air.

Chelan was a ghost town. The few cars that lined the street were empty. Most of the stores were shut. Normally at this time of day there would be people getting coffee and breakfast, opening shops and jogging. Cyclists would finish their early morning rides, gathering in front of the bakery. Kids sneaking out of the waterfront hotels across the street, jumping off the bridge leading into town, despite the *No Jumping* sign.

Carmen realized that the tourists were as much a part of this place as the locals. It was always a relief in September when the lake quietened, but when they returned, the tourists brought summer to Chelan with their noise, bright bathing suits and ridiculous inflatables peppering the lake. They kept things going. Carmen thought about the new-money people like Evan, with their fancy cars and expensive sunglasses. What would happen to those people if the town burned? Would they stay and rebuild, or would they take their toys and leave?

Carmen shook her head as Evan drove down Main Street. She couldn't think like that. They'd find Papi, and the fire would burn out or swerve. Evan pulled into the parking lot of the Apple Cup to see if any of the staff were inside, prepping for the breakfast crowd. Maybe someone had seen or heard from him. It was worth checking.

The blinds were down at the Apple Cup. A sign on the door said *Following evacuation plan. See you soon.* Lola called the phone number on the paper and got a recorded message. She asked them to call her if anyone had seen Juan Alvarez.

She climbed back into the car. "Let's file a report."

*

The sheriff's offices had become an impromptu command central for the Forest Service. They were studying maps on the wall and speaking loudly on their radios to water planes and helicopter pilots. Carmen decided it was hopeful, seeing all the activity surrounding the fire. All these men and women had so much technology at their fingertips. Although everyone knew that what ultimately stopped fires was good old-fashioned boots on the ground. The maps showed where the Smoke Jumpers were digging trenches. A mere twenty miles north of Chelan. Apparently, the winds blowing the smoke in their direction were faster up-lake. It made Carmen feel calmer, momentarily, to know that the situation was better than it looked.

The sheriff, Mike Granger, who had gone to school with Adella, said hello and led them back to his office. "Sorry, it's kind of nuts in here right now, but the Forest Service offices were maxed out. We've got the North Cascades crew in here." He waved an arm towards the office in general. Carmen could tell he liked the excitement. A small-town sheriff, who wouldn't be held responsible, probably enjoyed the change of pace, provided the fire stayed at a safe distance.

After finding chairs for everyone, Mike closed the door, handing Carmen the paperwork to fill out. "I'm sorry I didn't realize right away who your father was. Right after you called, Adella reached out, and I put the pieces together. I sent out an APB and had some people comb the town. We'll check places like the Safeway or the Starbucks, provided these were places he might habitually go."

Carmen looked up from the papers. "Safeway, yes. Starbucks, no."

Mike nodded. "Right. Old school. I get it."

"We've checked the Apple Cup," Lola said. "They're not open."

"That was my next question," Mike said. "Also, start calling anyone he might be friendly with. Someone who might have seen him in town. Who forgot to call or maybe doesn't have your cell number?"

Lola stood up. "The prayer group."

Carmen felt a flash of relief. Of course. He'd just seen those women. Maybe he'd decided to go check on them. That would make total sense. He would have wanted to make sure they were okay. "Why don't you start with the single ones first?" Everyone looked at her with raised eyebrows. "He would want to make sure they were okay."

Lola nodded. "Yep. That's what Papi would do."

Paolo stood up. "We need food. I go to make the breakfast and bring it back."

Evan nodded. "Good idea." He looked at Lola. "We can split the phone list."

"Thank you. Papi has a lot of friends."

Carmen glanced up from her paperwork to find Evan looking at her. Their eyes met and he smiled. "In medical schools, doctors are taught to look for the obvious first. If they hear hooves, they shouldn't think, oh, that's a zebra. It's probably a horse. Because horses are more common."

"And this is relevant why?"

"Because I think your father is hiding in plain sight and when we figure it out, we're going to wonder why we didn't think of it in the first place."

CHAPTER TWENTY-FIVE

Search Party

Paolo was a baker. His rustic bread came in thick crusty slices that he'd slathered with butter and marmalade, wrapping them in parchment paper. He also had small almond-scented cookies, ripe cherries and thick, strong coffee he poured from a thermos into mugs, mixing it with heated milk from another thermos. He spread his offerings on a small shabby side table beside a stack of snowy white linen napkins and small plates. "Mangiare! Mangiare! Eat! You need to keep the strength."

Carmen, who gratefully accepted coffee but couldn't eat, was stuck on the randomness of this beautiful breakfast, more suited to a food blog than a shabby sheriff's office. When did Paolo find time to bake? Did Italians eat cookies for breakfast?

How was it that her father was missing and all she could think about was food?

Carmen made herself a plate and when Paolo wasn't looking, placed it on Mike's desk.

Evan noticed and handed her some of his bread, placing a sticky slice on her napkin. "Eat," he said simply. "Or you'll hurt Paolo's feelings."

"God forbid Paolo's feelings get hurt." She rolled her eyes.

"He's Italian," Evan said as if this explained everything. "Food is a very big deal to him. Besides, we don't want you fainting."

Keeping her eyes locked on him, Carmen picked up the bread and took a bite, chewing aggressively.

"Very attractive," Evan said.

Carmen took another bite, stuffing her mouth. She really didn't care what he thought. But she did care if she choked. She took a drink of coffee.

Outside the door, Lola worked her phone, leaving messages and asking for numbers as she went.

Carmen pushed the sandwich away. "I can't just sit here. I need to be looking."

Even stood up. "Then let's look."

All afternoon they drove the streets of Chelan, looking down alleys, peering inside closed restaurants. After they'd finished the town, they ranged further, into the orchards and vacation homes on the east side of the lake. Although it was a long shot, they took an unpaved road up a steep hillside to check if Papi's truck was at the trailhead of one of his favorite hikes. There wasn't a single car in the dirt parking lot. On their descent, they could see the smoke blanketing the valley, obscuring their view of the lake. A family of deer ran across the road, kicking up dirt, heading south, away from the fires.

They'd reached the main road running down the east side of the lake when Evan's phone rang. He answered, assuring the caller that he was okay. "No, I'm fine. I'm not leaving. There's a voluntary evacuation for seniors and people with respiratory issues but they haven't ordered a mandatory evacuation yet. Yeah. I'm helping a friend. Okay, I'll call if I do. Thanks for checking in." He took a right onto the road, continuing up the lake towards the small town of Manson. Carmen wondered why he hadn't put the phone on speaker.

There was a lot about Evan that she didn't know. Other than his stellar career at Microsoft, she knew little of his previous life in Seattle. "Was that family?"

He shook his head. "No. Friends. My parents are on a cruise."

"Nice." She studied a dog boarding kennel and small hardware store from the car before shaking her head at the stupidity. Her father had probably never set foot in these stores. Was Evan just keeping her busy? Stopping her from spiraling into a sinkhole of worry?

Evan took a left before they reached Manson, driving past cherry orchards towards some lakefront homes. They reached the end of the road, turning around at a small marina. "Yeah. They spend more time on cruises than at home. Or golfing. They love golfing. When I didn't make my high school golf team, my dad didn't talk to me for two days."

Carmen couldn't imagine Papi not talking to her, no matter how mad he was. "Does it bother you?"

Evan looked at her sideways. "No. I'm an adult." They drove past a mini mall with a Thriftway, a hair salon and a sandwich shop. "You know, maybe it does. At Christmas and my birthday."

Carmen glanced at him, perplexed. "They don't come home for Christmas?"

Evan shook his head. "They invited me to come see them a couple of times. In Norway and Greece. It never worked out."

"Wow. Papi makes a traditional Mexican Christmas dinner with tamales and goose and tres leches cake. It's ridiculous. You walk in Orchard House and there isn't one spare inch in the fridge. He invites anyone who doesn't have a place to go." Her voice cracked with emotion, eyes brimming with tears. "It's really nice."

Evan nodded, looking wistful. "Sounds like it."

"Yeah. It's his favorite time of year."

Carmen thought about how, as a kid, she'd complained about wearing hand-me-downs and her mother being unwilling to pay for name brand snacks. She'd whined, saying one variety pack of Lay's potato chips from Costco wouldn't destroy their family. All those little things she'd complained about, when in reality, she'd had everything and more than she'd needed. There had always been an abundance of love and closeness. Of laughter, home-cooking, friends. All the important things that gave their lives depth and meaning.

Maybe she'd had to leave Chelan to realize it, but right now she felt it more than she ever had in her entire life. Mami's death had made Papi double down on the love. That first Christmas after had been sad, but breathtaking. Papi had gotten the biggest tree, showing it to them with such pride, overplaying the drama of how the tree had fallen in the wrong direction after he'd chopped it, nearly felling him in the process. He'd arranged a nonstop parade of friends and neighbors, stuffing everyone with tamales and his first glorious attempt at Mami's Polvorones de Canele, cookies laced with cinnamon, snowy with powdered sugar. He'd even taken them on a horse-drawn sleigh ride, their eyes bright with the cold, the bells jingling in the pine-scented air.

On Christmas Eve they'd all gathered by the fire, stunned by the food, exhausted from all the activity. He'd reached his arms around the three of them, kissing the nearest on the head. "Mis amores. Mami would want us to be happy. Feliz Navidad." Carmen's eyes teared at the memory.

They'd reached the tiny lakeside town of Manson, pulling into the park, directly across the lake from their houses. Through the smoke she could just make out the vineyards spreading up the side of the hills, vibrant and green. The harvest didn't seem to matter anymore. Keeping the vineyard seemed like a quaint idea from another era. The lake spread out before them with slightly better visibility. Smoke gathered on the far shore.

"Seems a little bit better," Carmen said. She'd been bargaining with God. If Papi was returned to her, she'd be kinder. Go to church every Sunday. Tithe. Her mother used to say that God didn't make bargains. Then again, Carmen thought, maybe he did.

"Would your father have any reason to go further?" Evan looked up the narrow road heading up-lake, where the fire raged. Beyond Manson was a string of houses and cabins clinging to a slender slice of land off the road, including a few stunners belonging to Seahawks players. When Carmen was a kid, they'd take their friend's boats down here to gawk at the things money could buy. The tennis courts, terraced gardens hanging from cliff walls, the European speedboats so sleek they look fast tied to the dock.

She shook her head. "No."

Evan started to turn the car around, but stopped. He pulled over, putting the car in park. "Carmen, I just want to say that I'm really sorry. I genuinely didn't know that your father had Alzheimer's. I thought he was ready to retire."

"I don't know. Maybe he was. Maybe he wanted to slow down and I messed everything up."

Evan shook his head. "No way. The man you just described wouldn't think a daughter taking over the family business was anything other than wonderful. You know, he told me about all of you. He's very proud of you."

Carmen wiped away a tear. "He probably told you I was mayor of Seattle."

Evan nodded. "Something like that. Governor of Washington State."

Carmen smiled. "Sounds about right."

Evan's phone rang. Although he fumbled to locate it, the call went to the car's speaker system. "Hey, Ev. I'm just calling to see if you got the land from that crazy Latina and her nutso family." Evan fumbled for his phone. "She sounds like a piece of work, man."

Evan found his phone, not daring to look at Carmen as he spoke. "She's sitting right here and you're on speaker phone."

"My bad," said the friend. "Hey, señorita, I hear you really know how to screw up a wedding!"

Evan glanced at Carmen with pleading eyes, swirling his finger at his temple, mouthing, "He's crazy."

Carmen shook her head in pity. *Poor Evan.*

Not.

Glaring out the window as he talked, she didn't bother looking at him when he hung up. She was afraid she'd haul off and punch him. *Crazy Latina and her nutso family?*

"I did not say those things. He's an old fraternity friend and a complete jerk."

Carmen spoke through gritted teeth. "Then you make a perfect pair."

"You have to believe me." Evan's voice quivered with emotion.

"Turn the car around."

On the seemingly endless ride back to Chelan, Carmen settled into a familiar feeling.

Hating Evan Hollister.

As they pulled up in front of the sheriff's office, Carmen ignored Evan's offer of help getting out of the car. She'd rather sprain both ankles than touch him again.

"Carmen, please!" Evan said as she hobbled past him.

She shook her head angrily. "Stay away from me."

Lola, Paolo and Stella were slumped in hard plastic seats. Through the sheet glass windows of the sheriff's office they could see Adella crossing the street through the late afternoon sun. A light breeze ruffled the trees, shifting the smoke, making it slightly easier to breathe. It could also, Stella said, fuel the wildfires.

Evan blocked Carmen's way to the office door. "I might have talked to Jake when I was tired. Right after I found out about the goats. Maybe I was, I don't know, letting off steam. I swear I didn't call your family crazy. Or you. Jake was calling to see if he could borrow money. He's that kind of friend."

Carmen leaned on a bike rack, her ankle throbbing. "Look, I don't care. Every time you're nice to me, I find there's some agenda. You hire away my cook or sabotage a wedding I'm hosting. Do you have any idea how hard it is for normal people to come up with the kind of money we need? I've had old ladies picking in our fields. You know what I've found out, though? People love us. People I didn't even know." She waved her hands at the town in a wild gesture that almost caused her to lose her balance until Evan stepped in. "I've also realized that they are the people I need to be around. Not new people, who care more about acreage than friendship." She patted her chest. "I belong here. I do." She stopped for a moment, noticing Evan's troubled face.

"And you don't think I do?" he asked, earnestly.

She shook her head. "No."

Evan sighed deeply. Without a word, he walked into the sheriff's office. Carmen saw him through the window, speaking to the assembled group.

A second later he walked past her. "Good luck finding your dad." He put his hand out to tenderly pat her shoulder, then held it in place, thinking better of it. "You'll find him. I know it."

He got into his car and drove off. Carmen watched as it turned the corner and disappeared.

She'd thought telling Evan off would make her feel better.

It had just made her feel worse.

*

Carmen limped into the sheriff's waiting room, hoping for good news. Her sisters remained slumped in their chairs, faces gray and tired in the dingy light. She brushed a strand of hair from her eyes, scanning their faces, looking for a scrap of hope. Something to cling to. All she saw was exhaustion. Every second that her father remained unaccounted for felt like an eternity. As if a piece of her was missing.

She waited for someone to say something, but they all found something terribly interesting on the linoleum floor. Carmen slid gracelessly into a hard chair, unable to avoid wincing in pain. She bent over to loosen the laces on her tennis shoes. It wouldn't make any difference, but it gave her something to do. She sat up, waiting for someone to break the unbearable silence.

"Well, this is awkward."

She was met by more silence. She crossed her arms, preparing to wait out whatever this was.

Adella came over, kissing her on the head. "Bob's got the kids." When Carmen raised her eyebrows, Adella shrugged. "He's trying to find a sitter. His boss Lorne offered up his eighty-five-year old mother. Can you imagine?" She shrugged. "Anyway, we're waiting for Mike to come out and tell us the next steps. The APB is out all across the state and Idaho."

"Idaho?"

Lola nodded. "It's standard."

"Hey, what did you say to Evan? He seemed pretty upset," Adella asked.

Carmen's eyes flashed. "I called him out on something and as usual, he blamed it on someone else. It's a pattern with him."

Adella and Lola exchanged looks.

"He said to get you off your feet," Adella said. "He's worried about your ankle."

"It seems like he really cares about you," Lola said.

"I know him better than both of you, and I can tell you the only thing Evan Hollister cares about is himself." Even to herself, she sounded bitter. Nothing mattered when the most important person in the world was missing.

CHAPTER TWENTY-SIX

Wonderful Chaos

Mike held the meeting in the conference room, temporarily vacated by the Forest Service people, who'd gone to find something to eat. He waited for everyone to be seated, removing his glasses to rub his red eyes. Clearly, the fire was taking its toll on everyone.

Mike wanted a narrower timeline. Had anyone noticed breakfast dishes or a brewed pot of coffee that could be attributed to Juan? Had their father been at the house the night after the festival? Had anyone seen him before he went to sleep? Every little detail would help.

Adella watched her sisters patiently answering Mike's questions. They all knew that Papi needed more supervision. Their minds raced to the worst possible conclusions, blaming themselves for what they all should have known. Smoke always led to fires.

"I'm sorry I don't have better news. We've had every kind of call come in, but nothing about your father. The most likely scenario is that he's with a friend, waiting out the fire, and his cell phone battery died. He's probably not thinking contacting the police is the first step you'd take, so he isn't taking any great measures at this point to get in touch. This happens more than you'd think. He might have been intending to get back by tonight and with the fire he just decided to stay hunkered down. This is likely. We've got people looking, getting the word out on social media. We can't search door by door under these conditions, and also as you can imagine, our manpower is way down due to the fire. The best thing for you to do is go home and keep calling his friends. The more people who know the better. I'll touch base with you later in the day but we're going to have to call off the search when it gets dark."

Adella spoke for everyone. "What if we don't find him by then? What if he's out there on his own? Possibly disoriented?" Her eyes filled with tears.

Mike nodded. "I understand. Believe me, I don't like it either. I'll call you later today and we'll reconvene in the morning if we have to."

Paolo stood up. "He's right."

The three sisters looked at one another. It didn't look like they had any choice.

Lola was crying. The sisters huddled in the reception area. Paolo and Stella waited discreetly by the door. Adella rubbed Lola's back while Carmen clenched and unclenched her fist. "It feels wrong to go home. We can call people from the car. He would never give up looking for any one of us."

Adella shook her head. "No. But where else could we look? We've covered the town. Carmen and Evan drove all over the east side of the lake all the way up to Manson."

"Is there anyone else in the county that he'd check on?" Carmen asked. "Someone we haven't thought of. I just don't think he'd go that far."

Lola sniffed. "There's that lady with the goats. She lives way out there by herself. Maybe he went out to see if she needed any help."

They all brightened at the thought.

Adella nodded, patting Carmen on the back. "We'll go there and then we'll go home, make some more phone calls, update Facebook. Mike is right. We'd be wasting our time randomly driving around."

Carmen wiped her nose. "Okay." Adella slipped an arm around her sister to help her limp out the door. "We should drop you at the house so you can get off your feet."

Carmen thought about arguing before realizing that her sister was right. Putting her swollen, throbbing ankle up to rest sounded wonderful.

Half an hour later, she hobbled into the kitchen, switching on the lights. "Papi! Papi!" she yelled up the stairs, before opening the freezer to dig for an ice pack. Half-expecting to find her father asleep in the living room, she plopped down on the empty couch, thinking of all the times as a kid she complained about her noisy family, her singing father, her squabbling sisters. At this moment, she'd do anything to hear that kind of wonderful chaos.

*

His living room was exactly sixty-five steps wide. He'd paced it enough times this afternoon to know exactly how many steps it took to cross from one side to the other. Evan was a counter. He knew exactly how many stairs were in every building he'd ever worked. How many steps it took from his parking spot at Microsoft to all three offices he'd worked in during his tenure. Someone told him once that counting was a way of framing the world down to size. Making sense of chaos. This was the most chaotic he'd felt in a long time.

He thought of calling that idiot Jake and yelling at him, but decided it would be wasted breath. Jake was a college buddy who wasn't someone he'd pick to be friends with now, but they'd been roommates freshman year and had been forever bonded by their mutual loathing of large crowds and love of Pop Tarts. Jake was the shaggy dog Evan couldn't seem to shake. Except today, Jake had wreaked havoc that Evan didn't think could be undone. It had come at a fragile time. Carmen would now always associate the search for her father with being called the crazy Latina. Nothing like being called a stereotype at the lowest point of your life. For turning a point of pride into a caricature.

Thanks, Jake.

Evan considered pouring himself a drink, but after filling the glass with ice, opted for water. There might be more he could do before night fell. The idea of the old man on his own was unsettling. Sure, he was a tough old buzzard, but nobody should be out of touch right now.

Maybe he should walk around the Alvarez property one more time? Had they covered every inch of the field? What if Juan had gone out to check on the irrigation and succumbed to the smoke? It wasn't a half-bad theory.

Evan switched his flip-flops for tennis shoes, donning a baseball cap. Low flying bats scared him a little bit. He was always worried they'd hit his head. That, he thought, would make Carmen laugh.

He'd have to stop thinking like this. Give up on Carmen. She'd given up on him.

In the kitchen, he called Barry, patting the dog's soft fur.

"Come on, boy. Time to earn your keep." He wished he had something that Juan had worn in case Jake could act as a search dog. He briefly entertained the idea of asking at the house, but thought better of it. He couldn't face Carmen.

Besides, Barry wouldn't know what to do with a T-shirt except rip it to shreds. He was a rescue mutt, not a search dog.

The walk through the fields wasn't yielding anything, but both Evan and his dog needed the escape. The smell of the freshly watered leaves and loamy soil coursed through his system like a calming sedative. As the late afternoon sun had slipped below the hills, streaking the smoky sky with deep pinks and vivid tangerine, Evan's mind went back to earlier that day. He thought of what Carmen had said about him not belonging.

What had he been wanting, moving here in the first place? Chelan was undoubtedly beautiful, but Washington State was bursting with beautiful locations. If he went back in his mind, Evan could recall one of the best family memories he had in Chelan. His parents had rented the same cabin a few years in a row. The place had golf carts that drove people down to the lake. There was a sandy beach where families camped out under umbrellas. Children played in the sand and splashed in the water. Red-faced adults blew up inflatables that were carried, with much hilarity, off the back of the golf carts at the end of the day. At night they'd reconvene, showered and fed, for bonfires with s'mores. There were loads of kids the same age to play with. The parents chatted, drank wine.

Had he been trying to go back to those happy memories? To reconnect with the place he'd felt a part of a happy family? Evan turned down another row of grapevines, smiling at his pop psychology.

Maybe he had.

Maybe it was a mistake.

Maybe he'd made too much of a mess of things with the neighbors. Truth be told, old man Alvarez was the person whose trust he'd really wanted to earn. When he'd met Carmen, his need to impress the old man had doubled. He stopped walking, shaking his head, looking across the lake.

Where was Juan?

The lake was shot through with color, reflecting the sunset. Those colors would leach from the sky as night fell with the old man still unaccounted for. He felt helpless, wracked by guilt that he'd aggressively pursued the business of a man suffering from Alzheimer's.

Movement, he decided, was the answer.

As Evan walked across the packed dirt, he saw something ahead of him on the ground. A small piece of paper. A card. He picked it up and flipped it over. It was illustration of a saint holding up his hand, wearing red robes and a golden halo. Saint Xavier. He tried to read what it said, before realizing it was in Spanish. Probably one of the ladies in the prayer group had dropped it. He tucked it into the back pocket of his jeans before stopping cold.

The prayer group.

Why had no one thought of this before?

It seemed so obvious. Had one of the girls already looked?

Evan started running down the field, heading at first to Orchard House and then, changing his mind, to his home. Barry followed, deliriously happy that Evan was running, racing ahead like a puppy. Evan didn't want to get the sisters' hopes up. He'd go by himself.

Dashing into his house to grab his keys, Evan noticed Barry panting beside him. He quickly filled the dog's bowl. Barry lapped it greedily as Evan left, closing the kitchen door.

A second later he reopened the door, looking at his hopeful dog. "Come on. Maybe we can do this together."

Man and dog climbed into the car and sped down the driveway into the thickening dusk.

CHAPTER TWENTY-SEVEN

What Evan Found

Adella and Lola found Crystal Huttinger in the narrow kitchen of her ancient Airstream trailer, drinking coffee. It helped her sleep, she said. She'd turned on the generator to power an old TV for a goat that was nestled onto a dog bed on the couch. Papi had insisted his little girls call Crystal "Mrs. Huttinger". Behind Papi's back, she'd always been the Goat Lady.

"He likes PBS." Crystal's Airstream was on five rocky acres with a serene view of the lake, surrounded by flowering beds of hydrangeas and lavender. "Only flowers goats won't eat," Crystal had explained.

The goat, named Spright, did seem to be watching TV. He was the sole casualty from the wildfire smoke and was inside recuperating from smoke inhalation and catching up on *Downton Abbey* reruns.

"Your father was here," said Crystal, nodding vigorously. "Early this morning. He helped me get the generator going. It's old." She laughed. "Everything around here is old, right Spright?"

The goat kept his eyes on the TV, where Lady Mary was giving a suitor a dressing-down.

Adella glanced out at the lake through the Airstream's foggy windows at the dusky sky over the lake. "Did he say anything about where he might have been going?"

Crystal shook her head. Her long gray braids snaked across her back. "No. He said they'd recommended people our age evacuating, so I assumed he was going home to pack up. I'm sorry he's missing, but your dad is very resourceful. I'm sure he'll be fine." She seemed convinced, which made sense. Crystal, older than Juan by at least a decade, was used to getting by on her own.

Adella smiled wanly. "Thank you. If you think of anything, I'll write down my number." She found a piece of paper by the landline.

"I definitely will. Call me when you find him, would you? I'm going to worry about him until he makes it home."

Adella nodded. "We will." The old woman's certainty was reassuring. She didn't have the same anxiety they did, but then again, Juan wasn't her father. She lived way out here with nobody for company but a couple dozen goats. Glancing at the old goat curled up on the plaid couch, Adella thought maybe that wasn't such a bad way to live. Goats had to be easier than children.

The sisters walked across a rocky field to their truck, parked next to the weather-worn barn, listening to the soft bleating of the goats settling down for the night. Adella drove back to Orchard House in silence, hoping that by some miracle they'd open the door and find Papi, waiting to tell them how silly they were to be worried.

*

Evan drove fast, wondering vaguely if there were any police around to give him a ticket. He was driving the Lamborghini. The hell with what people thought. The expensive car comforted him. The speed, the solidness, the way it hugged the curves of the lakeside road. He was a cop magnet in this flaming yellow car. It didn't matter. He'd take the ticket if he could find the old man. It had become imperative that he be the one to find him. To be the hero. To rectify everything with Carmen. It could have been the fatigue messing with his brain, but it felt like his entire future in Chelan hinged on bringing back Juan. If anything bad happened, he'd feel guilty for the rest of his life, wondering if he'd made the old man feel incompetent as a businessman by trying to buy his land. He shut that particular line of thought off, thinking only of the road ahead. He found the sign he was looking for and headed up the hill, west of Main Street. The smoke had cleared to a thin layer, leaving Chelan looking hazy.

The Lamborghini climbed the hill as he turned at a copse of trees. The houses here were older, smaller. Built when Chelan was primarily a farming town. Wooden bungalows with wraparound porches to capture the breeze. They'd been spared the fires of two years ago by a surprise change in winds. This was their second lease at life; the changing winds had once again granted them more time. The front yards were profuse with hollyhocks, lilacs and dinner plate-sized dahlias. Off to the sides, many of them had gardens. Evan thought if he stayed here, he'd put in a garden. Grow flowers himself instead of leaving it all to a landscaper. He laughed at himself, thinking of becoming the kind of man who grew flowers and talked about his zucchini. He could grow into that kind of man. His father hadn't, but that didn't mean he couldn't.

The longer he lived in Chelan, the more he wanted to become that man. Less ambitious, more in touch with the land. He'd learn about wine, instead of just using the vineyard as another form of competition. He'd spend time with Juan. Learn how to live.

Juan.

Evan reached the parking lot and jumped out of his car, letting Barry out of the back seat. "Find Juan!" he said pointedly, like he'd seen in movies. The dog looked at him plaintively, as if to say, "I'm a house dog," before wandering off on his own to explore.

Evan walked to the neat square inside a white picket fence. Most of the tombstones were basic marble, but a few had statues of angels. *Where was her grave?* The cemetery was small, but it was growing dark and hard to see the grave sites without streetlights. The closest house was a half mile away. Evan turned on the flashlight on his phone to read the gravestones. The last streaks of sunset were obscured by a cloud which promised rain. Evan hadn't looked at the weather app for the first time in days. Was there rain forecast? Wouldn't that be the answer to a million prayers?

"Juan!" he called into twilight, walking quickly into the heart of the cemetery, wondering which way to start looking, feeling a sudden urgency. "Juan! It's Evan. Evan Hollister. Your neighbor!"

For a second Evan felt silly, calling into the empty cemetery, wishing he hadn't let himself get so excited about the playing the hero. Barry sniffed nearby. Evan headed to what he hoped was the middle of the graveyard. Juan would surely be able to hear him from here. There couldn't have been more than forty grave sites in this whole place. No wonder Juan had buried his wife here. The graveyard had a panoramic view of the narrow lake twisting through the purple hills, vanishing into the craggy peaks of the North Cascade mountains. Stunning.

Evan called out one more time, letting his voice get whipped into the density of the smoky air.

Nothing.

So.

This was it.

No Juan.

An immense sadness pushed down upon Evan. He collapsed on a stone bench, burying his head in his hands. He wasn't going to make it in Chelan. Carmen would find her father, and Evan would be the one who'd disappointed her when she needed him the most. He'd wanted to be there for her. Be the hero. Right now, all he wanted was to find Juan. Not for himself.

For Carmen.

Wiping his eyes, he felt Barry nuzzle him. The dog walked expectantly towards the car. "Nice search and rescue, Barry. You just want to go home and have dinner."

The dog trotted forward, looking back to make sure his master was following.

Evan followed the dog to his car. Someone was standing there.

It was Juan, leaning down to pat the dog. "Your dog woke me up. I fell asleep."

Evan laughed, praising his dog profusely. Barry lapped up the affection, looking between the two men happily, as if his work was done.

The old man talked as though they'd run into each other on the street. "I went to see if my old amiga Crystal was okay, and then I decided to check in on Mercedes."

"Where's your truck?"

"Around the corner. I had it parked on the street facing downhill in case I needed to pop the clutch while it was running. Didn't work. Might need a new starter." He shrugged. "I took a little siesta."

"A siesta?" Evan didn't care what the other man would think. He walked right up to him and hugged him, patting him vigorously on the back. "Your girls are looking for you."

Juan nodded, looking baffled. He patted Evan's back awkwardly before they separated. "They worry too much."

"They called the police."

Juan raised his eyebrows. "The police? Maybe we can leave the truck here and you give me a ride home."

Evan laughed. "Maybe I should."

They got into the fancy yellow car with the slobbering dog poking his head between them and started down the road.

Sometimes, Evan thought as they wound down the hill, life was simple.

Sometimes you went looking for something and you found it.

*

At the winery, Evan opened the kitchen door for Juan, letting him simply walk through Orchard House into the living room. He was close enough on the old man's heels to see Carmen jump up from the couch on her sprained ankle and shriek, "Ow! Owwwwww!" as she hobbled over to fall on her father, who caught her.

"What happened to your ankle?" Juan asked.

Carmen laughed with tears in her eyes. "What happened to my ankle? Papi! Who cares what happened to my ankle? Where were you?!"

Her father looked around the room at his excited children, perplexed. "I went to see Mami. I wanted to make sure the cemetery wasn't going to burn down." He couldn't understand all the fuss. "It's not," he added, even though his children clearly didn't share his concern.

Adella hugged her father. "You had us worried, Papi."

Juan waved his hand in front of his face. "Hijas, your Papi isn't going to do anything crazy." He smiled contentedly. "You were the ones always making me loco." He clapped his hand over his heart. "Now you know what it's like to have teenagers. One heart attack after another."

The sisters clustered around him, hugging their father in one tight, teary knot. The sight warmed Evan's heart and made him a little wistful. While his parents cruised around the world on luxury liners, families like the Alvarez hugged and kissed and cried together. He wanted this, he decided. Exactly.

Evan's phone pinged. A notification on the forest service app. The evacuation for the south side of the lake and all of Chelan, Manson and surrounding areas was now mandatory. After taking Adella aside and agreeing that they should leave as soon as possible, Evan slipped out the back door to pack dog food, turn on his irrigation system and pack a few things if he had time.

Outside, he let Barry out of the Lamborghini, letting him run up the hill to his own patio while he drove down the winding orchard driveway and back up the neatly terraced Hollister Estate road. Barry greeted him, slobbering joyfully, his long tail thumping the car door. Evan bent down to reassure the dog, who seemed uneasy, crowding against him as if he sensed Evan's anxiety. Barry followed him up the hill, staying close as Evan flipped on every switch controlling the vineyard irrigation. Designed to minimize evaporation, the water system wouldn't help in a fire, but it could save plants during a prolonged absence.

In the quiet kitchen Evan measured dog food into Ziploc bags before feeding the dog, filling his water bowl before he hurried upstairs to pack. Evan heard the dog climbing the stairs, his nervous panting as he entered the room. He circled the room, his nails clicking on the tile as Evan shoved T-shirts and a clean pair of jeans into a duffel. "Dude, you need to eat. You're going to be packed into a van. I know it's early but it's chow time." Evan ran to the bathroom, grabbed his leather Dopp kit, tossing on his clothes and zipped it up. "Go. Eat."

He ran downstairs, gathered the kibble bags and dashed outside his car. Barry followed at his heel so closely that Evan nearly tripped. Evan threw the duffel and food into the trunk and opened the car door for Barry, putting the seat down. The dog sat there, staring at him before looking away.

"Barry, get in the car." The dog lowered his head, backing away and whining. Evan's grew annoyed, snapping his fingers. "Barry. Car." He lunged for the dog's collar, but the dog refused, running away, barking. "What's gotten into you? You love car rides. Barry, please. Get in the goddamned car."

"Help, I'm falling!" a voice shot out of the dusk. Evan was crouching down, dangling a piece of lunch meat as bait, trying to lure Barry within arm's reach.

It was Carmen. Evan tossed the lunchmeat to the dog, muttering that this wasn't over yet and ran from the driveway to the side of his patio. Carmen was sliding backwards off the hill that divided their properties. "Ow. Ow. Ow."

"Carmen, the evacuation is mandatory. Really not the time to be hiking." He looked at his watch. "I was just heading over."

Carmen pinwheeled her arms, trying to stay upright. "Don't let me fall."

He slid down the hill. "Stay there. I'll come get you."

Carmen looked like she had no intention of moving. She was balanced precariously, trying to keep her weight off her ankle, wrapped in an elastic bandage. He slid down the hill, wondering why she struggled up here on a hurt ankle when they should be fleeing.

By the time he reached her, Carmen was sweating from the effort of staying on the hill. He grabbed her arm by the elbow, pulling her up. "We should stop meeting like this," he quipped.

"Don't make me sorry I came over."

"You're not over yet." He pulled her up to the patio as she awkwardly hopped, wincing in pain. "There, now you are. I see you're taking good care of that ankle."

Carmen crossed her arms. "I wanted to thank you in private. So, thank you, from the crazy Latina."

He looked at his watch, offering his arm. "I never said that."

She declined, following him with a slow limp to the car. He waited, opening the door, glaring at the dog still at a safe, cautious distance. "You most certainly did. You also ruined my wedding business, hired away my cook—"

He lifted in a finger. "My housekeeper. Not me."

She ignored the distinction. "And never bothered to tell me while we were swimming in the moonlight. Every time I think I can trust you, you do something completely deceitful. And yet, I find myself here, thanking you for saving my father."

"You're welcome. If you really want to show your gratitude, you can get Barry into the car. He's been—"

Carmen simply snapped her fingers and pointed at the car. The dog obediently leaped into the back seat. "Anything else?"

Evan grinned at her. "Do you know how long Barry was running around here making trouble?"

"No idea, but we should be going."

He bent into the car to lift the front seat to make space for her. "Yes, we should. Thank you. I wasn't about to leave him behind." When he stood, she took his arm to get into the car. "Unfortunately, at this moment, Barry is the love of my life."

Carmen looked around his shoulder at the dog. "He's pretty adorable."

"Yeah. But in times like this it becomes painfully obvious what's important in life."

She looked up at him. "Such as?"

Her brown skin glowed. Her dark curls framed those Alvarez brown eyes. He leaned down until they were inches apart. Close enough to smell her lemony perfume. His throat was so tight he could barely whisper. "Carmen, we should go."

"Yes." She kissed him. One playful little kiss. Her eyes glinted mischievously as she leaned back against car door. "We should go." She wobbled unsteadily.

"Yep." He grabbed her, wrapping his arms around her, holding her up, kissing her with an intensity that blacked out his rational brain. She responded, kissing him, running her fingers through his hair and down his back.

She kept kissing him, muttering. "Should. Leave. Now."

"You're right." He placed his hands on either side of her face just as Carmen pulled herself away.

Her face flushed pink. "Okay. Wow. That was—"

He rubbed his chin, grinning. Every cell in his body wanted to kiss her again and forget everything. "Yeah. Exactly."

"I'm sorry. I shouldn't have." She slapped a hand over her eyes, hiding.

"I'm not sorry. Frankly, I'm stunned. What's happening here?"

Carmen remained quiet a while. She peeked through her hands before finally looking up. "I don't know. We're getting in the car. We're getting my family and we're evacuating."

She was right. Because of the situation with Juan, they'd ignored every sign until it was almost too late.

CHAPTER TWENTY-EIGHT

Spright

As Evan turned the van around in the Alvarez yard, there was a faint glow over the darkening hill above the winery. Wind whipped the fire into a frenzy. Barry whined in the backseat as Lola tried to calm him, stroking his ears, murmuring into his fur. Adella had left on her own to join her family. The remaining Alvarez family, Evan, Paolo and Stella had all managed to pile into the one vehicle. There hadn't been time to grab anything beyond a couple of photo albums.

Juan had been the one to insist they leave everything else behind. He kept muttering "Nos tenemos el uno al otro," as they loaded into the van, leaving behind everything he'd worked so hard to build over his lifetime. "Nos tenemos el uno al otro. Nos tenemos el uno al otro."

As they bumped down the driveway, Evan turned to Carmen in the passenger seat, whispering. "What's he saying?"

A fat tear rode down Carmen's cheek. "We have each other."

By the time they reached Crystal's property, she had released all her goats. They'd escaped to the foothills. Spright, still too sick to run, bleated plaintively on her leash.

"We can't take her," Evan said, pointing to the van. Every seat was taken.

Crystal firmly shook her head. "Can't leave her."

Lola insisted that everyone pile out of the van. "Come on, Spright."

The goat charged into the van, hopping back out when Barry snapped and growled. Evan stuck his head into the car, yelling at the poor dog. "Knock it off, Barry!"

Barry whined unhappily but made no further protest. The reluctant goat was lifted into the car. Spright's final protest was a spray of goat poop. It landed on Evan as he shoved the goat into the backseat. Carmen bent over in laughter.

"Not funny," Evan said, brushing the stinky pellets off his shirt.

Lola tried unsuccessfully to hold back her laughter. "No. Not at all."

"All right. Get in the car," Evan snapped.

Juan said something in Spanish that had his daughters giggling hysterically.

"What?" Evan growled.

Carmen shook her head, wiping the tears from her eyes. "You don't want to know."

They fastened their buckles. Evan started the van. "Yes, I actually do."

Carmen sniffed, snorting in an effort not to laugh. "Um, well, he said, 'At least I didn't poop on Evan when he rescued me.'"

Juan's daughters burst into renewed laughter. This time, Paolo joined them. Evan drove off Crystal's property, wondering how on earth he'd ended up ferrying a vanload of people, one dog and a goat through a wildfire.

*

It took three hours on winding back roads, some unpaved and pocked with fires, to make it to Wenatchee. Before they checked into a hotel, they needed to find a home for Spright. The shelters in Wenatchee wouldn't take animals. They'd called every shelter listed by the Red Cross, but all of them required that the animals be dropped at emergency rescue sites. None of them took livestock.

"Spright isn't livestock," sniffed Crystal.

Unfortunately, the Red Cross didn't agree.

Evan decided he'd throw his lot in with Crystal. Barry had grown fond of the goat during the journey. The two animals had slept wrapped around each other in the back seat, a tangle of cloven hooves and paws. The older woman clearly couldn't be separated from an animal that was family. And Barry, for better or worse, was all Evan had.

Evan tried to convince the Alvarez family that they could spend the night in the East Wenatchee High School gym, where there were spots for groups of four. But Juan didn't want the group to break up. They found a late-night burger place by the road, feeding the delighted animals their own meals and charming the small children at the road stop diner by walking the goat on a leash. Spright reveled in the attention, sneaking licks off ice cream cones and the occasional french fry. When dogs barked at him from cars, he turned back to Lola, who was walking him. After a few pets, he'd walk past, learning to conquer his fear.

Evan remained in the car, calling motels and hotels in the area. None would take animals. Finally, he called the Apple Inn. They had two rooms. "No. No pets. Just seven adults."

He glanced at Carmen, who whispered, "I don't care. We'll sneak in the animals. I just wanted to sleep and shower off the smell of goat." And in a louder tone, "Great. Yes. On my Visa card."

When he got off the phone and delivered the good news, Juan offered to pay for the second night. Evan waved him away. Juan insisted.

"Look, hopefully we won't need a second night," Evan said, glancing at Carmen and thinking the exact opposite.

Even with wildfire raging, a restless dog, a nervous goat and a van load of stressed people, being near Carmen Alvarez was turning into his lifelong goal.

*

The Apple Inn's website did not do it justice. It was far from the roadside motel Evan had expected. The modern inn was tucked into a canyon, surrounded by stands of fragrant ponderosa pines. Two luxury suites, the only ones available, put a serious ding on his credit card. He didn't care. When they pulled into the spacious parking lot, dotted by fluttering aspens and glowing clumps of end-of-season goldenrod and black-eyed Susans, a small hope fluttered inside of him. This might be exactly what they needed.

Small cedar-shingled units were spaced in a wide circle around a beautifully landscaped pool. The lobby featured a river stone fireplace, a deer antler chandelier and soft, deep red velvet couches. The night clerk offered to have someone show them to their rooms. Evan politely declined, intentionally neglecting to share that they were fire refugees. He didn't want to be anything but a guest wanting to collapse on a well-made bed. A guest without pets.

Yes, he was sorry they'd missed the happy hour featuring local wine. They could have used it. On second thought, Evan mused, maybe it was a good thing, keeping Carmen away from local wine. It would only remind her of their rivalry.

Evan strolled back to the van holding two room keys, wishing one was just for him and Carmen. The math was against it. In the rush to escape the fire, they hadn't had a second alone. He craved a private space to talk to her, nothing more. He reached the car, dangling a key in each hand.

Lola had sorted out the room arrangements. The men would have one room and the women the other. Evan nodded like it made sense. It did. It just wasn't what he wanted. Barry loped happily alongside Juan, who had fallen hard for the goofy dog. Carmen stayed behind with Spright, as everyone went to prepare a smooth transition for their noisiest guest. Evan lingered at the open door to the van. The parking lot was full of cars, which would make it easier to hide Sprite, provided he wasn't stubborn and loud. Carmen rubbed behind the goat's long silky ears. Spright shifted uncomfortably on the middle row of seats. It had been a long ride.

Evan leaned into the van to rub the goat's head. The goat glanced between him and Carmen, a child between tense parents. Carmen hadn't mentioned anything about the kiss, so he'd better mention it. He was sorry there hadn't been more time. Everything had been so rushed. "Hey, I just wanted to say I'm sorry—"

Carmen cut him off, shaking her head without looking at him. "Don't."

"Don't what?"

"Don't talk about it, okay? We can just go on about our lives and pretend like it never happened."

Later, Evan couldn't recall what his response had been. He ducked his head, not wanting her to see the crushed look on his face. The tumult of emotions he was feeling. He stayed, pretending like he agreed, probably saying something to that effect. As if it didn't feel like a chunk of him had been ripped away. He was far too good at hiding pain. He'd had a lifetime of pretending his feelings didn't matter, starting with his parents. Continuing with various girlfriends.

This time, it was worse. This time he'd invested. Put more on the table. Carmen wasn't a girlfriend, but somehow that had given him room to grow. He wasn't playing a role. Carmen had seen him at his worst. Maybe that was the problem.

He'd wanted to say that he was sorry they got off on the wrong foot.

He'd wanted a fresh start.

When Lola opened the hotel room door and gave them a thumbs-up, it should have been funny, sneaking a goat through a parking lot. They held tight onto Spright's collar, sticking to the path they'd agreed upon, behind a clump of trees with a water feature that would drown out the sound of clattering hooves on the cement. The goat bleated, lowering his head, trying to free himself from their grip.

Carmen kept up a steady patter of encouragement. "Come on, Spright. Almost there. Be a good boy and there's another hamburger in it for you. Maybe something from the mini bar. Do you know what a mini bar is, Spright? Tiny bits of food at stupid prices."

When they reached the room, they should have collapsed with relieved laughter, especially when Spright jumped up, bouncing gleefully between two beds until Crystal made him get down.

"Spright, mind your manners. This is a hotel," she scolded the happy goat, who thrived on the attention.

It should have been hilarious.

That's what Evan thought as he walked back to his room.

Instead, it was just sad. Simply because nothing was funny anymore.

Outside light leaked into the hotel room through the edges of the blackout curtains. Juan and Evan lay in their respective beds, motionless. Evan had thought Juan was asleep when he'd come in, so he washed up quietly, thinking it would be a relief to stop worrying about Carmen. Her feelings. Their arguments. The endless wondering about how she felt about him. It would be a relief, he thought, to go back to living for himself. Maybe the fire would be a fresh start. He didn't want it that way, but he'd already decided that if his house burned, he wouldn't rebuild. There would be too much to overcome.

He didn't want to wake up every day and think about Carmen Alvarez.

"The cemetery is in the path of the fire," Juan said into the dark.

Evan's head twisted on the pillow, looking at the old man, whose hands were folded on the white sheets. "Maybe."

"I'd still be there if you hadn't come for me."

Evan let that one sit a minute. "You'd have gotten out. You wouldn't have slept that long."

"Smoke might have gotten me. More people die of the smoke than the actual fire."

Evan nodded in the dark. "You don't know what would have happened. Crystal said you'd be okay. I believed her."

He saw the old man nodding. "It's hard to kill us old timers. You don't get to be this age without knowing a few tricks."

Evan knew the old man expected a laugh, but he couldn't muster one. Not tonight. "I'm sure. I could sure learn a lot from you."

Juan exhaled a long breath. "You know, my wife didn't want to marry a recolector migrante. A migrant picker. She thought nobody would ever let un hombre mexicano learn anything about the wine business." Juan pointed a finger at the ceiling. "All it took was one person to see my potential. Yes, it took a long time, but I never gave up. I knew what I wanted, and I kept working hard. Following my passion. Do you know what I'm talking about?"

Evan had underestimated Juan. "I think so."

"Carmen isn't the kind of girl you give up on."

Evan didn't want to explain that Carmen had told him, in no uncertain terms, that she didn't want anything to do with him. The last thing he wanted to do was tell the old man that he'd kissed his daughter and she wanted to forget all about it. That he'd felt everything, and she'd wanted nothing. "She certainly isn't, sir."

He'd leave it at that.

His best wasn't good enough.

Evan waited until the old man's breathing fell into regular, slow rhythms. He opened the mini bar. Inside was a full-sized bottle of wine. He couldn't read the label. It didn't matter. He grabbed the wine opener from the desk and slipped outside.

Tonight was a good night for drinking alone.

Tomorrow he'd deal with the pain.

CHAPTER TWENTY-NINE

The Girl Next Door

It was hard sleeping with a goat in the room. First, he snored. Then there was that funky, fusty smell, like a dog who came home reeking of eau de Something Dead. Then there was the heat. Air conditioning wasn't keeping up with the number of bodies in the room. Carmen slipped into the bathroom to don a bathing suit she'd already had in the bottom of her bag. It was old and stretched, but nobody would see her. The goat bleated softly as she opened the door.

"So long, stinky," Carmen whispered. She was already growing fond of the quirky, odiferous creature.

The pool lights were off. A sign said it was closed. The gate was locked, but Carmen found a way in through the landscaping. She brushed the peat from her soles and dove in, surfacing at the deep end. The water felt wonderful. Cool enough to be refreshing. She rolled over, luxuriating in the pool, enjoying the scattering of stars. Maybe that meant there was less smoke, less flames? She tried to enjoy the water on her skin, to not think of more troublesome things, kicking her way to the shallow end.

Someone was at the end of the pool. A man with a bottle on the table, slumped in a chair. *Is that Evan?* She dove under and surfaced at the edge, resting her elbows.

It was Evan.

"Whatcha drinking?"

He squinted in the dark, lifting his glass. "A Cab Sauvignon. Pretty good. Want some?"

Wine sounded good. She lifted herself effortlessly from the pool, wrapping herself in a towel. She saw his eyes appreciating her and then looking away. He offered his own glass. "I don't have another one."

She took it from him, taking a cautious sip. "Couldn't sleep?"

He shook his head, almost snorting. "No. Not tonight."

"Too worried about your vineyard?" She thought she was being solicitous, but he rolled his eyes.

"Um, no."

She handed back the glass. "It is good."

He took a long, greedy drink. "It'll do the job."

Carmen studied him, trying to understand this swift change in moods. He'd been elated when he'd delivered her father; then something had changed in the parking lot, after they'd talked about forgetting that regrettable, embarrassing incident. "Look, Evan, I just want you to know that I don't hold it against you."

He squinted at her. "Very big of you, I suppose."

She flushed, happy for the dark. "We've all done stupid things."

"As if you didn't make the first move."

"What?" Her voice carried in the dark. "By acting like—and I'm quoting here—a crazy Latina? Talk about a cultural stereotype.

Yeah, we're all completely loco with our big hoops and our sassy ways." She stood up, bending over to whisper, inches from his ear. "You think your friend is the one with issues? Look in the mirror, Evan. You're rattling around in your dream house, all alone. When someone gets the slightest bit close to you, you sabotage it or turn it into a competition. If you think I'm loco, think again. Tú eres el loco. Eres tú." She padded across the patio in her bare feet, stopping to give him one last look. "I'll pay you back for the room. This crazy Latina doesn't want anything from you."

It took Evan a moment to puzzle out what she was talking about. He jumped up so fast, he nearly fell into the pool. "Wait!" He rushed across the patio to her. She went around him. He dashed around her until she was nearly backed into the pool. He grabbed her by the shoulders. "Carmen, when you said forget about it—you meant the incident on the speaker phone in the car?"

She pulled herself away. "Yes."

"I thought you meant the kiss."

She rewrapped her towel, thinking about what exactly she'd said. "You thought I wanted to forget about the kiss?"

"Yes, in the driveway." As if there was any other kiss in the history of the known world.

"That's not what I meant." Her voice was guarded.

He put his hand up to touch her face, but stopped. Both hands lifted as if in surrender. "Carmen, we've gotten—no, wait, *I've* gotten—so many things wrong. I didn't respect your decision to run the winery. I didn't take it, or you, seriously. Even when I couldn't think about anything else but seeing your beautiful face every day, I was still trying to beat you. Trying to win. You're right. I don't know why."

"I do."

"Do I want to hear this?"

She shrugged. "Probably not."

He winced. "Okay. Tell me."

"You don't really know how to be close to a woman."

He sat with it for a moment, squinting, as if looking inward. He sighed. "Probably. But doesn't that just make me like ninety percent of the guys out there?"

She nodded. "I don't want ninety percent of the guys out there."

He rubbed his forehead. "What if…" He shook his head.

"What?"

"What if we started over? And I did everything differently? If I went against all my instincts and tried just being with you. Listening to you. Learning from you and your family?" He grinned. "I am nothing if not a fast learner."

She leaned in, smelling his soap and skin beneath the smokiness that clung to his clothing. "You want a do-over?"

He blinked, as if he couldn't quite believe what she was saying. "Seriously?"

"What would you do differently?"

"Well, I'd introduce myself properly and ask you out. I'd pick you up in the Jeep and burn the Lamborghini. I'd take you out to dinner at the kind of restaurants where they focus on amazing food and don't cater to pretentious wine snobs. I'd follow the best food trucks on Instagram and take you to them, hoping to convince you that I'm just a little bit cool. I'd make us picnics with sandwiches like Paolo's, but even better."

"Not possible."

He lifted a finger. "Not done here."

Carmen grinned. "Proceed."

"I'd take you on boat rides and get to know your family, especially your father."

Carmen nodded. "He'd like that. He also thinks I haven't been fair to you, and he's right."

Evan nodded, allowing himself a small grin. "I'd never tell you what I know about making wine because your father and Paolo are the experts. Maybe I know how to run a business and maybe I don't, because my work-life balance is not even a thing, as witnessed by how badly I screwed up with you. If I could do everything over, I'd spend every second of every day trying to make you laugh, just to see you happy."

Carmen rolled her eyes. "That sounds exhausting."

"I don't think I could tone down the intensity. We hard-driving tech types really don't know much about dialing it down."

"Neither do I, Evan. It's not like this has been all your fault."

He sighed. "I just want a fresh start."

"You know I'm not selling you Blue Hills."

He nodded. "That hurts, a little."

"It should. We're the best vineyard in the state."

He raised an eyebrow. "For now."

"We're not going to compete," she reminded him, knowing that they would. A little.

"I would love that."

Carmen sighed. It was no use. She did love a project. "So. You want to date?"

He nodded.

"Like normal people?"

"Yes. Absolutely. I want to date the girl next door."

She grinned. "That's me."

He bent down to kiss her. "That's you."

Her towel fell off as she embraced him, kissing him in a way that promised much, much more.

EPILOGUE

Nine Months Later

Carmen looked into her mirror, smiling at her reflection, listening for the crunch of gravel on the driveway indicating that her date had arrived. It was like high school, down to the concert stubs tucked into the frame of her mirror: Dave Matthews at the Gorge (his idea), the Mexican band Los Ángeles Azules in Yakima (hers). Except she was running the winery. Thanks to the prayer group, the grapes had been harvested in time and the wine, although not yet aged, had convinced the bank to refinance the loan, allowing them to make smaller payments. A cellar full of aging wine counted as an asset.

Downstairs, guests were on the patio for a tasting. Not one of them knew that the winery had been threatened by fire less than a year ago. They were blissfully unaware that a change of wind had saved the very land upon which they stood, sipping the latest vintage. They were more interested in selfies in front of the magnificent view and the chance to tell their friends they'd visited the hot new place.

Carmen was reluctant to leave on a weekend, but Lola had insisted. She would be fine running the new tasting bar, she said, even though Saturday was their busiest night. They had a great cook and wait staff thanks to the profit-sharing plan Adella had engineered.

Carmen gazed out her bedroom window. A car wound its way up from the lake. Evan in his new Jeep. The Lamborghini was now a source of humor: Evan had had an early mid-life crisis. Now, he didn't want to stick out, or scream, "I'm new. I'm rich. I'm an ass."

When Carmen came downstairs, she had to pull Evan away from her father. They could talk soil erosion and acidity all night. Carmen wanted a night off, if there was such a thing. Evan seemed to learn something from every glass of wine he drank. He'd gotten his first bronze medal. It didn't count, he said, until it was gold. Some things never changed.

Outside, the evening air was warm. Early spring was Carmen's favorite time of year in Chelan. A time of promise, new beginnings, rich with possibility. As Carmen got into the Jeep with Evan, she reached across and kissed his cheek. He smelled of soap and minty toothpaste. He started the car, asking her if she wanted to meet Paolo and Stella for an early drink or head straight to dinner.

"Whatever you want. I'm all yours." It was shockingly easy to say. As the Jeep passed through the orchard and down to the placid lake, Carmen felt something truly rare. An awareness that right now, in this very moment, she was utterly happy.

Sometimes, Carmen thought, life was simple. Sometimes you go looking for something and you find it.

A Letter from Ellyn

Hello and greetings from Seattle!

Thanks so much for spending time with *Summer at Orchard House*. Hopefully you enjoyed it. If you'd like to hear about my upcoming books, sign up below. Your email address will never be shared and you can unsubscribe at any time.

www.bookouture.com/ellyn-oaksmith

Sharing your thoughts in a review is a wonderful way to help authors and readers connect. You'd not only give me valuable feedback; you'd help new readers discover my books. (And reviews make authors ridiculously happy!)

Finally, I'd love to hear from you! Let's chat on Instagram, Facebook, Twitter, Goodreads or my website.

Happy reading,
Ellyn Oaksmith

ellynoaksmith
EllynOaksmith
@EllynOaksmith
EllynOaksmith.com

Acknowledgments

Thank you to everyone at Bookouture, especially Hannah Bond, whose enthusiasm, positivity and energy has made the drudgery of editing so much more bearable. Also, thanks to Peta Nightingale, Gabrielle Chant, Kim Nash, Natasha Hodgson and Alexandra Holmes. You ladies are the literary equivalent to Spanx and make everything look much, much better.

Thanks to Mary Oaksmith Nichols and family for sharing your beautiful Lake Chelan house with my family, without which this book and so many good times, never would have happened.

My fellow authors: Melanie Bates, Angela Curran and Jesse Ewing-Frable. You're all game changers in your own talented and hilarious way.

Thanks to SMS/AMS/CES for everything, always.